"So you adm̱

D0342895

"Don't start, Re_____se I care." He cupped his large hand against Diana's cheek, a gesture so tender it made her throat tighten. "All the years I've been a cop, and I never got personal with a case. Cops who get personal, they burn out. I never did that." One finger gently caressed her cheek. "But this *is* personal. You know I don't want to care much about you."

"It's a human tendency to resist that which we need the most." She could stand here and stare into his beautiful eyes all day long.

"No games, okay? We're friends. Good friends, but just friends...."

Diana guessed where he was leading, and tamped the urge to argue. He needed to say what he needed to say.

"You're right. I do think you're sexy. I've thought about asking you out. I even dream about you. But I don't want to wreck our friendship. I don't want to hurt you."

Or himself.

"But you still want to kiss me."

His chest rose and fell in a heavy breath. "Yeah."

Dear Harlequin Intrigue Reader,

Got a bad case of spring fever? Harlequin Intrigue has the antidote for what ails you. Breathtaking romantic suspense to blast away the cold of winter.

Adrianne Lee brings you the next title in our TOP SECRET BABIES promotion. Tough-guy cop Cade Maconahey could face down any foe, but he was a fish out of water with a baby. Good thing Joanna Edwards showed up when she did to help him out…but what was her real motive? Find out in *Undercover Baby*.

Passion ignites in Debra Webb's next COLBY AGENCY case. Ian Michaels and Nicole Reed go head-to-head in *Protective Custody*—the result is nothing short of explosive. Charlotte Douglas follows up her cross-over Harlequin American Romance-Harlequin Intrigue series, IDENTITY SWAP. Sexy lawman Dylan Blackburn had loved Jennifer Reid from afar, but when he had the chance to love her up close, he'd learned there was a *Stranger in His Arms*.

Finally, Sheryl Lynn winds up her two-book McCLINTOCK COUNTRY miniseries with *Colorado's Finest*. Tate Raleigh combines urban street smarts with a rugged physique and stalwart principles that stand the test of time. He's a devastating opponent to any criminal—and totally irresistible to every woman.

So we hope each one of these fantastic stories jump-starts the season for you. Enjoy!

Sincerely,

Denise O'Sullivan
Associate Senior Editor
Harlequin Intrigue

COLORADO'S FINEST
SHERYL LYNN

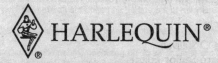

HARLEQUIN®

TORONTO • NEW YORK • LONDON
AMSTERDAM • PARIS • SYDNEY • HAMBURG
STOCKHOLM • ATHENS • TOKYO • MILAN • MADRID
PRAGUE • WARSAW • BUDAPEST • AUCKLAND

ISBN 0-373-22612-8

COLORADO'S FINEST

ABOUT THE AUTHOR

Sheryl Lynn lives in a pine forest atop a hill in Colorado. When not writing, she amuses herself by embarrassing her two teenagers, walking her dogs in a nearby park and feeding peanuts to the dozens of Steller's jays, scrub jays, blue jays and squirrels who live in her backyard. Her best ideas come from the newspapers, although she admits that a lot of what she reads is way too weird for fiction.

Books by Sheryl Lynn

Don't miss any of our special offers. Write to us at the following address for information on our newest releases.

Harlequin Reader Service
U.S.: 3010 Walden Ave., P.O. Box 1325, Buffalo, NY 14269
Canadian: P.O. Box 609, Fort Erie, Ont. L2A 5X3

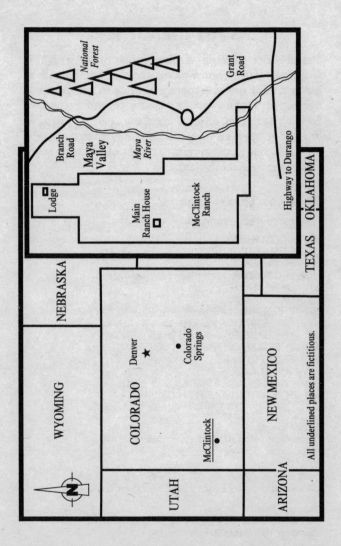

CAST OF CHARACTERS

Deputy Tate Raleigh—Formerly one of New York's finest, this tough cop owns the historic Track Shack Bar and Grill and is desperately trying to escape his past.

Diana Dover—She's been reborn, and found peace and balance in McClintock, Colorado. Lessons from the past must be dealt with, even if it puts her in danger or causes her to lose the love of her life.

Bernadette O'Malley—Unrepentant thief and liar who has finally gone too far, and only her twin sister can possibly save her.

Sheriff Gil Vance—He takes care of his town, even if it means going head-to-head with the FBI.

Farrah Montgomery—Deadly avenger or murder victim?

Special Agent Andrew Albright—An FBI agent with an agenda. He'll get what he wants no matter who gets hurt.

Thank you, my little chicks, Becky, Khrys, Kitty and Sara. We have entirely too much fun.

Chapter One

Trouble, Tim had told her. Like one of them jinxes, turning gold into lead.

Bernie was beginning to believe it. Or maybe she'd known it all along and only now had a name for the bad luck that had dogged her all her life. She was a jinx.

She stared up at the security guard. Most gated communities in the Phoenix area hired geezers to check traffic moving in and out. Forty Palm's residents employed a tough looking man who wore a sidearm and looked capable, and willing to use it.

Bernie tried to turn on the charm. Her hands ached from how tightly she clutched the steering wheel. Her wounded arm throbbed. A bullet seemed too small to cause such a huge misery, but the pain radiated the length of her arm and across her shoulder blades. Heat outside the open window clashed with the car's air-conditioning and made her woozy. Charm eluded her. "Can't you just double-check? Please? Ruth O'Malley, 1421 Paloma Way. She's lived there over twenty years. I'm her daughter. Call her, she'll tell you."

The guard held a clipboard. After giving it a cursory scan, he shook his head. "Sorry, ma'am, no O'Malley at that address. No O'Malley on the list at all."

"Call the house."

"I'll call the police." His tone was mild, but his expression wasn't.

Bernie couldn't afford official intervention right now. She shoved the transmission into reverse and backed into the street. She kept backing up until she was out of the guard's line of sight, then put the Buick into park.

She rested her forearms on the steering wheel and her head on her arms. She hurt all over. Her eyeballs felt like sandblasted marbles. Her stomach was as hollow as a deflated balloon, but the mere idea of shoving snack food into her mouth made her ill.

She didn't know where to go, what to do. She'd already been to her sister's condo. A stranger lived there now. She'd found her sister's husband living at another address. Good old Dr. Jeff had coldly informed her that he and Diana were divorced and he hadn't seen her in years. He'd hung up on her. Hard. Big priss must still be mad about the Porsche, she thought.

Diana's divorce didn't surprise Bernie, but it did worry her. If she'd remarried, she could have changed her name, or moved out of state. Bernie could understand Mom turning her away—it had been five or six years since Bernie had talked to her, and the old lady liked to pout and punish—but Diana would help her. No matter how angry she got, Diana always helped. Dear sister never held a grudge.

She turned her baleful gaze on Tim. Wrapped up in a blanket despite the heat, he slept. Worthless. This was all his fault.

A car drove past and turned into the community entrance. Bernie glimpsed the passenger's profile. There was an ugly mug she'd never forget—a bullet from his pistol had torn a chunk out of her arm. Her heart thudded.

"What are these guys?" she wailed. "Psychic?"

She whipped the car in a U-turn. The front wheels thumped hard on the median curb. Tim's head lolled and smacked against the glass. The bumper plowed through blooming bird-of-paradise, then thumped again when it hit the street.

A minivan swerved and honked. Bernie punched the accelerator.

Half a mile down the road she remembered the wires hanging from the steering column. All a cop had to do was look in the window and he'd know the car was stolen. She searched the rearview mirror; the road was empty behind her. She slowed the car to the speed limit.

"This is all your fault, you jerk," she snarled. Tim slumped on the seat. Only a seat belt kept him from crumpling onto the floor. His face was gray. "You didn't have to kill her. We got the money. Everybody cooperated. Damn you, she was my friend!"

He muttered and struggled weakly against the blanket. A fresh, red stain spread on the wool. He was bleeding all over the car.

"You hurting?" she asked. "Good, because I am, too. And you know what? Phoenix isn't big enough. They're here! I don't know how they know, but they know and they're right behind us!" She slammed a fist against the steering wheel.

She couldn't find her family. Friends had given up on her long ago. Those murderous bloodhounds seemed to be anticipating her every move.

Tim groaned. She should dump him in an emergency room. Then he'd be arrested, and he'd talk like he was being paid by the word. He'd put the blame for the whole screwed-up mess on her.

She turned east. If her family couldn't—wouldn't—

help her, she'd have to help herself. "We're going to Colorado."

Tim groaned again.

"McClintock, Colorado." Memories of wide open spaces, towering mountains and ranch country populated by goat-ropin' hicks lifted her mood. "The land that time forgot. They'll never find us there. Not in a million years. Do you hear me? Once we get across the state line, all our problems are solved."

"Do you know what your real problem is?"

Don't smile, Tate Raleigh warned himself. Smiling only encouraged Diana. He tapped a pencil against the messy sprawl of paperwork on the bar.

"Well?" she asked. "Do you?"

It occurred to him that the Track Shack had grown quiet. He swiveled on the bar stool, and was surprised to see the dining room was empty. He'd been so engrossed in trying to figure out how to stay out of bankruptcy, he hadn't noticed that the lunch crowd had cleared. The only noise came from the kitchen where Consuela banged pots, pans and dishes.

With a questioning look, Diana raised a coffee carafe. He pushed his cup toward her. He rested his chin on a fist. The Track Shack Bar and Grill was a money pit, and he was drowning.

Diana filled his cup. The aroma curled around his nose, soothing him. For someone who never touched the stuff, she made fantastic coffee.

She grinned at him. A yellow pencil stuck out of too-wild hair. Her blue eyes sparkled with good humor. That's what he liked most about her. She was her own little patch of sunshine. Despite himself, his mood lifted.

"How many times have I told you to not give me advice, lectures or analysis?"

Her face scrunched in concentration. "Let's see. I've worked here about six months, five days a week. That's, um…approximately ninety-six times."

"Okay, for the ninety-seventh time, mind your own business."

"You're mistaking quantity for quality. You work too hard."

Once Diana had it in her head to counsel him about improving his life, a machine-gun nest and barbed wire couldn't keep her at bay. "Is that so?"

"Workaholics don't put in the hours to get more done." She shook her head, setting her curly hair bobbing. "It's a way to escape yourself. An impossible goal. Still, that's not your real problem. Negative energy. That's the *real* problem."

Giving her a dry look, he sipped coffee. "Don't you have tables to bus?"

"Everything in its time. I'm worried about you." She stretched a hand across the bar and used a fingertip to lightly rub the worry lines between his eyebrows.

"Not now, Red." He jerked a thumb over his shoulder. "Get this place cleaned up."

"Negative energy attracts negative energy. Whatever you put out, that's what comes back. You don't want to sell the Shack. That's why you've got headaches and heartburn. Even this building can feel it. All the vibes are off-kilter, energy flows are disrupted. That's why things keep breaking."

"Huh. And here I thought it was because this building is almost a hundred years old. Dry rot, a leaky roof and ancient plumbing is the problem. Not to mention, my suppliers upping costs every time I turn around." He lost his grip on the good mood and snarled at the paperwork. "The Feed Bag turned into a sports bar with not one, but two big-screen televisions. How am I supposed to compete with that? McClintock isn't big enough to support all the restaurants we've got. It's survival of the fittest, Red, and quite frankly, the old Shack is on her last legs."

He looked around at the grease-darkened, pine-panelled walls, the garish neon signs advertising brands of beer and the 1950s era tubular steel dining tables. A fixture in McClintock, Colorado, the Shack had history and Wild West charm. It hurt his heart knowing he had to let it go.

"I messed up buying out Junior's share of the business. I'm in hock up to my eyeballs." He turned a critical eye on the floor. The linoleum had to be fifty years old, and was worn through in places. "If I thought it would do any good, I'd renovate the place, but then I'll chase away my regulars."

"Have you tried prayer?"

"Me and religion parted ways a long time ago."

"You don't need religion to pray." She touched his hand. "All you have to do is ask."

"Right." He studied her hand. Her fingers were long, slender, work-roughened, but graceful. He liked it a tad more than was wise when she touched him. He lifted his gaze to her face. Her skin was milky-white, emphasizing the angularity of a very Irish heritage. Taken individually her features were ordinary. All together they somehow added up to a peculiar beauty.

Not for the first time, he debated asking her to dinner. Not for the first time, a warning voice told him not to go there. He and Diana had a great relationship just the way it was.

A woman strode into the bar and called out a cheerful hello. "Marlee!" Diana called in return.

Within seconds Diana and Marlee Crowder had their heads together, giggling like girls. Their friendship baffled Tate. Marlee, a veterinarian and daughter of the richest woman in the Maya Valley, was almost twenty years younger than Diana, a forty-something retro-hippie. Yet, whenever they got together, it turned into a laugh fest.

A grown man didn't need a buddy who was privy to every little aspect of his life. Still, a pang of envy tightened his diaphragm. Stupid.

Diana went to the kitchen to fetch Marlee's take-out order. Marlee slid onto a stool next to Tate.

"How's the animal doctor business?" he asked.

"Couldn't be better. How's the barkeep slash deputy sheriff business?" Her grin sparkled in the gloomy light. "Have you ever considered the irony of what you do?"

Marlee loved to tease him. She reminded him of his younger sisters. Sassy, uncowed by his superior size and strength, and secure in the knowledge that he'd never strike back no matter what the provocation.

"The bulk of law enforcement around here deals with the effects of alcohol," she said. "Drunk drivers, domestic brawls, underage drinkers. Yet, you own a bar."

"It isn't ironic," he said, straight-faced. "It's symbiotic."

She frowned for a few seconds, then comprehension dawned and she laughed. She quickly sobered and looked around the place as if it were a sick animal she needed to figure out how to tend. "I heard a rumor that you're going to sell the Shack."

He covered the paperwork with his forearms. It was impossible to keep anything secret in this town, but he had his pride. "No rumor. It's a fact. I'm getting everything in order so I can list it on the market."

"Be a real shame if the Shack shut down. Do you know this is the oldest original building in McClintock?"

As fast as it was falling apart, he could believe it. "I did not know that."

"It used to be a railroad station."

That much he knew. He also knew the Shack would go the way of the dinosaur if he didn't find a buyer. The land it sat on was worth more than the business, so if he lost it through bankruptcy, it would in all likelihood be bulldozed. That hurt too much to think about.

Diana returned with a paper bag. Marlee paid and tossed a breezy goodbye to Tate. He returned to figuring out how to tweak the budget in his favor.

Diana cleared tables, washed them down, wiped off chairs and refilled condiment and napkin dispensers. She served lunch to some stragglers, and coffee to a pair of old farmers who were arguing about drought conditions. Tate almost yelled at them to shut up so he could concentrate. With all the rain they'd had this spring, drought was the last thing anyone should worry about. The place emptied again, and Tate had tweaked as much as humanly possible. He couldn't make payroll unless he came up with five hundred bucks in the next week.

He rubbed his aching temples with the pads of his fingers.

"I know why you're really so grouchy," Diana said. She refilled his coffee cup.

"Because you're a pain in the butt?"

She winked. "Close. It's because you have the hots for me."

He arched an eyebrow.

"Sexual tension." She wiggled her hands. "It makes the air shivery. Crazy vibes."

It took him several seconds to catch up to the fact that

she was teasing him. Seconds where he flashed onto the wide, graceful fullness of her hips and those long legs that he'd love to see in a skirt. Where he considered plunging his hands into her corona of coppery hair to see if it was as lush and soft as it looked. Where he'd really like to kiss that wide mouth, in the hopes of finding out if her kisses were as fiery as her hair. He brutally shoved away that nonsense.

"Sorry, you're too old for me."

"Ha!" She fluffed hair against her palm and batted her eyelashes. "You know what Ben Franklin says about older women. Not only experienced, but grateful."

He nearly spewed coffee all over his papers. He coughed and thumped his chest. "Don't say things like that when my mouth is full!"

She leaned her arms on the bar and lowered her head so she peered up at him. A look both sexy and disconcerting. "I've seen how you look at me."

That sounded way too serious. And way too true. He pretended they still continued the lighthearted banter. "Hate to break it to you, Red, but you aren't my type."

An eyebrow lifted in a skeptical arch. "I've seen the women you've fooled yourself into thinking are your type."

"Then you know you aren't it."

"Tourists, here today, gone tomorrow. Or those high-maintenance women you wine and dine. They genuinely like you because you're a nice guy. Only it doesn't take long for them to figure out that you work sixteen-hour days, and you always have too much important stuff to do. Then, when they get too close, you convince yourself they're being unreasonably demanding. So when you dump them, it isn't your fault."

She wasn't funny anymore.

She shook a finger. "You deliberately pick a type that's absolutely wrong for you. You won't risk anyone getting close enough to look at that big hole in your heart."

Rippling back muscles accompanied the tightening of his diaphragm. Diana Dover was an insightful woman. He wasn't the only one who'd noticed her double dose of feminine intuition. Some folks went so far as to call her psychic. The last place he wanted her was inside his head. "I pay you to waitress, not psychoanalyze me."

"It's about time somebody did. It's pathetic. You live alone behind a bar and you're determined to work yourself into an early grave." She leaned in close enough for him to catch the scent of honey that always surrounded her. It was as if she bathed in the stuff. Her voice lowered, as smooth and smoky as her mesmerizing eyes. "Unless you acknowledge your grief, give it voice, it's never going to heal."

Lost in the depths of her eyes, he wanted to tell her all about his wife and how he'd let her down and how it wasn't grief that gnawed his guts, it was guilt. Or maybe grief and guilt. Or maybe he was just a lousy human being who'd forfeited his right to pursue happiness.

He never talked about that with anybody. Ever. Period.

He jerked back so roughly he nearly slipped off the stool. "You're full of crap, Red. My only problem is where I'm going to get the five hundred bucks I need for payroll."

She straightened. Her smile bugged the dickens out of him. Planting a big, wet kiss on her would wipe that knowing grin right off her smug face. He'd show her sexual tension.

"All prayers are answered," she said. She swiped a finger diagonally across her chest. "Honest."

"So I raise my hands to heaven." He did so, his fingers

splayed. He forced his features into a pious expression. "God, gimme five hundred bucks so I can make payroll."

"You're lucky the universe forgives sarcasm. But yes, that's all there is to it. And don't forget to say thank you."

"You make me nuts," he muttered.

"We all have a purpose in life." She reached behind her to untie her apron. "I have to run home and check on my kids. I'll be back in an hour. Can you manage without me?"

Kids? She kept bees, chickens and a horse, but other than that he'd been under the impression that she lived alone. "You took in foster kids or something?"

"When I say kids, I am speaking literally. I bought a flock of goats. Young wethers. They're adorable."

"Why did you do that?"

"Fiber. Cashmere comes from goats. I'm going to learn to spin and weave wool. Pretty cool, huh? I'm thinking about getting a llama, too."

He stacked paperwork. "You're a laugh a minute."

Sheriff Gil Vance entered the bar. He swept off his big Stetson hat and slid onto the stool next to Tate's.

"Hello, sheriff," Diana said. "Coffee?"

"To go. One cream, three sugars."

"Did you bring your cup?"

"Just make him a coffee to go," Tate said.

"Styrofoam is hard on the environment. If everyone brought in cups, we wouldn't contribute so much to pollution."

Gil chuckled at the ongoing argument. He was half Southern Ute, and his face was round, almost childishly soft. People who believed him soft quickly learned the error of their ways. "She's right, Tate. I'll make sure I bring a cup next time."

"Thank you." She tossed Tate a snotty smile and rummaged under the counter for a to-go cup.

"I got a problem," Gil said. "Hate to spring it on you like this, but Bill Yarrow came down with shingles."

"What's that?"

"Heck if I know."

Diana placed a large styrofoam cup of coffee in front of the sheriff. "Chicken pox," she said. Both men turned to her. "It's the same virus that causes chicken pox. Sometimes it flares up in adults, affecting nerves. It's extremely painful, and can be quite debilitating."

"Oh," Gil said. His face creased in a broad smile. "Ever thought about going on *Jeopardy?*"

"I don't believe competition is good for the soul."

"So, anyway," Tate said, interrupting what could turn into a long discussion, "Bill has chicken pox."

"Shingles. And he says he can't even wear trousers, much less a gun belt. I know it's your week off, but I've got no one else who can pull night patrol."

Tate worked part-time for the sheriff, one week on, and one week off. Pulling the night shift meant screwing up his sleep. Plus he had a thousand and one small chores to do around the bar.

"I'd do it myself, but I'm already pulling double shifts. And you know I can't put a volunteer deputy in a cruiser."

Tate waved a hand. "All right, all right. I can do it. Ten tonight?"

Gil hopped off the stool and clapped a hand against Tate's back. "If it wasn't the start of summer, I'd forget regular night patrol. But you know how it is."

Tate did. The Maya Valley's year-round population was around ten thousand people, tops. The sheriff's budget was tight, his staff small. He depended heavily on part-time deputies and volunteers. When the weather warmed and tourists poured into the Rocky Mountains to hike, fish, camp and mountain climb, the sheriff's resources were stretched to the limits.

After Gil left, Tate rested his face in his hands. He had to reseat the toilet in the ladies' room, climb onto the roof and find the source of a leak, clean out the drain trap in the kitchen—the list went on and on. Plus he had a meeting with a real estate agent to discuss how to price the business and how to market it.

Diana touched his arm. She had her jacket on and a backpack hanging from one shoulder. "Not to be nosy or anything, but how much do you get paid for a week of night patrol?"

"That is nosy." He grinned ruefully. "After Uncle Sam takes his pound of flesh, I clear about five-fifty. Why do you ask?" Then he knew why she asked. He stared openmouthed at the stack of bills. He'd just made payroll.

"Don't forget to say thank you," she said breezily and headed for the door. Her hair bounced against her shoulders, catching fluorescent light, sparking red and gold.

He watched her go and wondered how it was she so easily got under his skin and why her observations bugged him. He liked his life. He wasn't looking for change.

"Sexual tension," he muttered and rolled his eyes. Maybe if Diana were a cool blonde instead of a nutty redhead who couldn't keep her opinions to herself, he'd follow up on the flirtation.

Him and Diana? Ha! Not in a million years.

Chapter Two

Yawning and scratching, Tate wandered into the kitchen. He inhaled the aromas of braised pork, roasted green chilies and fried batter. He was going to miss the smell of this place.

He'd spent an uneventful night on patrol. Two speeding tickets, a minor accident involving a car and an elk—in which the animal suffered less damage than the car—and two DUIs. A stint in the Marine Corps had taught him how to fall asleep at any time, under any circumstances, but he disliked daytime sleep. It gave him outrageous dreams. This morning he'd dreamed Diana had been naked in a murky pond, urging him to jump into the water with her.

The cook turned from the sink. Soapsuds dripped off her rubber gloves. Consuela had been cooking at the Shack for close to thirty years. Tate had inherited her when he bought the place. She scared the hell out of him, but made up for it by working magic in the kitchen.

Her eyes glittered like shards of obsidian.

"What did I do now?" he asked warily.

She tossed her head, sweeping glossy black hair off her shoulders. She had dozens of grandchildren, but seemed to have stopped aging around twenty-five. Tate never had figured out how old she was and never dared to ask.

"Not you," she said, "Diana."

He looked uneasily at the batwing doors separating the kitchen from the dining room. If Diana had missed work, and Consuela had to take care of the lunch crowd by herself, he'd never hear the end of it. "What did she do?"

Consuela shook a gloved finger. "You! What did you do to her, eh?"

"Nothing, I swear."

Diana pushed backward through the doors. She lugged a bus tray piled high with dishes and glassware. She gave Tate a feeble smile and carried the dirty dishes to the sink.

"Good afternoon, Red," he said.

"Hi," she murmured and returned to the dining room.

"See!" Consuela exclaimed. "All day she's been like that. Sad as a mama that lost her babes. And I want—" The words turned into a stream of rapid Spanish. Tate couldn't interpret the speech, but understood the sentiment. He beat it out of the kitchen.

Three elderly men, dressed like triplets in dusty jeans, snap-front shirts straining over pot bellies and grimy baseball caps marked with the local feed store logo, occupied a table. Tate lifted a hand in greeting.

Shattering crockery made him jump.

Diana stood rigidly, head down, fists clenched. She stared at broken plates.

An uneasy feeling told Tate she was about to burst into tears. He grabbed a broom and dust pan.

"Sorry," she said. "You can take it out of my pay." She crouched to pick up the larger pieces.

"Accidents happen." He crouched next to her. "What's the matter?"

She shook her head.

In the year he'd known her, he'd never seen her worried or upset. "Don't lie to me."

She lifted her face. Her normally serene eyes were strained. "I'm okay."

"If you're sick or something, scoot out of here. I can handle the place."

"Hey, Red," a customer called. "Got my change, honey?"

"Oh, sorry." She jumped up, and knocked a chair with her hip. Tate shot out an arm to steady her. Usually she seemed to float rather than walk, so her clumsiness baffled him. She hurried to the table, and dug into the pockets of her apron. She handed over a fistful of money.

He waved a bill. "I gave you a ten, Red. Don't need a twenty in change."

She groaned. "I'm sorry, I'm sorry," she muttered and exchanged the twenty-dollar bill for a one-dollar bill.

"Hey, Tate," the man called. "Give this poor girl a vacation. You're working her near to death."

Tate finished cleaning up the broken dishes. After the customers left, he asked Diana again what was wrong.

"I'm fine. Don't worry about me." She disappeared into the kitchen.

He didn't know how to stop worrying. Especially when on the following day, she was even more distracted and upset than the day before. After the lunch crowd cleared out, he snagged her by the elbow. He took a wash rag out of her hand and urged her to sit at a table. He swung a chair around backward and sat on it, facing her. The old vinyl seat creaked beneath his weight.

She hung her head. Hair draped over her face.

He used a finger to part the coppery curtain. "Aside from the fact that I'm a cop and I know when people are lying, I'm your friend. So if you don't want me interrogating you, tell me what's the matter.''

She cocked her head as if listening to Consuela bustling around in the kitchen. ''It's not your concern.''

''It is when my dishes get broken.''

Her lips twitched as if she tried to smile, but couldn't quite make it. She sighed heavily and averted her gaze. ''Well, hypothetically speaking then.''

He hated it when people spoke ''hypothetically.'' It generally denoted very bad news. Eyebrows raised, she stared wide-eyed, pleading silently for understanding. He shoved down his impatience. ''Okay, hypothetically, what's your problem?''

''Let's suppose,'' she began, ''a person has a family member. Let's say, a sister. And this person hasn't seen the sister in many years. Mostly because the sister is really bad news.''

He didn't know she had a sister. Then again, he didn't know much about Diana Dover outside of the bar. ''How bad?''

''Oh…'' She hummed and rolled her eyes toward the ceiling. ''Say, going to jail kind of bad? Hypothetically, of course.''

''Of course.''

''This person knows the sister is involved in something. It's only right to contact…authorities, but it's her sister. What would you do in a situation like that?''

He conjured a mental map of her property, knowing he'd be visiting before this day was over. Her home was five miles north of town, abutting national forest, on land too rocky for either raising cattle or growing hay. ''It would depend on a number of factors.''

''Such as?''

Her sad expression ate at him, made him want to haul

her onto his lap and pet her. A hole in the vinyl chair back gave him something to fiddle with. "If this person has knowledge that the sister is a fugitive, then she is legally obligated to contact the law. Otherwise, she could be charged with accessory after the fact, or hindering prosecution."

It didn't appear to be the answer she was hoping for. "What if this person only *suspects* something bad is going on?"

He'd run into this situation too many times to count. Law-abiding people wanted to do the right thing, but it was difficult when it meant blowing the whistle on a loved one. No matter how he hardened himself, he always felt the heartbreak of mothers, fathers, siblings and spouses who gave up fugitive relatives or testified against them in court. He'd often asked himself if it were something he could do. Her misery told him she was struggling hard with her conscience.

"If it was me, and I only suspected a problem, I'd consider it gossip. No sense passing on gossip without any facts to back it up."

She looked relieved.

"If I had actual knowledge of a crime, it would be my duty to report it to authorities. I might call in an anonymous tip. Or encourage the sister to do the right thing."

Her shoulders sagged. She sighed again.

"Cut the crap," he said. "What's going on?"

She looked at the ceiling, the floor, the table—anywhere but at him. "It's my sister, Bernie—Bernadette. She's at my place. I think she's in some kind of trouble." She lifted her shoulders. "She's always in trouble."

He tossed a significant look at the telephone hanging on the wall behind the bar. "A deputy can be up there in fifteen minutes."

"No! I mean, like you said, if I don't know any facts then it's gossip."

He checked his watch. "Oscar and Susan are coming on at five. I don't have to report in to the sheriff until ten. How about I pop over to your place and have a chat with your sister? Low key, no pressure. Then if nothing is going on, you can show me your baby goats."

A mingling of worry and relief filled her eyes. "You're a good friend, Tate."

He pushed off the chair. "Okay then. So quit breaking my plates."

"Deal."

He stepped away, then stopped and turned around. "You're sure it's your sister bugging you? Sure it isn't that sexual tension thing? All that unrequited love stuff must be rough on your system."

Her mouth bloomed with the first genuine smile he'd seen on her in two days. "You have it backward," she said. "You're the one who has the hots for me."

"Whatever. Get back to work."

ON THE DRIVE HOME from work, Diana made up her mind. The days of enabling her sister to escape the consequences of her actions were past. She would resist Bernie's charm, ignore the sweet talk, refuse to let emotions override good sense. Bernie had to take responsibility for herself.

Her chest still ached with guilty anxiety. Guilt she didn't deserve, but suffered anyway. On the plus side, if Tate did arrest Bernie, she'd get proper medical attention for her gunshot wound.

Balance, she mused. Good and bad, dark and light, joy and sorrow—none was possible without the other. The universe abhorred imbalance as much as nature abhorred a vacuum. Life had been entirely too placid lately. So the universe gave her Bernadette.

She parked the pickup inside the shed that served as a garage. Bernie's car, looking road-weary and neglected, was pulled off to the side of the driveway, untouched since Bernie had arrived.

Her puppy squirmed from beneath the porch and galloped across the driveway. Wriggling, squirming and whining, the young Border collie let Diana know how much she'd been missed. Diana crouched to love up the dog, cooing, "Sweet Tippy, darling Tippy. Is him a good boy, hmm?" She received an enthusiastic face washing in return.

With Tippy on her heels, Diana entered the house. She called, "Bernie?" She opened the bedroom door. "Bernadette?"

The bedclothes were rumpled. A streak of blood stained a sheet. The air was heavy with the smell of antiseptic and sage smoke. The first-aid kit was missing from the side table. The bathroom was empty. She fingered a towel. Dry.

"Where did she go?"

Tippy wagged his tail.

Diana had a sick feeling that more than her sister was missing. A look inside the closet proved her suspicions. Two flannel shirts, jeans and a pair of boots were missing. So was her heavy winter coat. In the kitchen she discovered the pantry stripped of everything that could be eaten without cooking. A camp kit was gone, too. The jar where she deposited tip money was empty.

She closed her eyes, envisioning her sister gathering warm clothing and food. Supplies that would serve a person who intended roughing it in the wilderness.

"Oh, no," she breathed and ran outside.

Behind the house was a two-stall barn. The corral gate stood wide open. Shoulders sagging, Diana slowed to a walk. The barn felt as empty and deserted as the house. No friendly snuffle welcomed her. "Smoky Joe?" she called, and whistled hopefully. Her horse, and all his tack, was gone.

Guilt about sharing her concerns with Tate Raleigh winked away.

"I should trade you in on a rottweiler," she told the dog. Tippy wagged his tail and grinned.

She was so disgusted, and embarrassed, too. This same thing happened the last time she'd seen her sister. Bernie had shown up bruised and battered, needing a place to hide from an abusive boyfriend. Diana had fed her, tended her, made appointments with social workers, then arrived home from work to find Bernie gone, along with blank checks, jewelry and Diana's ex-husband's Porsche. Diana had convinced Jeff to not press charges about his stolen car, then had written off the stolen jewelry as a loss and made good on forged checks.

It seemed neither sister had learned from the past.

"I'm going to have her arrested," she told the dog while she stomped back to the house. "Enough is enough."

TATE STEERED THE CRUISER around deep potholes and rocks poking through the long driveway. Locals called Diana's property the O'Malley place. He never had figured out why. He did know the driveway needed grading and filling in the worst kind of way. He topped a hill. A tire dropped into a deep rut, and he bounced on the seat, striking his head on the roof. Rubbing his smarting crown, he wondered how she made it to work when it snowed.

Off to the right, goats grazed a boulder-strewn field. As

one they lifted their heads to watch the vehicle. Four were white, two were black and one was tricolored like a calico cat.

He'd had it in his head that she lived in a shack or a teepee or even a cave. The house proved to be a log cabin with a stone chimney. The porch was painted forest green to match the shutters.

A dirty Buick LeSabre with Arizona plates was parked next to a shed. The sister's, he guessed.

There was a barn behind the house. Red chickens pecked in the dirt inside a wire enclosure. A barbed wire fence surrounded a garden plot. High altitude, low precipitation and a short growing season discouraged many gardeners. Those who persisted were plagued by deer and elk that found salad fixings and bean plants irresistible.

A glint of metal caught his eye. Beyond the barn and corral was a curious sight. It looked like a chain-link dog run. Instead of dogs, it held a row of white boxes. It must be the beehives she talked about. He wondered why she fenced them in.

He parked behind the Buick. Through a shed's open door, he spotted Diana's pickup truck.

A high-pitched yip accompanied a black-and-white streak. Then a young dog was curling around Tate's legs and wagging its tail so hard, Tate feared the pup's spine might break. The dog barked and whined while Tate petted him and thumped its ribs. Its wriggling deposited white hairs on Tate's uniform trousers.

Diana stepped onto the porch. "Tippy, come!"

The dog whined and wagged, torn between obedience and greeting his new friend. Finally, he loped to Diana and sat at her feet, panting and bright-eyed. Diana waved to Tate.

He called in to dispatch and reported his location. The

dispatcher chided him about overtime. He responded with, "10-4. It's only a minor health and welfare. No charge. Over and out." Cool air raised goosebumps on his arms. He breathed deeply, expecting to smell the stench he'd heard goats were infamous for, but inhaling only clean, dry air and a hint of wildflowers.

"Hello," she called. "Fancy seeing you here."

"I figured it was time I saw how you spent your paycheck. Nice place." Her mood appeared much improved, but the strain was there. If he didn't know her so well, he'd say she was angry.

"Come on in."

The house was even nicer inside than outside. The hardwood floor was polished, with a patina of age and loving care. Throw rugs were scattered like flower petals. The sofa facing the fireplace took him aback. He couldn't be certain, but it looked to be made of fine leather. Prints and paintings, all with a circle and spiral theme, were professionally framed.

A not unpleasant acrid smell hung in the air. He wondered if it came from one of the pots on the stove.

Other than the Buick, he didn't see or hear indications of anyone else. He slid a hand over the back of his neck. "Okay, I'm here. What's going on?"

With a graceful wave she indicated a chair. "It's a long story."

A wall-hanging next to the front door caught his eye. Made of cloth, feathers, bits of wood and stone beads, it reminded him vaguely of a female body, but lacked hands, feet or features. Below it was a pile of rocks stacked neatly and topped with a lavender ceramic bowl filled with water.

She followed his gaze. "My prayer altar."

He lifted an eyebrow.

"It helps me focus. Would you care for tea? I have some raspberry that is just luscious."

"Okay." The house felt comfortable, with an open kitchen and exposed ceiling beams. Homey, but with a genteel air that didn't fit his preconceptions of how she lived but suited her anyway. Artistic bowls filled with smooth stones, beaded candle holders, and exotic sculptures decorated tables and shelves. Violets bloomed on the kitchen table. Ceramic lizards hung from the edge of the pot.

She had a lot of books. It looked like most were about spirituality or feminist studies. Quite a few were medical texts. Novels begged for his attention. It had been months since he'd been able to buy any books, and McClintock didn't have a library. He was hungry for a good read.

As soon as he sat down, the puppy sat on his feet and leaned against his shins. He stared up at Tate with one adoring brown eye and one adoring blue.

Diana filled a tin ball with loose tea, then hung it inside a squat teapot. She poured boiling water into the pot and a fruity aroma filled the air. She brought the pot, two mugs and a bowl of dark honey to the table.

"So what's your story?" he asked. "Where's your sister?"

She gave him a woebegone look. "She stole my horse."

On sunny days she rode the horse to work. She tethered him in the small field behind the Track Shack. "Are you sure? Maybe she went for a ride."

"She also stole clothing, food, camping supplies and about three hundred dollars in cash. She is definitely gone."

"Huh."

Shaking her head, she chuckled, a rueful note. "It isn't

my place to judge, but merely to experience. But darn it, I am sick to death of her ripping me off!''

Well, well, she *was* angry. He thought he'd never see the day. "She's done this kind of thing before?''

She rolled her eyes and made a sound full of disgust.

He took that as a yes. "Why would she steal your horse?'' He nodded toward the driveway. "That is her car, right?''

"That's what she drove up in, but whether or not it's hers, I have no idea. She's running from something.''

"What? Or should I say, who?''

"I suppose she's running from whoever shot her.'' She lifted the teapot lid, sniffed, then poured steaming, fragrant, reddish tea into two mugs.

This was getting interesting. "How did she get herself shot?''

"I don't know. She claimed she tripped and hit a sharp rock. Which is a lie. It's definitely a bullet wound, a few days old, with signs of infection.'' She tapped her left arm. "It took a chunk out of her triceps. I should have told you yesterday. I should have told you as soon as she showed up!''

"Why did she come to you?''

"She didn't.'' She waved a hand in a slow circle. "She came to this place. She was as surprised to see me as I was to see her.''

"I don't get it.''

"This cabin has been in my family for years. We used to come here for vacations. Hiking and such in the summers, and skiing in the winters.'' She smiled, her gaze gone distant. "Anyway, Bernie didn't know I was living here.''

His curiosity about Diana's background upped a notch. "Is O'Malley your family name?''

"Yes. Dover's my married name. I'm divorced." Her brows lowered. "Did you know my father? Peter O'Malley? No, you haven't lived in McClintock long enough. He died twelve years ago."

"Before my time. I was just wondering why people call this the O'Malley place." She began grinning at him.

"What?" he asked.

Her grin took a wicked turn. "I've seen you in uniform a lot of times. But this is the first time I've ever seen you acting like a cop." She wagged her eyebrows. "It's kind of a turn-on."

She was kidding, expressing gratitude in her own weird way. Still, his ego puffed a bit. "You're a real clown, Red. Back to your sister. You're positive she took off into the wilderness."

"It's not as crazy as it sounds. Bernie is an accomplished outdoorswoman. She's familiar with this country."

He pulled out a notebook and flipped it open to a blank page. "Do you want to file a complaint?"

"No. But I'm going to anyway."

He was happy to hear it. "What's her full name?"

"Bernadette Marie O'Malley…." Her voice trailed and she frowned. "Who knows what alias she's using. She's even impersonated me before."

"How about a description of her?"

"Look across the table. She's my identical twin."

Chapter Three

Tate radioed in a request to run the Buick's license plate. The state patrol had handheld computers that could run plates in seconds; McClintock couldn't afford the gadgetry.

While waiting for dispatch, he studied the horizon. A few stars were visible in the east. To the north, west and south spread the Maya Valley with its rolling hills and boulder outcrops. To the east, across the road from the farm, was a thick pine forest, rocky and cut through by steep ravines and the Maya River. If Bernadette had taken off right after Diana left for work this morning, she could have reached the mountains by now.

Tate had taken part in search and rescues. Half the time, searches ended tragically, or never ended at all. The Rockies had a habit of swallowing people. Bernadette couldn't have chosen a better place to disappear.

Diana had her lower lip caught in her teeth.

"Worried?" Tate asked.

"I shouldn't waste energy worrying about her. She certainly doesn't concern herself with me."

"Stock theft is taken seriously around here. We'll get your horse back."

"It's not just the horse. Bernie's arm is infected. It was

a through and through wound, but if the bullet nicked bone... I should have dragged her into town. She needs antibiotics.''

He scanned the horizon again. Pinpoints of lights indicated other ranches and farms. "She didn't drop any clues about who might have shot her?''

Diana leaned against the cruiser and folded her arms. Dusky light made her eyes seem bigger, luminous. She reminded him of a woodland nymph creeping from the shadows of the forest and into the moonlight. He shook the whimsical thoughts away. Her and her damned talk about sexual tension!

"She gave me a story about having to quit her job in a Las Vegas casino because her boss was sexually harassing her. It was a lie. I believe the part about Las Vegas, but nothing else. She probably robbed a liquor store or something.''

If the Buick was hot, ditching it made sense. What would also make sense would be to wait for Diana to fall asleep then steal the pickup truck. To steal a horse and head for the hills, however, didn't make sense—unless the woman was a desperate fugitive. "Does she have a habit of robbing liquor stores?''

"As a teenager, Bernie was busted for burglary. She'd done a lot of petty crimes before that, and always talked her way out of trouble. The burglary put her in a juvenile facility. It's been downhill ever since." Her eyes held a distant expression, as if she saw beyond the stars. "Mother wanted to save her, Dad wanted her to sink or swim. I've tried to resist helping her, but..." She shrugged. "I can say no to Bernie in the abstract, but not face-to-face. She's so...Bernie.''

He listened with half an ear to the radio traffic.

"I haven't heard from her in years. Until she showed

up day before yesterday, I didn't know if she was dead or alive."

"I thought twins were close," he said. "Psychic connection and all that."

She cocked her head, her smile faint. "Nobody in my family was ever close to anyone." A wistful comment that made Tate want to pat her shoulder, or even hug her. "We were afflicted by anger."

"You don't strike me as an angry person."

"I used to be." She looked around the farm. "It's pathetic. She consistently makes poor choices. She takes and never gives. She lies, steals...all she has to do is smile and I fall all over myself to bail her out of trouble."

Tate heard his call letters. He brought the mike to his mouth and told the dispatcher to go ahead. She informed him that the Buick had been reported stolen last Sunday, in Kingman, Arizona.

"Well?" Diana asked.

"Car's hot. Did she leave keys?"

"No."

He reported to the dispatcher his intention to process the vehicle. She dropped the official language and said, "You're *still* not on duty, Tate. Sheriff will squawk about overtime."

"Can't be helped, Ellen. Call the garage for a tow truck. Then contact the state boys and see if they have a forensic tech available. I might have a real crime scene for them to look at."

Ellen's laugh came through tinny and sharp. "You just can't stay out of trouble, can you?"

"I try, but it finds me anyway. Over and out."

He fetched an evidence kit from the cruiser's trunk. He pulled on latex gloves, then took out a nine-volt flashlight and a slim jim. He flexed the thin metal. Before he jimmied the Buick's driver door, he tried the handle. It was unlocked. As soon as he opened the door, he caught a whiff of a disgustingly familiar stench. Recoiling, he snorted. He'd know that stink anywhere.

Diana clapped a hand over her mouth and nose. "There's a body in there!"

The certainty in her voice stunned him. The vast majority of civilians went their entire lives without smelling a corpse. He noticed the puppy creeping closer, his nose working. "Better tie up your dog."

The Buick had a blue cloth interior. The flashlight beam picked up fast-food wrappers, discarded clothing and large stains that might be blood. The reek gagged him. He'd processed a lot of corpses, some of them in advanced stages of decomposition, but he never got used to the smell. A blanket-shrouded bundle lay on the back seat. He opened the back door. He carefully lifted a corner of the blanket and saw hair and a human ear.

"Bet the Buick's owner won't want this back," he muttered and lowered the blanket.

Diana appeared curious and concerned. "Is it a man or a woman?"

"Don't know yet. Can't touch anything until forensics gets here." He returned to the cruiser, but instead of using the radio, he called Gil Vance on a cellular phone. When the sheriff answered, Tate said, "I've got a body. Possible homicide, maybe even a murder."

Gil breathed an obscenity. Murder was rare in the Maya Valley. Tate had investigated very few since he'd been working for the sheriff's department. Only one had required real detective work. Tate gave the location and particulars; Gil ran down the list of authorities and technicians he would contact. Tate asked for an APB on Bernadette O'Malley. "She's Diana Dover's identical twin."

"I didn't know she had a twin sister."

"I didn't, either. She has a gunshot wound that needs medical attention. And she stole Diana's horse."

"Now that was a mistake, wasn't it? I'll put the state police and forest service on alert, and be there quick as I can."

THE BUICK WITH ITS macabre cargo drew Diana's gaze, as compelling as an itch. Having a body on her property was bad. Much worse was the memory of Bernie sitting at the kitchen table, making small talk and complaining about her sore arm, then sleeping in Diana's bed, all the while aware that there was a dead person in her car. It was as if Bernie were from a different planet.

Diana focused on Tate while he talked on a cell phone and paced thoughtfully around the Buick. Lantern light reflected off the equipment attached to his belt. His khaki shirt fit snugly over broad shoulders, the shirt sleeves stretched over massive biceps. His size alone made him stand out in a crowd. He was at least six feet four inches tall, and she estimated his weight at around two hundred and forty solidly muscular pounds. Add to that jet-black hair and a rugged face, and he was not only imposing, but very attractive, too.

He thought she was kidding about the sexual tension between them. Or maybe he was just scared.

Something beyond the physical drew her to him. The first time they'd met, she'd sensed his sorrow. Deep wounds scabbed over by time and force of will, but unhealed. He smiled, he joked, he walked with the proud stride of a confident man, but the sorrow was always there.

She supposed sorrow was part of her life path. She'd

certainly had enough of it in her life. She'd healed her wounds, and perhaps she was fated to help him heal his.

He finished talking on the telephone. For all his size, his step was graceful and sure while he walked toward the house. It was easy to imagine him melting hearts on a dance floor.

She looked past him to the Buick. Bernie had eaten heartily, and even joked around. It boggled her mind, and scared her, too. How dead did a soul have to be in order to act so callous? "What happens next?"

"A forensics team is on the way. The medical examiner needs to take a look before we move the body." His smile turned apologetic and he urged her inside the house. "It'll take some time. So let's talk about your sister. When exactly did she show up?"

She went to the stove to prepare a fresh pot of tea. She turned off the flame under a pot of soup. She didn't have much of an appetite. "Day before yesterday, not too long after I got home from work. Five-thirty?"

"Is she armed?"

"With a weapon? Bernie is not violent." She felt like an idiot. She knew what her sister was and what she was capable of doing, and still, she hadn't heeded her instincts. "I'm sorry for not telling you about her earlier."

"What's done is done. Did you ask her why she was here?"

"When she lied about the gunshot wound, I knew it was useless to ask questions. I don't think she knows the difference between fact and fantasy." It was always this way with Bernie. Heartbreaking love, boundless sorrow, pathetic hope, raging fury. Turmoil unsettled her blood and soured her stomach.

"Diana?"

Her eyes burned and her throat ached. A good cry

would flush the toxins from her system, but now was not the time. "She said she'd gone to Phoenix to visit Mother. She didn't know Mother had died."

"When did she pass?"

She sniffed back the urge to weep. "Five years ago. When Mother was ill, she asked me to find Bernie. I was the good daughter, taking care of Mother, seeing to her every need. And all she wanted was Bernie." She swiped a hand across her eyes and drew a deep breath. The past was past. Life was now. "It's not up to me to decide how others should feel."

"How did Bernie take the news about your mother's death?"

"She asked if Mother had left her any money."

"Did she?"

"Certainly. Mother left me a house and this property. The bulk of her estate goes to Bernie." She lowered her face and focused on the emotions climbing through her chest. "When Mother was sick, Bernie called collect several times. I refused the calls until she stopped trying. Pretty shabby on my part. I'm still ashamed of what I did."

"How can Bernie get her hands on her inheritance?"

"By contacting the executor. His name is Hugh Bardenow." She spelled the name for him. "I don't have his telephone number or address. Sorry. He's a partner in the law firm of Beatty, Brush and Bardenow in Scottsdale, Arizona."

"So she's in Vegas, then makes it to Kingman where she steals the car. How old do you think the gunshot wound is?"

Bernie's injury worried Diana. If the bullet had nicked bone, the infection could be originating from there. That type of infection could easily turn into gangrene. "It was scabbed over, but inflamed. The bruising was turning green. I'd say three or four days old when she arrived.''

God, she prayed, all that happens is part of Your greater plan. Help me remember I have the strength to deal with whatever comes. She scrunched her eyelids. And please, please, please keep Bernie safe.

Tate touched her arm. He had lovely eyes, dark velvety brown, framed by thick black brows. Intelligent, expressive eyes, quick and sharp. She drew from them strength and sympathy. He patted her hand. ''We'll find her.''

She poured tea, and added a dollop of honey to hers. She sipped, focusing on the sweet warmth and soothing fragrance. Bernie chose her own path. When it happened to cross Diana's, all she could do was ride out the tempest.

''This isn't making sense,'' he said.

''You wouldn't say that if you knew Bernie. She's a, um, chaotic personality.''

''She's got a hot car and a corpse. It makes sense to ditch both. But if she has a lot of money waiting for her in Phoenix, why steal a horse?'' He grinned widely. ''Ha! Because the campgrounds are filling up and folks in the great outdoors aren't that careful about their property.''

''She'll steal another car and head for Phoenix?'' Her belly lurched queasily. ''Oh my lord, did she kill the person in the Buick?''

''I have no idea.'' He focused on the notes he wrote. ''Does she have friends around here?''

Diana gave the question careful consideration. Her family spent many vacations in the Maya Valley. Her father had meticulously planned their days, as ferociously driven in recreation as he had been about his career. There had been no time for either sister to make friends with the locals.

''I can't think of anyone.''

A vehicle's lights flashed across the windows. Tippy leaped to his feet and pricked his ears. Tate went to the door. ''Is there anything outdoors you absolutely have to do?''

''Not really.''

''Hang out in here then. It'll take hours to process the car. Are you all right?''

She flashed her most reassuring smile. ''Don't worry your pretty head about me.''

He went outdoors to meet the sheriff.

Before too long, official vehicles and people filled the driveway and yard. Halogen lamps illuminated the crime scene. A rattling generator disturbed the silence of the night. When an ambulance arrived, Diana watched through the window. A man examined the corpse. The medical examiner, she supposed, officially declaring the body deceased.

As morbidly fascinating as the crime scene was, Diana pulled away from the windows. She tried to read, but after catching herself reading the same paragraph over and over, she gave up. She tried some housework, but kept ending up at the windows. Finally, she threw herself into the task of making bread. She mixed ingredients by hand, stirring the increasingly stiff dough until her arm ached. Kneading the dough further eased tension from her aching soul.

She was dozing on the sofa when Tate knocked on the door. ''Come in,'' she called, and stretched. She yawned mightily and pushed off the sofa. Chilled, she rubbed her arms. ''Are you finished? What time is it?''

''After midnight. I didn't mean to wake you.''

She waved off his concern.

He sniffed the air. ''Is that bread?''

"Honey whole wheat, my specialty. I always do my best baking when I'm upset. So what did you find out?"

"Victim's a male. Fifty-two years old. Brown hair, slight build. A parole card identifies him as Timothy James Robertson of Las Vegas, Nevada. Ring any bells with you?"

She gave it some thought, useless as it was. "No. Cause of death?"

"You don't want to know details."

"I'm not delicate."

He looked over his shoulder at the blaze of lights. "He was shot, at least twice. Looks like he bled out. He's been dead maybe four days, maybe five. We'll know more after the autopsy."

She intuited he held back something important. "Did Bernie murder him?"

"Too soon to tell." He closed the door. "We found an empty ammunition box. We have to go with the assumption that your sister is armed and dangerous."

Diana dropped onto a chair. She rested her face on her hands. She knew what Tate implied. If Bernie did anything reckless when approached by law officers, she could end up dead.

"I'm sorry," Tate said.

"She chose her path. She'll have to deal with the consequences. Want some bread?" Without awaiting his reply, she walked to the stove. It had taken months to learn how to properly use the old propane fueled stove and how to deal with the altitude. She rarely burned anything these days. She pulled a serrated bread knife from a wooden holder. There wasn't enough bread to slice in all the world to lessen her worry about her wayward sister.

"Do you have a photograph we can circulate?"

"No."

"What about of yourself?"

She paused in the midst of slicing. The few photos she'd kept from her former life seemed to be of a total stranger. "You can take mug shots of me. If I pull my hair back, I'll look pretty much like her. She's thinner than me, though. I'd say she doesn't weigh more than one twenty. I'm closer to one forty."

He made a strangled sound.

"Did I say something funny?"

He shook his head, but the way he fought a smile said otherwise. "I've never had a female volunteer her weight before."

She looked down at herself. She'd put on a few pounds and felt healthier for it. "It's only meat. More or less of it doesn't change who I am." She piled sliced bread on a plate and opened a jar of homemade apple butter.

He inhaled deeply, his eyelids lowering. "I shouldn't..." He slathered apple butter on a slice of bread and bit into it. "Does Consuela know you make bread like this?"

"I wouldn't dare even suggest messing around in her kitchen. So what happens next?"

"I'd like for you to stay in McClintock. It isn't safe here."

"In case Bernie comes back?" She shook her head. "She'll steal from me, but she won't hurt me." She almost claimed that her sister had never been violent, but Bernie sported a gunshot wound and there was a corpse in a stolen car. "At least, I don't think she would. And, I have to take care of my animals. Not to mention, there's that darned bear."

"You have a pet bear?" His face wrinkled in comical confusion.

She laughed. "No! A bear destroyed two of my hives

last fall. He came back this spring. I put up a fence, but you haven't seen persistence until you've seen this bear.''

"Have you contacted the wildlife people?"

"I don't want him hurt. I just want him to leave my hives alone.''

He swung his head and his big shoulders shook with silent laughter. "Your welfare comes before the animals. You need to leave.''

The sheriff knocked on the door and Diana invited him indoors. He was about her height, but stocky and powerfully built. She watched him take in the house. Unlike Tate, whose expressive face had registered surprise, bemusement and amusement, Gil Vance merely swept the place with his impassive gaze. She invited him to sit and offered him some bread. He refused both.

"The state police and forest service are checking out camp grounds and trail heads. If she runs into searchers or road blocks, she may double back. I want you to vacate this house until your sister is in custody.''

Diana bit back protests that Bernie wasn't violent. She no longer felt certain about anything concerning her sister. "Even if Bernie doesn't believe I'd report my stolen horse, she has to realize I'd eventually discover the body. She won't come back.''

"Depends on how desperate she gets. If you can't afford to stay in a hotel or a bed and breakfast, I'll find someone to put you up until your sister is taken into custody.''

"No.''

"We're hoping it won't take— No?'' His eyebrows drew into a deep frown. "This isn't a matter for debate, Diana.''

"I already explained to Tate. I can't leave my animals.''

"Diana," Tate said, "Be reason—"

"I'm not being unreasonable. I understand your concerns. But I can't leave."

The sheriff scowled and shifted his stance into one of aggressive authority with his shoulders back and his fists on his narrow hips. "There's protective custody."

She smiled. "If you're trying to scare me, Gil, it won't work. I know what a big softie you are." She noticed Tate pulling his chin and pointedly not looking at the sheriff. "If you'd like, I'll sign a waiver, releasing you from any responsibility for me in this matter."

"Is she always this stubborn?" Gil asked Tate.

"Usually she's worse."

Gil muttered under his breath, then shook his head. "Whether you're here or not, I'm posting a man on this property in case your sister returns."

"She won't."

"For her sake," Gil said. "I hope she does."

Chapter Four

Tate strode into the Track Shack and stopped short in amazement. It wasn't even nine in the morning and all tables were occupied, and people lined the bar. The air was heavy with conversation and the smell of bacon and huevos rancheros. Both weekend waitresses were circulating with coffeepots. Unable to account for why the place was so busy, he blinked at the sight.

He was wired, buzzing, itchy for action. He'd worked all night on the Robertson homicide, cursing the sketchy information available, but excited by it, too. Before he'd moved to McClintock, he'd been a New York City homicide detective. Investigating was in his blood, and he was fired up—even if Gil couldn't decide if it was their case or not.

No one knew where Robertson had been shot or where he'd died. Gil wanted to hand the case over to the state police; they had the budget for a proper investigation. Tate had convinced the sheriff to hold off playing musical-jurisdictions until after they picked up Bernadette.

He needed sleep, but doubted if he could shut off his brain. A decent cup of coffee was the next best thing.

Diana pushed through the kitchen doors. She balanced

a laden tray on one hand. He spotted her, she spotted him and in unison they frowned.

People shouted questions at him about the homicide. He recognized regulars, but quite a few customers were people who'd never stepped inside the Shack before. He waved off the curiosity, telling people he couldn't discuss an active case. He guessed the major topic of conversation throughout the valley was the body found on Diana's farm.

Finally, he said, "Read about it in the newspaper," and escaped into the kitchen.

Diana brought him a cup of coffee. She looked him up and down. He still wore his uniform. He needed a shower.

"What are you doing?" she asked. "I thought you were in back, asleep."

He gulped a slug of coffee. *Ahh*. The sludge Gil insisted was coffee tasted like motor oil. This was manna. "Haven't been to bed yet. And I could ask you the same thing. Isn't it Saturday?"

"I couldn't stay home. Too antsy. I saw how busy Susan and Anne were, so decided to help. Which was a mistake, since everyone wants to talk about Bernie and the body. I don't know what to say." She tugged his tie. "You look awful."

He saluted with the coffee cup. "Thanks.

"Have you learned anything?" she asked.

He rubbed the back of his neck. At the moment, all he had were questions with not a single answer in sight. Consuela was giving him the evil eye. He leaned in close and spoke for Diana's ears only. "Come on back to my apartment. I'll fill you in."

"Is it that bad?"

"Afraid so." He glanced at his watch. "Give me ten minutes to shower. See if you can sweet-talk Consuela into making me up something to eat. I don't care what. I'm so hungry, I'd eat sawdust.''

In the relative quiet of his apartment, the shower relaxed him almost too much. He caught himself drowsing under the spray. He cut off the water and stepped out. He wiped steam off the bathroom mirror and stared into his bleary eyes. At thirty-eight, he wasn't a kid anymore, able to run non-stop for days at a time. He thought about shaving, decided not to, and dressed in a clean T-shirt and jeans. Diana knocked on the door and he welcomed her inside.

She set down a tray loaded with a bowl of stew, a hamburger on a whole wheat bun and a salad. The brown bread made him curl his lip. She was always badgering him to stop eating white flour and sugar. At the moment, he was too hungry to gripe.

Diana sat across the table from him. She appeared to be in no hurry to hear whatever bad news he had to share. She looked around the efficient apartment. Her gaze lingered longest on the overflowing bookshelves.

Odd embarrassment trickled through him. This apartment was functional, nothing more. A place to sleep, store his belongings and work on his computer. Compared to Diana's pretty house, it was a slum.

Who cared? he told himself harshly and concentrated on the food.

He finally leaned back and patted his belly. A yawn escaped before he could stop it. "So, about your sister."

Her chest rose and sank in a silent sigh.

"She's got quite a rap sheet. Most of the charges are for non-violent crimes. Drugs, kiting bad checks, prostitution."

"Most?" she asked.

"She did some hard time in prison. Armed robbery. That's where she was when your mother died."

She placed a hand over her mouth.

"Robertson is quite the gentleman, too. Lucky him, he won't be going back to the slammer. Not that he'll be missed. He's a serial sex offender."

"A rapist?"

"That, too."

"Why did they let him out of prison?"

"I don't believe those scumbags are ever rehabilitated, but parole boards don't share my views. Anyway, it's not the sex offenses that makes this interesting. It's armed robbery. He has a habit of hitting places where he can take hostages. Specifically, young female hostages. I put in a query to Kingman to see what kind of trouble they've had lately."

"Was Bernie that man's hostage?"

"I doubt it. There are signs that she tried to stop his bleeding. It looks like they've been together for a while. We found receipts in the car that show she went from Kingman to the Phoenix area, then up the back way through northern Arizona and into Colorado."

"They were shot committing a robbery?"

He popped a pickle slice in his mouth. From where he sat the futon that served as both bed and couch was visible behind Diana. The futon cover was dark green; the way her hair looked against it distracted his fuzzy brain.

"Tate?"

He blinked rapidly. She repeated the question and he replied, "Anything is possible."

Her face was calm, but she was folding a scrap of paper into increasingly tiny squares.

"I put out inquiries. Nevada, Arizona, Utah and Colorado. We'll hear sometime today if she's wanted."

She picked at minuscule crumbs on the tray and deposited them in the salad bowl. Shaking her head, she huffed through her nose. "I need to be more careful what I wish for. Just the other day I was thinking I needed a bit of excitement."

"The forest service, state police, tribal police and our sheriff's department are blanketing the area. We put flyers into circulation. I got through to the attorney in Arizona. If she contacts him, he'll let us know immediately. Bernadette has nowhere to go. That makes her dangerous."

"You don't think I should go home."

"Right."

"What about my animals? The goats and chickens need to be fed twice a day. I can't leave Tippy all alone. He's just a baby."

He didn't know whether to express disgust or laugh. He did intuit that neither reaction would change her mind. He rubbed his scratchy eyes. "Pray," he said.

"Hmm, you're right," she said agreeably as if she hadn't noticed his sarcastic tone. Her eyelids slid closed. Her lashes were short, lush and copper-colored.

Maybe, he mused, she had a point about not wearing makeup. It would be a real shame to goop up those pretty eyes and flawless skin.

TATE STARTLED, CAUGHT inside a dream. He held on tight to a rope or a vine while Diana, naked and glowing, stood on the far side of a wide canyon. A river roared through the canyon. White water pounded the canyon walls. Diana was yelling at him to swing across. And God help him, but he wanted to try. Her voice rose higher and higher, shrill and louder than the roaring waters.

The dream released its hold and he propped himself on an elbow.

The telephone jangled. He groped for the handset and gave his head a shake. He couldn't tell by the light if it was morning or evening. "Raleigh."

"Hey, jarhead, did I catch you napping?"

It was his friend, Ric Buchanan. No official emergency. Tate flopped back down on the futon. He brought his wristwatch close to his face. He'd caught almost three hours of sleep. Not enough, but it would have to do.

"Pulled an all-nighter, man." He yawned noisily. "What's up?"

"I heard you were working a big case. A problem up at Diana's. Is she okay?"

"She's fine. What's up with you?"

"I wanted to know if we're still on for tomorrow. Your roof?"

"Oh, right." He scrubbed his eyes with the heel of his hand. He forced himself to a sitting position. His whole body ached. *Almost forty,* a nasty little voice reminded him, *getting old.* "Truth is, buddy, I don't know if I'm coming or going right now."

"Tell you what. Drop off the keys with Uncle Walt, then he and I will come over tomorrow and work on the roof."

"Good of you, man, but—"

"Never turn down an offer, jarhead. 'Sides, it's not like I have anything better to do. Nothing good on television, and the girls went with Lillian to Denver for the weekend."

Tate grinned. Ric's mother-in-law liked nothing better than roping her two daughters and granddaughter into a major shopping spree. Then it sank in who exactly he was talking to. He sat straighter and his toes curled, catching the shabby carpeting.

"Is your old trailer still hooked up to utilities?"

Ric lived on McClintock Ranch with his wife and daughter. He also owned ten acres north of town. Before he married Elaine, he'd lived up there in a trailer. He'd built a barn on the property, and someday intended to build a house. The property also boasted the fanciest hot tub setup Tate had ever seen.

"It's got electricity, and I can turn on the propane. No telephone, though. Why?"

Tate explained Diana's situation.

"If she needs to," Ric said, "she and her animals are more than welcome to hang at my place. I don't mind. In fact, if you need help moving her, let me know."

Tate almost asked if the hot tub was operational, but bit back the words. He had no intention of using the thing, or inviting Diana to use it with him. He refused to even imagine her soaking and sweating in the steaming water. "You're too good, my man. I'll call you back after I clear this with Diana."

He disconnected and stared at the telephone. Diana's prayers were mighty powerful things.

He dressed, pulled on shoes and tamed his hair the best he could. As soon as he opened the apartment door, the noise from the dining room hit him. It wasn't even a pay-day weekend, or after dark, and the place sounded packed to the rafters. Who'd have imagined a corpse in a stolen car would be good for business?

In the kitchen, Consuela shouted at a skinny young man who was chopping onions. Another young man scrubbed dishes. They were Consuela's grandsons, recruited to help out. A waitress, bearing a tray of dirty glasses and a hand-ful of order tickets, banged through the batwing doors. She spotted Tate and shot him a dizzy smile.

"Busy?" he asked innocently.

"Half the town has been in today, and I think the other

half is coming.'' She laughed. ''You go out there and you'll be mobbed. Everybody wants to know about the big fugitive hunt.''

Consuela snatched the order tickets out of the waitress's hand. ''You gonna stand there while my chilies get cold, girl?''

''Is Diana still here?'' Tate asked.

''I have never seen her frazzled like that. Guys were actually grabbing her so they could ask about her sister. She split a while ago.''

Consuela turned blazing eyes on Tate. ''You gonna waste this girl's time all day? Rellenos shriveling, hamburgers drowning in cold grease. What kind of way is that to treat good food, eh?''

Tate held up his hands and backed away. ''Okay, okay, I'm out of here.''

''We can manage, Tate,'' the waitress assured him. ''Go on back to sleep or whatever. We'll call if the place catches fire.'' She loaded plates on a tray and hustled out of the kitchen.

Tate decided now would be a good time to visit Diana and tell her the good news. He holstered a Glock 9mm on his hip, and affixed his cell phone on the other side of his belt. He slipped out via the back door.

On the drive to Diana's farm, he called the sheriff. Gil hadn't heard back on Robertson's autopsy yet. Bernadette seemed to have vanished off the face of the earth.

''If we find out,'' Gil said, ''that Robertson died before he hit the Colorado border, I'm finding somebody to dump him on.''

Tate laughed.

''You think I'm kidding. I'm not. I can't afford a murder investigation.''

On that happy note, Tate hung up, then turned into

Diana's sorry excuse for a driveway. Despite the lack of sleep, he felt great. Nothing fired his engines faster than a good investigation.

He topped the hill and spotted a man seated on Diana's front porch. Even at a distance, Tate recognized the huge yellow straw cowboy hat with a bright red band as belonging to Moe Sherwood, a volunteer deputy. Diana was in her garden plot. A floppy purple hat shaded her face from the sun. She sat back on her heels and waved to him.

Holding a rifle, Moe stepped off the porch. He had the loose walk and bowed legs of a horseman. When he wasn't volunteering for the sheriff's department, he grew hay and outfitted big-game hunters.

Tate parked his old Bronco. The truck shivered, the engine rattling to a stop. Tate tensed at the sound. He couldn't afford repairs right now. The door sagged when he shoved it open—the hinges were nearly shot. "You on watch, Moe?"

"10-4. Any sign of the perp yet?" Moe loved cop lingo. He wore his silver deputy badge with pride.

"Not a hair. I take it things are quiet here."

"No problems." A smile creased his leathery face. "That Diana is one heck of a cook. Consuela best watch her back."

"I'll tell her you said so."

The smile vanished, and Moe's eyes widened. "Just joshing. Don't you be ratting me out to Consuela. She'll spit in my stew."

Tate gave him an evil grin. He wasn't the only man in town who ran scared of the hot-tempered cook. Heading for the garden plot, he whistled a sappy tune.

Diana knelt in the dirt, using a hand rake to scrape up weeds. Her puppy was helping by digging enthusiastically. His snout and forelegs were black with dirt.

"Get enough sleep?" she asked.

"No, but I did find a place for you to stay."

"Gil is shipping me to Siberia?"

"He probably considered it, but no. Ric Buchanan has land north of here. It's got a trailer and barn. He says you can use it as long as you like. And all your beasts, too."

"Isn't that sweet?" She rose and swiped dirt off her cotton gloves. "You did tell him my beasts are goats, right?"

"No problem."

"I am most grateful then." She pulled off the hat and armed hair off her forehead. She left a smudge on her skin. "As I imagine you are. Will you continue to post people here in case Bernie returns?"

"Yes."

"Good. They can feed and water my chickens. It only takes a few minutes."

He turned his back on her distracting smile and called Ric. His friend promised to hook up the propane for the trailer.

Tate slid the phone back into its holster. He held barbed wire strands apart for Diana to leave the garden.

"Guess I ought to pack a few clothes and supplies. Ever rounded up goats before?"

"I've never even touched a goat."

"You're in for a treat then."

With Moe's help, they loaded Tate's Bronco with supplies. Diana would transport the goats in her pickup. Tate noticed the way Moe seemed starry-eyed around Diana. Moe had never been married, never intended to marry and, like many old bachelors, was innately suspicious of all things female. Yet, he grinned like an idiot whenever she smiled or spoke.

Tate didn't like it. He didn't like that he didn't like it.

It almost felt like jealousy, which was crazy since he didn't have a jealous bone in his body. Not that he had any proprietary interest in Diana to jealously protect. And the way his thoughts kept returning to things like *that* annoyed the devil out of him.

Hands on her hips, Diana frowned at a roll of wire fencing. "I better bring this, just in case. Those little boogers are escape artists. A regular stock fence won't hold them."

Moe all but tripped over himself in his rush to grab the fencing and hoist it on his shoulder. He grunted with the weight and staggered toward the Bronco.

Show off, Tate thought darkly. He helped Diana wrestle a stock rack into place around the bed of her pickup.

Diana started her truck. "I have to drive in on the far side. I'll meet you boys in the pasture."

It was only after she headed down a rutted path that it occurred to Tate that goats could be dangerous. He turned to Moe. "Do goats bite?"

Moe scratched beneath his hat. "Don't rightly know." He walked up the rocky hill toward the pasture.

Tate had never owned a pet. He liked dogs, tolerated cats, but until he moved to Colorado, the closest he'd ever come to livestock was in a butcher shop. Goats. Shaking his head in trepidation, he followed Moe up the hill.

By the time the men reached a gate, Diana had already pulled the pickup into the pasture. The puppy was chasing the goats. Belly nearly to the ground, he stalked across the rocky field, then darted in and out. The tricolored goat bleated and shook nubbin horns threateningly at the dog. Head and tail low, the dog faced the goat squarely.

"She's got herself a good pup there," Moe said.

"Because it chases goats?" He made sure the gate was

closed securely behind them. He hoped the dog kept the goats far away from him.

"He ain't chasing, he's herding. Look at that! Just like he knows what he's doing."

Tate realized Moe was right. The puppy was trying to intimidate the goats into moving where he wanted them to move. He was almost succeeding.

Diana's laughter rang across the rocky pasture. "All right, Tippy, cut it out. Come!" She held a bucket. She shook it hard. As one, the goats turned to her and began bleating. They ran toward her, their legs stiff, rocking along like windup toys.

By the time the men reached her, she was surrounded by seven goats of various sizes, all trying to get their heads into the bucket. Their tails flipped furiously. Tate thought they were cute. Especially the black goats with their big floppy ears.

Then he saw their eyes. The pupils were dark rectangles in yellow irises, expressionless and alien. They reminded him of cat's eye marbles he played with as a boy. They gave him the willies.

"Do they bite?" he asked.

"No, but they do nibble," Diana answered.

As if to prove the point, a white goat began chewing on Tate's gun holster. He shooed it, but it merely stared with those creepy eyes and went after the holster again. Exactly what he needed, his Glock 9mm eaten by a goat. "Are you sure they don't bite?"

"No front teeth. But don't stick your fingers in their mouths. Those molars will take your skin off."

He couldn't think of anything in the world that could induce him to stick his hand in a goat's mouth. He shooed the persistent animal again. "How do we do this?"

Diana spread grain on the ground, then climbed into

the truck bed. "If you gentleman will hand them up to me, that will work. They don't weigh much."

Tate tried to dodge the white goat. It seemed enamored of the taste of the holster. It bleated at him and followed, lips flapping and tail flipping.

Moe grabbed a black goat around the belly. It *baa-ed* and bleated and kicked its hooves, but the man hoisted it over the truck gate to Diana. She eased it onto the metal bed. Its hooves rang and rattled.

Tate cast Moe a look askance. If the old coot could do it, then Tate surely could. He grabbed for the white goat. It skipped away. "C'mere you," he growled and lunged for it. It sprang into the air as if made of rubber. The puppy joined the game, cutting off the goat's escape. When the animals engaged in a staring contest, Tate grabbed the goat. It bleated in surprise. Grinning, Tate lugged it to the truck. As he lifted it over the gate, it flung its head back and struck his jaw.

The damn thing's head felt like a brick. Tate grunted, but hung on. Diana pulled it out of his arms.

"Good job," she said.

Rubbing his sore jaw, he turned for another goat. Moe grabbed a white goat. Tate picked up a black one. It was so fixated on the grain its neck strained and its lips nibbled even as Tate hoisted it into the truck.

A piercing shriek rent the air. Tate froze, staring toward the house where the scream had originated. Another screech ripped the sudden silence, then another which trailed into a strangled wail.

Diana jumped out of the truck and hit the ground running. Her speed astonished Tate. He wasted precious seconds gawking. Then it hit him that she could be rushing into danger. Drawing the Glock, he flicked off the safety and ran.

Chapter Five

Tate topped the ridge and bounded downhill. Jutting rocks and hummocks of grass threatened his footing. He kept the Glock held high and his eyes wide open. Once past the garage, he took in the scene in a sweeping glance. The front door of Diana's house was wide open. Diana stood in the middle of the driveway. A man ran down the driveway, toward the road.

Tate planted his feet in a shooter's stance and yelled, "Halt! Sheriff's department! Stop!"

The man stumbled and turned. Tate automatically assessed the man's appearance. Average height and weight, dark shirt, dark trousers. Dark glasses formed a featureless band across his upper face. Sunshine glinted on something metallic and black he held in both hands. *A gun!* Tate dived for Diana.

He locked an arm around her shoulders and sent her spinning toward the porch. He braced for the sound of gunfire, but the man was running again and disappeared over the hill. "Take cover! He's armed!" He ran after the intruder.

He hadn't even reached the hilltop before Diana screamed his name. He dug in his heels, torn between the chase and her cry for help. She was leaping in the air, waving both hands wildly.

He could catch the guy. He knew he could. But Diana needed him. "Damn it," he ground through his teeth.

Diana ran past the house, waving and yelling his name, her cries frantic. He ran back to join her. Sweat stung his eyes. His heart pounded. He hated letting that scumbag get away. Moe reached the driveway. He'd retrieved his rifle, but lost his big yellow hat.

Moe ran to the corner of the house. He dug the heels of his cowboy boots into the ground and skidded to a stop. He held his rifle across his chest. His eyes were as round as quarters. Tate would have run past him, but Diana yelled.

"Stop!" She faced the men, both hands thrust forward. "Don't move!"

Adrenaline pumped through his veins, souring his mouth and sharpening his senses. He smelled his own sweat and sun-warmed earth. Diana's eyes were wide, but not panicked. Behind her a dark cloud swirled and broke and gathered.

"Bees," Moe said. "Lots and lots of bees."

The gate on the dog run stood open. One of the hives was overturned. Bees swarmed around Diana, their angry buzzing vibrating the air. About ten feet from the fence, a man lay face down on the ground.

"Are either of you allergic to bee stings?" Diana called.

A shudder rippled through Tate's muscles. He hated bees. "No."

"Positive?"

"Positive."

"Moe?"

He swallowed hard, but answered that he was positive he wasn't allergic to bee stings.

"I need your help." She spoke calmly now, as if she didn't notice the bees swirling around her. "Tate, take off your shirt."

"What?"

"Black excites the bees. You're better off without the shirt. Please. Then walk normally and don't swat or wave your arms around. They're calming down. Let's keep them calm. Okay?"

He looked at Moe, Moe looked at him. No matter how creepy this was, that mope on the ground needed help. He holstered the Glock, grasped the hem of the black T-shirt he wore and ripped it over his head. He called himself an idiot for giving up even the thin protection the shirt offered. Moe gulped, his adam's apple bobbing, then placed his rifle gently on the ground. They walked into the swarm.

"These are honeybees," Diana said. "Gentle. They won't pursue us. It's important not to swat them. Okay?"

Tate felt bees crawling in his hair—his black hair. He forced down a groan. Moe's weathered face had turned pasty. The men grasped the downed man's shoulders. A bee stung Tate's palm. He gritted his teeth and pulled.

"Move slow," Diana said, her voice calm and assuring. She was gently scooping bees off the man's back and legs. "Pull him slow. Are you sure you aren't allergic?"

If he was, he was in trouble. Along with the sting on his hand, he had a sting on his back, and at least two on his forehead. A bee writhed in a frantic circle on Moe's forearm, trying to free itself from its embedded stinger. They pulled the man toward the house. As Diana had promised, the bees didn't pursue them. Those insects that could, flew away from the fallen man.

Diana urged them to roll the man over. The grotesque sight made Tate recoil. The man's face was purple and blotched, with his eyes swelled shut and his tongue protruding. He sported a shoulder harness holding a .22 automatic. Tate pulled the weapon free. It was fully loaded.

"Is he dead?" Moe asked.

"He will be. We need paramedics, right now." Diana dug in her pocket and produced a folding knife. She cut off the man's tie, then unceremoniously ripped open his shirt. His chest was as blue as his lips. She jerked the man's head back, exposing his swollen throat. Tate could see he wasn't breathing. She looked around. "Either of you have a ballpoint pen?"

Moe fished in a shirt pocket and brought out a pen. He handed it over and she unscrewed the barrel then flung the insides away. She clamped the nib end of the barrel between her teeth, then stretched taut the skin over the man's adam's apple.

"Diana?" Tate suspected what she meant to do, but didn't believe it.

"I said, call the paramedics. Now! Move it!" Sure and swift, she cut into the man's throat. Dark blood seeped and trickled. She jammed the pen barrel into the hole. Air rushed out. She held it in place with two fingers.

Tate flipped open his cell phone and dialed 911. He told Moe, "There's a first-aid kit under the passenger seat in my truck." Moe took off at a run. Tate reached emergency services.

"Tell them we have a man in anaphylactic shock and cardiac arrest. Get down here, hold the pen." As soon as he did so, she began compressing the man's chest. Tate relayed information from her to emergency services. His gut churned when she blew into the bloody pen barrel.

Brave woman. When Moe returned, she explained to Tate how to tape up the pen so it didn't shift.

She never broke rhythm in performing CPR. Sweat poured from her brow and dripped from the end of her nose. Her face turned bright red. Fifteen compressions, then two big breaths into the pen.

"Two man CPR is easier," he said. "I'll compress, you breathe." Even for a woman as fit as she was, CPR was hard work. She sat back on her heels, shook her hands and rubbed her biceps.

He folded his hands, found the man's sternum, then began compression. She counted five beats, then breathed into the pen.

It finally caught up to Tate that Diana had reacted like someone trained in emergency response. Not only did she know exactly what to do, but she was in total command. It felt perfectly natural to hop to when she ordered it.

"Hey, Red." He kept his eyes on his hands. His back and shoulders were burning with effort. One, two, three, four, five—Diana breathed into the pen. Sweat made bee stings burn like drops of molten metal. "Are you holding out on me? Are you a copper?"

"I've never been a police officer. Stop. Let's see if there's a pulse."

Tate sat back on his heels and flexed his aching hands. She probed the man's swollen throat and then his groin. She shook her head. He renewed CPR.

"Moe," she said, "don't pick at the bee stings. Use a credit card or driver's license to scrape them off. How does your tongue feel? Any shortness of breath?"

"I'm okay," Moe said.

Tate's stings burned like crazy. He didn't even want to know how many times he'd been stung. But he was able to assure Diana that he wasn't having an allergic reaction.

He strained his ears for the sound of sirens. Television shows made CPR look like a stroll in the park, but in reality it was exhausting work. His underarms grew greasy with sweat. His shoulders ached. He might have to keep this up for a long time until the paramedics arrived.

He waited for her to breathe for the guy again. Then he asked, "How'd you know how to help this clown?"

Moe leaned in close, his eyes bright with curiosity.

Diana sighed. "I'm a physician. Keep compressing, three, four, five…"

DIANA STOOD NEXT TO HER truck and fed bits of bread to the goats. She watched the ambulance drive away, its emergency lights flashing. Now that the excitement was over, her knees felt watery, and her chest ached. Her salivary glands were tight. She'd rinsed her mouth with straight peroxide then with vinegar. A useless exercise if the bee-stung man carried some blood-borne disease, but it made her feel a little better anyway.

Tate approached. He'd put his shirt back on, which she considered a shame. He had a body that could make an anatomy professor weep in ecstasy. Examining his well-defined pectorals and heavily muscled shoulders would make a fine diversion from her fugitive sister and gunmen invading her farm.

He stopped out of range of the goats' inquisitive nibbling. Clucking her tongue, she lightly fingered the bee-sting welts on his forehead and the developing bruise on his chin. "Poor Tate. My critters are giving you a working over today."

She rested a hand against his chest. Hanks of black hair fell boyishly over his forehead, and somehow made his flinty eyes look dangerous. His temperament was mellow, good humored. He didn't need excessive noise or bluster to call attention to himself. If, however, the man who'd run away ever got a good look at Tate's expression, as it was now, he'd flee the state and never look back.

"I'll live." He cocked his head, his gaze probing. "Guess that explains the couch."

"What?"

"I was wondering how you afforded that leather couch on what I pay you. How come you didn't tell me you're a doctor?"

She looked past him to Gil. The sheriff sat inside a marked Range Rover. He was writing up the incident. Moe sat inside the Rover, too, probably filling in details.

"It doesn't have anything to do with waitressing," she said.

"You saved that guy's life. The paramedics are way impressed."

She'd never heard this tone of voice from him before. It occurred to her that he might be angry with her. She drew her head aside. "If he lives, it'll be God's doing, not mine." She shoved her shaky hands in her pockets.

"So what gives? If you're a doctor, why are you working in a dive and living in the middle of nowhere?"

The past was gone, an illusion, nothing to dwell on, nothing to talk about. She walked her dharmic path now. "Let's just say I wasn't supposed to be a physician."

"Your hands looked pretty good to me."

He *was* angry. This felt like an interrogation. "My hands were never the problem." She dropped her gaze to his sidearm. The man who'd been stung by bees had been carrying a weapon. The man who ran away probably did, too. Thinking about them made her shiver. "I'm suddenly in a hurry to get out of here."

He scratched furiously at his ribs. "Right."

"Are you mad at me?"

He turned his head, revealing a set jaw and thunderous brow. He grabbed her shoulders and gave her a little shake. He was trembling. "Damn it! That mope had a gun! I know you're nuts, but I didn't know you're crazy! You scared the hell out of me. I don't believe you took off running like that!"

She blinked rapidly. Reviewing what had happened, she conceded that his anger was justified. Years as an emergency room physician had trained her to react. Personal danger had not even entered the equation.

She could have been killed.

"I'm sorry," she whispered. "I didn't think."

He gave her another little shake, but as his hands slid off her shoulders it almost felt like a caress. "You... you're...you're the best waitress I ever had. I don't want to lose you."

So the anger was more personal than professional. She was contrite, but pleased, too, that he cared so much. She hugged herself.

Gil and Moe left the Rover. In unison, they settled broad-brimmed hats on their heads. Gil stared in the direction the ambulance had gone. He handed a cell phone to Moe and said something that caused the old cowboy to nod. Then Gil beckoned to Tate and Diana. He walked toward the beehives. The bees had settled, but he stopped a good thirty feet away. "What the heck is your sister into, Diana?"

"I wish I knew," she said. Bernadette's criminal behavior had begun early. In grammar school she'd been a liar and a thief, a chronic truant and troublemaker. She'd only been twelve years old when she discovered illicit drugs, alcohol and older men. Perhaps Bernie understood what went through her mind, but Diana did not. She never had. "Right now, my queen concerns me. If she's dead, I could lose the hive."

Gil's normally placid face turned dark and furious. "I've got dead and wounded men, a nut with a gun running around, and you're worried about bees?"

"What can I say? I'm their caretaker. Besides, you don't need speculation, you need answers. I don't have any." She took two steps then stopped. "Don't you want to know why those men were raiding my hives?"

Diana fetched her beekeeper hat and smoker from the barn. She settled the broad white hat on her head and draped the veiling over her shoulders. She'd been stung enough for one day. She checked the fuel in the smoker can, then lit it and pumped until pale smoke curled from the spout.

Tending a hive required slow, almost dance-like movements. The work soothed her shaken soul and settled her thoughts. She smoked the fallen hive until the bees stopped flying. Each hive rested on cinder blocks so air could circulate. Last year's tall grass formed a tawny curtain around the blocks. A dull silver-colored case had been hidden beneath the fallen hive. She pulled it free—it was very heavy—and set it aside. Then she righted the hive onto the cinder blocks and worked off the lid. A few more puffs of smoke further quieted the bees inside.

Gil was shouting questions, but she ignored him.

The combs were dripping honey, many of the cells broken, but the forms were intact. She lifted forms one by one until she found the queen. Workers circled the much larger queen, grooming and fussing over her.

"Good girl. So sorry about the excitement," she murmured. She gently settled the form back into place and replaced the lid. Left alone, the bees would soon have the hive back in order.

Only then did she turn her attention to the metal briefcase. "Oh, Bernie, what have you done now?"

"What have you got?" Tate called.

She left the enclosure and fastened the gate securely behind her. Anger rose, hot and disturbingly familiar. Hadn't she left all this behind? The endless drama, the useless anger, the agony of watching loved ones self-destruct. She'd learned her lesson and walked away. And trouble followed.

She lifted the veil off her face and scanned the horizon. Bernie knew darned well her pursuers might come here. Men with guns. Bernie didn't care.

Diana gave the case to Gil. He looked worried, which worried her.

Her anxiety increased when the sheriff placed the case on the hood of the Rover and snapped open the latches. It was packed tight with fat bundles of twenty- and hundred-dollar bills. Tate whistled, soft and low. Moe asked if the money was real. The sheriff muttered a curse. All Diana could do was shake her head.

"You're out of here, Diana," Tate said. "Right now."

THE SHERIFF STOOD BEFORE a large topographical map of the Maya Valley and surrounding mountains. He rocked on his heels. "What the hell is going on, Tate?" He turned his head. "I don't like bodies dropping in my jurisdiction."

The metal briefcase sat on a desk between Tate and the sheriff. It lacked identifiers and clues to its origins, but somebody wanted it back.

The station was quiet except for the tapping of a secretary typing up a report and the dispatcher handling the radio. All available personnel were either involved in the fugitive search for Diana's sister, or looking for the man who'd run away from Diana's farm, or transporting evidence to various labs. Gil had banished reporters, but that didn't stop the phone from ringing off the hook with journalists in search of headlines.

Hands on his hips, Tate glared at the briefcase. All the staring in the world couldn't force it to give up its secrets.

Bernadette had chosen a good hiding place for her stash of cash. So how had those mopes known where to look?

"Sheriff?" the dispatcher called.

"Yeah, Ellen, what?"

"The forest service guys want to know if you have more flyers."

"My budget is shot to hell," Gil muttered. Then louder, "Tell them I'll get something to them tomorrow morning."

Nearly sixty percent of the county was made up of either national forest or Indian reservation; the sheriff's jurisdiction was fairly small, and so was his budget. Bernadette was gobbling up the sheriff's budget like cheap chocolate.

Gil checked his watch. "You look beat. Go home and get some sleep. I still need you on patrol tonight."

Tate waved off the concern. He dropped onto a chair and rested his chin on his fist. He shifted his attention to the pistol he'd taken off the injured man. It was tagged, nestled inside an evidence bag. Its serial number had been acid-burned off. Crooks eradicated serial numbers when they meant to dispose of a weapon. The only reason to dispose of a perfectly good firearm was because it could be used as evidence in a crime.

"Any empty vacation cabins with the phone service hooked up?"

"Maybe. Why?"

"Those guys knew right where to look."

"Do you think Bernadette tipped them off?"

Tate couldn't think of another explanation.

Gil perched on the desk edge and crossed his arms. "Doesn't make sense. Why go to the trouble of hiding the money if she meant to give it up?"

A call came in for the sheriff. Gil listened, responding with the occasional "uh-huh" and scribbling on a sheet of paper. He hung up. "That was Jimmy, down in Durango. Mr. Bee-sting is officially deceased."

"Sorry to hear it," Tate said dryly.

"Sure you are. His ID says he's Richard Taylor from Los Angeles, California. Jimmy gave his prints to the Durango P.D. They're running them through the computer for us."

California added more geography to the mix, Tate thought and rubbed his weary eyes. This just kept getting better and better.

"And Jimmy checked the airport. Two passengers fitting the descriptions of our guys came in on a morning flight out of Denver. Taylor rented a car."

Tate straightened on the chair and snatched up Gil's notes. "Jimmy needs a promotion. Hey, Ellen! Need an APB on a rental car." He read off the rental's make, model, color and license plate number to the dispatcher. Then he called the Durango–La Plata airport and spoke to the head of security. He soon learned that Taylor's partner was listed on the manifest as John Williams. Richard Taylor, John Williams—common enough names, and probably phony.

In any case, if Williams showed up to turn in the rental car or make a flight, he'd be detained. Tate called the airport in Denver and spoke to the head of security there. The man promised to check manifests.

Tate glowered at the telephone, mulling over his next step. "We need to do a door-to-door."

"You're joking."

Tate dropped a hand on the metal briefcase. "Our girl isn't looking for money. She's looking to hide. Only she can't find her mother, so she shows up here. Then our guys, supposedly out of L.A. turn up via Denver. How'd they know Bernadette would be here? How'd they know to look at the beehives?"

"She's tired of running, so she tips off the boys from L.A.?"

"Not probable, but possible. She may have broken into an empty house or talked her way into an occupied residence in order to use the phone."

Gil dragged a hand across his eyes, then opened a desk drawer. He brought out the book that contained the volunteer deputy alert roster. Grumbling to himself, he took it into his office and shut the door. Hard.

Tate studied the case notes, searching for any lead he might have missed.

Diana walked into the station. Tate's heart leaped at the sight of her, taking in every detail from the soft bobbing of her hair to her curvy hips. Then it sank in that she was alone. He jumped to his feet. "You really are crazy!"

Clutching a brown paper sack to her chest, she backed a step.

"You're supposed to be at Ric's place. There's a gunman running around."

A not-quite-chastised expression pulled her features. She looked as tired as he felt. Crow's feet were apparent around her eyes, and her shoulders sagged. "If I'm not safe in the sheriff's station, then what's the use of hiding?"

He opened his mouth to yell at her, but she held up a hand and shook her head firmly.

"Save it." She placed the paper bag next to the briefcase. She dropped onto a chair with a thump. A heavy sigh escaped her.

He felt bad for losing his temper. It had been a long time since he cared enough to yell at anybody. Diana had him rattled every which way. "Is everything okay up at Ric's place?" He opened the bag. It contained clothing and two matchbooks. He dumped it all on the desk.

"Ric hooked up the propane, then he helped me put up temporary fencing for the goats. He even showed me how to work the hot tub." Her smile was strained. "That man? Did he make it?"

Tate shook his head.

She closed her eyes for a long moment. "I didn't think he would. Hope his next life is better." She pointed at the clothes. A shirt was bloody. "Those are Bernie's. She stuffed them in with my laundry. I found the matchbooks in the jeans."

One matchbook was from the Sparkle City hotel and casino in Las Vegas, Nevada; the other was from the Blue Heron restaurant, also in Las Vegas. A telephone number was written inside the Blue Heron matchbook.

He met Diana's eyes. "I could kiss you."

She smiled, close-mouthed and seductive. Her eyelashes fluttered. From the corner of his eye he caught the dispatcher watching the exchange with open interest. His ears burned.

"I'm out of here," she said and started to rise.

"Stay." The word was out before he realized it sounded like a plea. "I mean, it's not a good idea for you to be alone right now."

"Gee, and I was hoping you just enjoyed my company."

He glanced at the dispatcher. Ellen was grinning like an idiot. "We've got a make on the shooter. We should have him in custody before too long."

"Who is he?"

"John Williams, supposedly from Los Angeles. Know him?"

"Yeah, right." She turned a frown on the briefcase. "How in the world did they know to look under the beehive? It's driving me batty."

"Only thing I can come up with is that Bernadette told them about the farm. What's your mother's old address? Where would Bernadette go to find her?"

She gave him an address, then added, "But the house was sold years ago."

"What about your old address?"

She gave him an address in Scottsdale, Arizona. "It doesn't make sense for Bernie to hide money only to tell those men where to find it." She caught her lower lip in her teeth and her brows drew into a deep V. "Unless they were friends of hers. If so, why head for the hills?"

He reached for the telephone. "Questions, questions. Ask me again when I have some answers." He got through to the Scottsdale police department. He asked to speak to a major crimes detective and was put on hold. "Your sister could have tossed a bone, hoping the mopes would stop chasing her."

"She didn't have to do it on my farm," Diana grumbled. She huffed a humorless laugh. "There's half a million dollars in there. Toss a bone, yes, but the entire side of beef? That is not the way my sister operates."

An Arizona detective came on the line. Tate identified himself and explained his problem. The man sounded interested enough for Tate to believe that his request wouldn't get shoved beneath the get-around-to-it pile. When Tate read off Diana's previous address, there was dead silence on the line.

"Hello? Detective, are you still there?"

"Can you repeat that address, deputy?"

Tate did so. "What do you have?"

"Mind if I call you back?"

Every nerve went on alert. The detective's request meant he had something hot and needed to confirm Tate's official status. "No problem," he said and didn't offer a phone number. The detective would look it up.

Within two minutes the secretary informed him he had a call on line two.

"Sorry about that, deputy," the detective said. "I don't know if it's related, but it's a helluva coincidence. Day before yesterday the woman who lived there was murdered."

Hairs lifted on his nape. "What happened?"

"Middle of the night, no sign the victim struggled. Looks like she answered the door and bam, right through the heart. Then a neat little shot through the back of her head. The weapon was a .22."

His blood chilled. Amateurs liked big guns, making big messes and a lot of noise. Pros favored .22-calibre pistols. The round made a small hole going in, bounced around ripping up soft tissue, and rarely exited, especially when shot into a skull. Neat, clean, effective and relatively quiet. He stared at the bagged and tagged .22 on his desk. "Sounds like an assassination."

Diana started, her eyes going wide.

"Looks like it. Except, the victim is clean. No involvement with drugs or gambling. No ex-husbands or boyfriends gunning for her. No disgruntled employees or coworkers. She wasn't sexually assaulted. She had some nice electronic equipment, a purse in plain view, but they were untouched. Her place was tossed, but if the perps stole anything or left any evidence, we haven't found it yet.''

"Hold on a sec." He placed a hand over the mouthpiece and smiled at Diana. She sat rigidly, her face pale. "Mind getting me a cup of coffee? It's down that hall, first door on the right." She acted more than happy to get away from his side of the conversation. "Is there any way you can check out the other address?"

"I can do that. What do you have?"

Tate elaborated on his situation. He promised to send Richard Taylor's fingerprints along with particulars on Tim Robertson and Bernadette O'Malley. Almost as an afterthought, he added, "Oh, and would you like to look at a .22 semi-auto?"

The detective whooped and Tate grinned. He told the man about the weapon taken off Taylor and promised it would be flown to Phoenix by special courier first thing Monday morning.

Holding a coffee cup, Diana lingered near Ellen's desk. The dispatcher appeared to be explaining to her how the radio system worked. After Tate hung up, Diana brought his coffee.

"Did Bernie murder someone?" she asked.

Her plaintive tone made his heart hurt for her. Even when he was angry with his siblings or disapproving of their actions, he still loved them. "I don't know. The woman who was living at your former address was murdered. It might be related."

Gil stalked out of his office and at seeing Diana, stopped short.

Tate held up a matchbook. "Might have a lead. Diana

found these in her sister's clothes.'' He made a quick mental assessment of the situation. John Williams either realized the sheriff had the briefcase, or he was lurking around Diana's farm—where a pair of deputies stood watch—trying to figure out how to get past the bees. Diana should be safe. He worked a key off a ring. He handed it over. "Key to my place. Catch a nap, watch some television, read a book. I shouldn't be more than an hour. Then I'll escort you up to Ric's place. Okay?"

She smiled gratefully, confirming his suspicion that she was scared to be alone.

He watched her walk out, allowing himself a few admiring thoughts about her backside. Then he turned to Gil. "This might be a whole lot uglier than we thought. Let me tell you what I just found out about Arizona."

Chapter Six

Diana cruised Main Street. She hardly ever came into town on the weekends and never this late on a Saturday night. The small parking lot behind the Track Shack was full. Vehicles, many with out-of-state plates, lined both sides of the street. Pedestrians strolled along on the sidewalks. It was easy to tell the tourists from the locals. The locals were in short sleeves, unaffected by the temperature that had dropped into the forties after the sun went down. Tourists wore sweaters and jackets.

She found a parking place on a side street a few blocks from the Track Shack. She yawned mightily and rubbed her gritty eyes. A nap sounded good.

She walked past the arcade. It was packed with teenagers playing electronic games. Sweet innocence, she thought sadly. In her youth she'd been too busy trying to meet her father's expectations to ever have any fun. No wonder her life had been so out of balance.

An RV as long as a Greyhound bus took up three parking places in front of the drugstore. She stepped off the sidewalk in front of the RV and waited for a break in traffic. The Track Shack was lit up, the tinted front window glowing amber. She bet it was even more crowded than it had been earlier. A car passed, and she stepped into the street.

Brake lights flared on the car. Tires screeched. She tensed for a collision, which didn't come. Back-up lights glowed, the engine roared. The driver must have spotted a parking place. Diana stepped out of the way.

The dark sedan stopped in front of her. The passenger side window lowered with a faint mechanical sound. Every hair on her body lifted. Her scalp tightened. An inner voice said *Run!* Her legs refused to obey until a movement in the shadowy car interior reached her brain. She pivoted, slamming her back against the flat grill of the RV.

Crack!

Aftershock smacked her eardrums. Her nostrils caught a whiff of gunpowder. *Crack!* The ping of a ricocheting bullet spurred her into action. She darted into the street, around the RV, out of line with the sedan's passenger window. *Crack!* People screamed. Diana ran like hell.

She raced around the back of the RV and leaped over the curb onto the sidewalk. A doorway beckoned, and she grabbed for the handle. *NO!* Trap! She ran downhill, dodging people who were frantically looking for a place to hide. The car backed up recklessly; oncoming traffic honked, screeched and veered out of the way.

She darted around a corner, away from the street lights and into the shadows.

Metal crunched metal. Glass shattered. A man shouted, "Get him!" Other voices rose in a furious cry to battle. A siren wailed.

Diana pressed herself into a dark doorway, trying to make herself small, invisible. Her heart pounded. Her mouth was sour with adrenaline.

"I've got him, dammit!" a man roared. "Back off!

Hey! Yeah, you! Get off him. He ain't going anywhere. I mean it, put those rifles away! All of you, move!''

Red and blue emergency flashers bounced off the buildings. People milled about on a street corner, seeking a better view. Diana sagged and patted her chest and upper arms, assuring herself she wasn't wounded. A panicked voice in her head told her the noises and lights were all part of a trick to make her run into the open. Reason told her otherwise, but still she couldn't make herself move.

If it's my time... She couldn't finish the prayer.

A beam of light swept the doorway niche. She bit off a squeal and pressed against the wall, feeling the texture of brick through her shirt. She clenched her teeth to keep them from chattering.

"Diana?" Tate called. "Diana!"

"Here I am." Her legs gave out, and she slid down the wall. Thank you, God, thank you, thank you, thank you.

"Hey, are you all right?" He shone the flashlight at the ground near her feet. "Are you hit?"

"No. Just scared."

He grasped her arm and hauled her upright. She stumbled against his chest and buried her face against his shoulder. He wrapped an arm around her. So big and safe—she didn't want to ever let him go. He murmured soothing words against her hair. At long last the trembling stopped. Her legs felt strong enough to hold her. She lifted her face to his.

His features were hidden by darkness, but his eyes caught lights from Main Street. He smelled hot and dangerous.

"Tate? Did you find her?" the sheriff called. "Is she all right?" He appeared in silhouette on the street corner. He aimed a big flashlight their way.

"I've got her. She's fine."

Tate guided her back to Main Street. The sedan was crushed like a demolition derby loser between two pickup trucks. Farmers and ranchers strutted in the street like wolves circling a fresh kill. Many carried rifles. Tourists and townsfolk lined the sidewalks. Gil's official Range Rover blocked the street.

"I saw everything," a woman cried. She pointed at Diana. "That's who he shot! That's her!"

Diana caught a few words from the murmuring crowd. "Shooting up our town..." "Showed him..." "Stupid sumbitch..."

Tate tightened his hold around Diana's shoulders. They followed Gil. A man, his hands locked behind him, sat in the back seat of a cruiser. His head lolled. He had a bloody nose, swollen jaw and a split lip. Either he'd hit the steering wheel when the trucks smashed his car, or townsfolk had gotten in some blows.

"Little tip for you, boy," Gil said. "This is a real bad place for a drive-by shooting."

The man moaned. "I need a doctor."

"You'll need more than a doctor before we're through with you."

A shudder racked Diana's body. She'd seen crazed patients attack hospital staff, experienced the terror of gang members carrying feuds into the emergency room, and lived through a nurse's ex-boyfriend shooting up an X-ray lab in an attempt to get at her. No one had ever shot at her before. Aimed a gun, gave chase, *tried to kill her!*

"You all right?" Tate whispered in her ear.

"He thinks I'm Bernie, doesn't he?" she whispered back. "He wants to kill my sister."

DIANA PLACED A HAND in the small of her back and arched against the ache. She studied the surrounding forest. The sun had risen an hour ago, but still hadn't topped the trees. Ric's property sat near the end of a dirt road, and from where she stood there wasn't one sign of neighbors. Tippy raced around, eagerly sniffing bushes, tufts of grass, rocks and tree stumps. Unseen birds cawed, whistled and screeched.

Logic told her she was perfectly safe. The man who'd shot at her was locked up in a jail cell. She wasn't hurt, and no one else had been hurt. Even if Bernie looked for her, she didn't know about Ric's place.

Still, she'd slept poorly. Wind had rocked the old trailer throughout the night, making it groan, creak and rattle. Every noise had jerked her to nervous wakefulness.

A nearby woodpile had scraps of lumber among the split logs. She picked up a four-foot length of two-by-two and hefted it. It wasn't a baseball bat, but it would do. While she fed the goats and made sure the temporary fencing would hold them inside the corral, she kept the two-by-two handy.

She entered the trailer and latched the flimsy lock. Irritation rasped her frayed nerves. She hadn't bothered locking a door since leaving Phoenix.

She lowered her face and closed her eyes. "A gift," she murmured. "All is Your gift. It is up to me to open my heart and see it. Help me remember I have the strength to deal with everything that is happening."

She stood still, closing off her thoughts, leaving her heart open. Her nervousness eased.

Hoping a shower would wake her up, she ran water until it was steaming and stepped into the tiny stall. She stood under the hot spray, letting it pound the tension from her bones. She soaped up, scrubbed, rinsed, then lifted her left arm over her head. She did a breast exam, her fingers probing for lumps or changes in the breast and armpit. All was well. She raised her right arm. She traced the scar where her right breast used to be, then checked her armpit for lumps, nodules or tenderness.

She wondered what Tate would think about the mastectomy. Such a self-conscious thought made her wonder if she'd truly come to terms with what breast cancer had done to her body.

"It's only meat," she whispered. She looked down at herself and grinned. Even in her twenties, she'd barely filled an A-cup bra. Age had softened her remaining breast, making her almost as flat on the left side as on the right.

Buttoning a shirt made the self-consciousness return. Once upon a time, she'd showed off her toned figure with tailored suits and clingy blouses. She'd possessed drawers full of expensive lingerie. Now she wore elastic sports bras or undershirts instead of lace brassieres, and men's shirts that made it impossible to tell how many breasts she had.

She dressed for comfort, not sex appeal. Maybe she was fooling herself.

She unbuttoned the shirt and studied herself in a mirror. Her ex-husband, a plastic surgeon, had badgered her to have reconstructive surgery. As if perky boobs would make up for the cancer and the pain and the fear. As if she weren't a real woman unless she possessed breasts men could admire.

Anger at her ex-husband, at a shallow society, at magazines that worshipped cleavage and two-dimensional sexuality, had dissipated into the realm of vague memory. She thought the fear and self-consciousness had left her as well. Apparently not.

She caressed the left side of her chest, tracing soft cotton and softer skin. She loved her body, scars and all. It allowed for the expression and exploration of her spirit. To finally understand the essential truth of her life, made the sacrifice of a breast a small price to pay.

Knocking startled her. She clutched the shirt plackets. Tippy lay on the bed, one ear up and the other flopped over. He stared in the direction of the door, but didn't bark.

"That's it," she muttered. "I'm trading you in for *two* rottweilers."

Buttoning the shirt, she tiptoed to the small bedroom window and peered out. The sight of Tate's battered old Bronco softened her tense muscles. He must have driven up while she was in the shower, otherwise she'd have heard him. Knocking made the trailer shake.

"Coming!" she yelled.

She opened the front door. Tate stood on the metal stoop. He wore a dark blue T-shirt tucked into blue jeans. His sidearm gleamed on his hip. His eyes were bloodshot, his complexion drawn.

Her throat tightened. "Did you find Bernie?" Her voice emerged weak and fearful. It was one thing to understand intellectually that her sister chose her own path, quite another to actually realize Bernie could end up shot to death or be tried for murder.

He shook his head. "Not a clue to her whereabouts."

"Why are you here?"

He ran a hand through his hair. His mouth twisted. "Gil ordered me out of the station. Said he'd shoot me in the foot if I didn't get some sleep. I don't report in for regular duty until Tuesday." His scowl deepened. He shifted his weight from foot to foot. He added, gruffly, "And I was worried about you."

Last night he'd escorted her to Ric's place and gave

her a cell phone in case of emergency. This visit went far above and beyond the call of duty. She didn't know why she did what she did next, except that she was happy to see him, and glad she could stop jumping at shadows.

She slid her hands over his shoulders and gazed into his eyes. He exhaled audibly through his nose, a sound akin to surrender. He canted his head. Her eyelids lowered in tacit acquiescence. He kissed her.

His mouth was soft, his upper lip bristly. He tasted of coffee. Kissing created a pleasant tightness in her jaw that spread to her throat, her chest, her belly and finally settled in her pelvis. Her hips went heavy and loose. When he put a big hand on her back, electric tingling delighted her spine. He wove his other hand into her shower damp hair, gently pulling her scalp.

She'd imagined such a response to him. His response to her thrilled her to her toes. He pressed her tightly against his belly and chest. His thigh nudged hers, urging her backward, over the threshold, into the trailer. The flooring creaked. His damp mouth was as sweet as summer rain, his tongue erotic and demanding, exploring her mouth as hotly as she explored his.

When he lifted his head, she touched her tongue to her lips. They felt full and lonesome. She forced her eyes open. He appeared dazed, solemn, hungry. He turned her loose and her whole body felt as lonesome as her mouth.

"Thank you," she said.

He scowled. "That wasn't pity."

She placed a hand on his broad chest, flat over his heart. "I wasn't exactly thanking *you*." She turned away. "Have a seat, I'll make you some breakfast."

"I shouldn't stay."

Diana knew fear when she heard it. She sensed in him a heart not easily mended once broken. Who or what had broken his heart, she hadn't a clue. Not even the biggest gossips in the valley had any ideas about Tate Raleigh's life before he left New York City and settled in Mc-Clintock, Colorado. While in his apartment she hadn't seen any clues to his past, not even a photograph. All she knew was that he'd been a police detective and he had a large family.

Tippy was winding and wriggling around Tate's legs, his happy noises growing increasingly frantic. Tate finally dropped onto the sofa and bent over to pet the dog. Tippy practically swooned in ecstasy over the attention.

"Ric left some coffee." She pulled a small can from a cupboard and looked for an expiration date. Not finding one, she decided it smelled all right and set about making a pot. Then she put water on to boil for tea.

"So why'd you give it up?" Tate asked. "Being a doctor." Tippy draped over his lap, his paws in the air, his tongue lolling. Tate rubbed circles over the puppy's belly.

His question surprised her. She'd never heard him asking personal questions of anyone. "Dharma."

"What's that?"

"Each of us has a place and purpose in life. When one discovers what that is, there's balance and bliss. Dharma."

"Huh."

She placed a bowl of brown eggs on the counter. The kitchen held an assortment of mismatched pots and pans. She rummaged until she found a cast-iron skillet. After rinsing off the dust, she put it on a burner. "My father was a cardiac surgeon. A brilliant man. To please him, I went to medical school. I was first in my class. After I finished my residency, I received offers from hospitals all over the country."

"Sounds like you were good."

"I was driven. There is a difference." She cracked eggs into a bowl, and whisked them with a fork. "So driven in fact I never realized how ill-suited I was for the path I chose. I worked in an emergency room at a large county hospital. That way I stayed so busy I didn't have time to think. I even married a fellow doctor. We spent our honeymoon at a medical convention."

His eyebrows lifted.

"I didn't have a social life. My husband and I discussed case histories when we bothered to talk at all. Patients were nothing but body parts and diseased or injured flesh. Nurses and orderlies were mere staff." She chuckled, a self-deprecating note. "They called me Dr. Do-it-over, or worse. All that time I thought I had a good life, but my soul knew better. My body knew better."

"What happened?"

She ran her tongue over her lower lip, imagining his taste, wanting to taste him again. Now would be a good time to tell him about the cancer. How she'd survived, but sacrificed a breast in order to do so. Except, it didn't feel like the right time.

"God gave me a gift. I paid attention."

Maybe she was afraid of running him off, of never feeling those muscular arms around her again. Her ex-husband, medical degree notwithstanding, had been repulsed by her illness and scars. His sexual rejection had hurt; his emotional desertion had crushed her. She'd survived, emerged stronger for the experience, but she needed some time to explore her reticence about telling Tate.

She poured clarified butter into the pan. While it heated, she sliced bread and cantaloupe. She poured the eggs into the hot pan, whisking them fluffy while they cooked.

Fear was a cold fire she needed to walk through. If Tate

was repulsed, then so be it. She wouldn't think less of him. They'd still be friends. "A tech was in training at the hospital, learning how to operate and read mammography results. All female staff had—"

Chin to chest, hands folded over his belly, he'd fallen asleep. She smiled, lifting her face to the heavens. "Fine," she murmured, "I'll tell you about it later."

TATE PUSHED HIMSELF upright. He vaguely recalled Diana urging him to remove his shoes and pistol. He didn't remember her sliding a pillow under his head or covering him with an afghan. He'd forgotten how pleasant it was to have a woman fussing over him.

He stretched and yawned. He'd slept so hard, he hadn't even dreamed. He checked his watch, incredulous about how long he'd slept.

He wandered around the small trailer in search of Diana. He made a stop in the bathroom. A bar of soap rested in a dish. He brought it to his nose and sniffed, smelling honey. Desire jolted him, and he quickly put the soap down and rinsed his hands. Shouldn't have kissed her. It was stupid, reckless. He didn't want that kind of relationship with her.

He desperately wanted to kiss her again.

A plastic box caught his attention. It was filled with pill bottles. Vitamins, herbs, calcium tablets—brown prescription bottles. He clenched his fists at his sides. He refused to stoop so low by snooping.

He holstered his weapon, put on his shoes and looked around for his telephone. It wasn't on the coffee table or the bookcase. He pawed through the cushions on the couch, shook out the afghan. It wasn't there. Muttering obscenities, he lifted the couch. There were jackrabbit-sized dust bunnies on the floor, but no telephone. He knew he'd had it when he arrived.

Any number of developments could have occurred while he'd been sleeping. Bernadette could have been apprehended. The mope who'd shot at Diana could have talked. Lab results could have come in. This was no time to lose his telephone.

He rushed outside. The sun had lowered to the treetops. He looked around wildly. He opened his mouth to shout when he spotted Diana. She was down the meadow where she sat on the ground with Tippy next to her, watching the goats graze.

He jogged down the slope. The goats lifted their heads to watch him. Tippy ran to meet him. Diana turned her head and smiled.

"I lost my telephone! Have you seen—?"

Wordlessly, she pulled the small unit out of her shirt pocket and offered it.

Dumbfounded, he took it. It was activated.

"I didn't want it to disturb you," she said. She patted the grass next to her. "Have a seat."

"Excuse me," he said, "but I'm in the middle of a homicide investigation and a fugitive search." He shook the phone at her. "It's my job to answer calls."

Her smile quirked.

"This is serious," he said.

She held a two-by-two piece of lumber across her lap. She rose, then leaned on the stick as if it were a staff. Smiling gently, she faced him. "When everything is important, nothing is important." Her serene blue gaze heightened his temper.

"What the hell is that supposed to mean?"

"It means, if I answered a call that was a true emergency, which absolutely required your attention, I would have awakened you. But your sleep is important. You were dead on your feet.''

"Who are you to decide what is important?"

"Somebody needs to."

"That somebody ain't you!" He leaned in close, but she didn't even flinch. "Who called?"

"Nobody."

"Liar."

Her eyebrows arched. Then, she laid a hand on his cheek. He was so astonished by her boldness, he didn't move. "Haven't you figured out by now that no matter how many miles you travel, no matter how many hours a day you work, you still can't run away from yourself?"

He pushed her hand off his face. "I am not in the mood for your touchy-feely crap. I have a job to do. I decide what's important and what's not."

Her smile faded. "Whatever you say."

His gut ached. He felt as bad as if he'd kicked Tippy. Unable to bear the disapproval on her face, he turned away. He stomped up the hill. Dried grasses and weeds snapped and crunched beneath his shoes. He punched in the number for his voice mail. No messages.

He was an ass.

He turned around. Leaning on the stick, she watched him. He shoved the telephone into its holster, then raked both hands through his hair. She'd let him sleep—not exactly a class-A felony.

He should go home. The Track Shack was closed on Sundays, so he could make much-needed repairs without customers to worry about. He could pop over to the station, make some phone calls, light a few fires under lab technicians.

Grumbling, he walked back down the hill. He jutted his

chin at the goats. "Did they escape? Need some help rounding them up?"

"Apology accepted."

"When I'm sorry, I'll say I'm sorry." He glowered at his shoes. "I'm sorry."

"Okay. And to answer your question, no, they didn't escape. I let them out. No sense all these lovely weeds going to waste. And Tippy and I need goatherd practice."

"Thanks for letting me sleep."

"You're welcome. Are you hungry?"

His gut felt like a raw hole. "I'll go home, fix a sandwich. I've got some work to do."

"Don't be silly. It's Sunday, a day of rest. I have plenty of food. Let me put the babies in the barn." She thrust the stick at him. "Here, keep the wolves away." She headed for the barn.

A white goat bleated and trotted after Diana. The others took up the cry and broke into their funny, windup toy gallop. Tippy barked and raced after them. Bemused, Tate followed. The goats darted into the barn, their hooves scrabbling on the concrete floor.

Diana's laughter echoed through the small barn. It was impossible not to smile. Impossible to remain grumpy around her.

She held a bucket and the goats were going nuts trying to get at it. The tricolored goat reared on its hind legs, arched its neck, then head-butted a white goat. Diana called to Tate to shut the door. He did so, latching it securely.

"They sure like you," he said.

"They sure like grain," she answered. She poured small piles of grain on the floor.

He leaned against a stall door and watched her fill a water tank. The barn was fairly clean, smelling faintly of raw wood. Tippy sneaked around a goat, trying to get it to do something, but the goat was preoccupied with vacuuming up food.

"Are they girl goats or boys?" he asked.

She chuckled. "The proper terms are bucks and does. And these are wethers. Castrated males."

He tightened his thighs. "Oh."

"I don't know if I want to breed goats. So I bought wethers to see how we get along." She turned off the water hose. "By next winter, I should be able to comb them for cashmere. Come on, let's get you fed."

Once inside the trailer, he said, "I really am sorry for acting like a jerk."

"It's okay, really. I know where you're coming from." She laughed, a saucy sound. "Besides, you're a coffee addict. Lack of it makes you grouchy."

He knew better than to ask, but he did anyway. "Where exactly am I coming from?"

"Fear." The word and her direct look challenged him to say she was wrong. "The real problem with overwork is that you get into the mindset that the whole world rests on your shoulders. That if you miss a call or don't supervise every task or do it yourself, then the world will collapse."

He gave her words some thought. She had him pegged cold. "I actually understand."

She opened the small refrigerator and peered at the contents. "I've been there." She brought out bowls and set them on the counter. "If your hours are filled with a million and one supremely important tasks, you never have to spend any time with yourself. You don't have to listen."

"Listen to what?"

She waved an arm in an expansive arc. "God, the Universe. Your own heart." She set a large frying pan on the stove. "Life doesn't have to be as hard as we make it. Ever wonder about the meaning of it all?"

He snorted. "I'm too busy to worry about it."

"You're so funny." She dumped cooked rice into the hot oil. It sizzled and popped while she stirred it. After a minute, she added chopped vegetables to the rice.

The sight of her cooking made him as hungry for her as he was for food. Her hands were deft and sure, her arms strong. The young dog sat hopefully at her feet. The kitchen light bounced and danced off her hair, sparking it with a range of golds, reds and rich browns. A pretty picture all the way around. He wondered what she'd do if he walked up behind her, slipped his arms around her waist and buried his face in her hair. If he kissed her neck.

She turned her head, her smile soft and knowing. Positive she knew exactly what he was thinking, he broke eye contact.

"While I was sitting out there with the goats, I thought of something," she said. She cracked two eggs and dropped them into the pan and gave them a stir. Then she shook a glass jar that held dark liquid. After the eggs had cooked a while, she poured liquid into the pan. Steam wreathed her face and filled the trailer with a spicy aroma.

"What?" he asked.

"I don't think Bernie means to steal another car. We would know it by now, right? Somebody would have seen her or Smoky Joe. She's hiding until it's safe to retrieve the money."

"Okay."

"There's a place where Dad used to take us fishing. A lake or a pond. There's an old mining camp nearby. Falling-down buildings and such. I'm fairly sure it's on private property."

"Where is it?"

She shook her head and lifted the pan. She scraped the rice and vegetables into a large bowl. "It's been so long, I can't remember exactly. What I do remember clearly is that there's a mine shaft. It was boarded up. Dad caught Bernie and me trying to pull off the boards." She rolled her eyes. "Blew his gasket. In any case, it would make a great place to hide. That is, if nobody built a house on it, or turned it into an RV park."

The mountains ringing the valley were pocked with old mine shafts. At least once a year he could count on some knucklehead falling into one and requiring rescue. "If you had a good map, could you remember where this place is?"

"Maybe."

She set the table for two, and put the steaming bowl of fried rice in front of him. His mouth watered at the smell. When she placed a basket of sliced homemade bread in front of him, his belly rumbled embarrassingly loud. She urged him to dig in.

He didn't care for broccoli or carrots, both of which were present in abundance. The vegetables were crisp and nicely seasoned with soy and ginger; they were almost tasty.

His telephone rang. A knowing look from Diana quelled his eagerness. He really was married to the telephone, addicted to busy work. He took his time answering. It was Gil.

"Get enough sleep?" Gil asked.

"Yeah. What's up? Did you get a statement from Williams?"

"He's taking seriously his right to remain silent. He used his one telephone call to contact an attorney. We did find the motel where he was staying. Found something interesting.''

"What is it?"

"You'll have to see it to believe it."

"I'll be right there."

"No hurry. It'll be here tomorrow."

"Yeah, right," he said. "I'll be there in less than an hour."

Chapter Seven

Tate parked in front of the sheriff's station. He cut the engine, and the old Bronco shimmied and rattled before wheezing into silence.

Diana patted the dashboard as if soothing a child with the hiccoughs. "Poor baby. Got the pre-ignition blues."

"The what?" he asked.

"I don't know why it's called pre-ignition. It should be post-ignition. It's a timing problem."

He knew his mouth was hanging open, but he couldn't help it. "How in the world do you know that?"

She lifted a shoulder in a lazy shrug. "I've always had a thing for mechanical stuff. When I was a kid, I built a lot of clocks and crystal radios. It's probably why I did so well in med school. Thought of human bodies as machines." She grinned, still caressing the sun-cracked dash. "I've always done my own car maintenance. It infuriated my ex-husband when he caught me changing oil. He didn't think it was dignified, but it was one of the few things that actually relaxed me."

He was impressed. "So, this ignition problem, is it bad?"

"It isn't good. The engine timing is off. So when you turn off the engine, the gas is still pumping and it's combusting because of pressure. That's where the vibration comes from. You could need a new distributor, or a timing chain. Or, considering the age of this thing, you could need a whole new ignition system.''

"Expensive?"

"Could be. Think positively."

He chuckled. "So you're not just blowing smoke when you offer to help me out at the Shack. You actually know how to fix things."

"Who do you think repaired the dishwasher and put a new thermostat in the oven? Fairies?"

He focused so much on problems, he had no energy to notice positive occurrences. Maybe she was right about negative energy. "You? First a doctor, now a mechanic. Amazing."

"That's the problem with labels. Once you label a person, you limit yourself. People aren't what they do. They are what they are with unlimited potential." She slid her hand across the seat, almost but not quite touching his leg. Awareness of her made him tingle. "Once upon a time I used to label people. A clerk, a housekeeper, a nurse, an orderly, an appendicitis. It made it easy to dismiss them."

She slid her fingers in a feathery caress along the seam of his jeans. He swallowed hard. "The worst thing of all is when we label ourselves." She offered a graceful hand to the sky. "What we are isn't out there." She placed the hand between her breasts. "It's in here."

No matter how many times he told himself her New Age-babble was bunk, he was—always—utterly fascinated by what she had to say. At the moment he was dying to know what she saw when she peered past his defenses to the man inside. He fiddled with his keys. "This shouldn't take more than a few minutes. You can look at a map of the area, see if you can remember where your dad used to take you fishing.''

Yellowish light from the tall lamps around the station made her mysterious, her eyes dark, gleaming with inner fire. ''Do you even know why you're so afraid of me?''

He didn't deserve her interest, her tenderness and, most of all, he didn't deserve her acceptance. ''Do all our conversations have to turn into shrink sessions?''

''Anger is fear.''

''I am not angry!''

''Hmm.''

He shook a finger at her. ''Cut it out, Red. I mean it. I don't know why you have to pester me all the time. But cut it out.''

She gazed evenly at him. He was rattled and she knew it.

''Do you know,'' she said, ''why wild animals are rarely neurotic? Aside from the fact that predators are very quick to eliminate the weak?''

He didn't want this conversation; he couldn't make himself leave the truck.

''Animals in their natural state have an instinctual awareness of when the times are right. Mothers know when to wean their young, when to punish, when to reward, when to eat, when to sleep. They know when it is time to grieve, and when it is time to let go and go on. We humans don't listen so well to our instincts. It makes us neurotic.''

''Now I'm neurotic?''

''Are you?''

''Not a neurotic bone in my body.''

''If you say so.'' She opened the door. The dome light highlighted sparkling eyes and a smug smile.

He caught her upper arm. "Why do you do this to me?"

"Do you recall the first time we met?"

The heat spread from his ears to his neck. "No," he lied.

"Yes, you do. You knocked over an entire display of spray-paint cans." She touched the center of her forehead. "We smacked heads when we bent over to pick them up. I had quite a goose egg."

He lowered his face to hide a sheepish smile. They'd been in the hardware store. She'd been buying fence staples; he'd been looking for primer. Her hair had drawn him like a magnet. Then she looked at him with those incredible crystal-blue eyes, and he walked straight into the spray-paint display.

"I knew that day our fates are entwined. We're meant for each other."

"We're too different."

She made a neutral sound, neither agreeing or disagreeing.

"After I sell the bar, who knows what will happen. Gil can't afford me full-time. I'll probably have to move to Denver or Colorado Springs, or maybe even back to New York." The excuses sounded lame. He puffed his cheeks and released a long breath. "I'm not interested in fate."

Again, a noncommittal *hmm.*

He sank lower, drawing in his chin. He'd been getting on along just fine until she stumbled into his life. Before she started in with her nonsense about sexual tension. Then to kiss him! She might be a nut, but she sure knew how to curl his toes.

"You know what they say," she said. "Without pain, pleasure isn't possible." She hopped out of the Bronco.

Refusing to look at her, he escorted her into the station.

The place was quiet, even for a Sunday evening. The weekend dispatcher was reading a paperback novel. Deputy Bill Yarrow, having recovered enough from shingles to wear his uniform, sat before a computer, hunting and pecking his way through a report. A volunteer deputy was on the telephone.

"Where's the sheriff?" Tate asked.

"In and out," the volunteer replied. "What are you doing here?" He smiled at Diana.

"Sheriff's downstairs," Bill said. He swiveled his chair away from the keyboard. "Our shooter's mouthpiece finally showed up."

"On a Sunday? He can't be local."

"Never seen him before. Looks pretty high priced." The deputy cast a speculative look down the hallway that led to the stairwell. The jail was in the basement. "The sheriff is not impressed."

John Williams and Richard Taylor, who'd died from bee stings, were carrying false identification. Tate checked the fax machine. No hits on fingerprints from either man. Maybe with his attorney present, Williams—or whatever his name was—would provide a few answers.

Tate guided Diana to a topographic map affixed to a wall. He put his finger on McClintock. "You are here. See if you can find the fishing pond."

A metal door slammed. Gil Vance, garbed in civilian clothes, emerged from the basement. He was grinning and shaking his head as if he couldn't believe what he'd seen or heard.

"We've got that boy cold," he said. "Illegal firearms possession, illegal discharge of a weapon, attempted murder, assault, trespassing, carrying false identification and reckless driving. And you know what that yahoo lawyer says to me? 'I'm sure we can clear up this little misunderstanding.'" He barked a harsh laugh. "Idiot thinks I'm Deputy Dawg."

"What's Williams's real name?"

"Couldn't tell you." He turned a business card in his fingers, examining it front and back. "Mr. Lloyd Johnson, Esquire, attorney-at-law, the firm of White and Morgenstern, Denver." He pointed his chin at Diana. "What's with the esquire?"

"It's a courtesy title. I'm unsure why attorneys use it. Maybe it's because the word means shield bearer."

Gil harrumphed. "Truth in advertising laws ought to make them use bloodsucker."

It bugged the crap out of Tate that he hadn't gotten a hit on either mope's fingerprints. It didn't make sense. Taylor and Williams didn't just wake up this week and decide to take up a life of crime. Unfortunately, not every law enforcement agency entered local fingerprint files into the national database. Figuring out who they were might take a while.

"So how can he afford a big-shot lawyer?" Tate asked.

Gil gave him a dry look. "Maybe he's one of the rich and famous." He beckoned. "Come on in my office and look what we found."

"I'm telling you," Gil said, as he left the door open enough so he could hear what was happening in the station, "we should get Diana on *Jeopardy.* She'd clean up, do this town proud."

The metal briefcase sat on Gil's desk. It was empty, the money now locked up in the evidence locker. Gil picked up what looked like the control unit for a radio-controlled toy car. He grinned at Tate and twisted a dial. A high-pitched squeal made Tate flinch.

"Okay, Mr. New York detective. What have we got? Or do we need to ask Diana?" Gil backed a few feet from the desk and pointed the unit's antenna out the window. He turned a dial. The unit squealed. When he swung it toward the briefcase, the squeal increased in pitch and volume.

"I'll be damned," Tate breathed. "A bird dog."

Gil handed over the tracking device. It was heavy, the face covered with dials and meters. Tate realized this was what Williams had been holding when he ran away from the farm.

"We also confiscated a fairly decent arsenal, all of it untraceable, by the way, and about five grand in cash."

"Professional hitters."

"That's not funny."

Tate placed the unit on the desk and turned his attention to the case. He poked and prodded at the interior and exterior. It all seemed solid and of a piece, without any type of liner or hidden compartments. He examined the handle. With a letter opener, he pried at the plastic sheath covering the grip. It was stuck, as if glued, and the plastic cracked when he pried at it. He finally got it off and found a tiny transmitter.

"Is that the bug?"

He held the transmitter up to the light. He hadn't seen anything this fancy outside of a law enforcement trade show. The FBI and CIA had the money to buy this kind of equipment; local law enforcement generally did not. Any private citizen with the bucks to burn could purchase it, too. "Let's ship this to Quantico. The FBI might be able to trace it."

Gil planted his fists on his hips. "What have we got? A drug deal gone sour?"

Tate showed his palms. "If it is, it doesn't make sense."

"Makes sense to me."

"Drug dealers don't use bird dogs. Bernadette's made a powerful enemy somewhere along the line."

The dispatcher's voice came over the intercom: "Sheriff? The Kingman, Arizona, police department is on line three."

Gil waved a magnanimous hand. "Your call."

Tate picked up the phone and identified himself. "What do you have?"

"We had an incident last week." He laughed sheepishly. "Took me a while to make the connection. Had a shoot-out at a little motel on I-40. Not far from there we found an abandoned vehicle. A Lincoln Continental registered to Farrah Montgomery of Las Vegas, Nevada. It has bullet holes in it and matches a witness description from the motel."

"Who the hell is Farrah Montgomery?" Tate asked. This thing just kept getting more and more complicated. "Reported stolen?"

"Uh-uh. Turns out Ms. Montgomery owns and operates a casino called Sparkle City. Las Vegas."

Remembering the matchbooks Diana had found, Tate sat straighter.

"That's not the interesting part."

Tate caught a strained note in the man's voice. "What's going on?"

"The FBI. Suckers swooped in like vultures, confiscated the Lincoln and our case file. Questioned everybody." He laughed, but didn't sound amused. "Made us all sign confidentiality statements. Put a blanket on everybody, cops and civilians."

"What are they looking for?"

"Couldn't discuss it even if I knew. But it's big, deputy, real big. Have you heard from the feds?"

Tate suspected they would in the very near future. He

stared at the metal briefcase. Money, a transmitter, the FBI. It added up to either extortion or a kidnapping. "Looks like I better contact them. You've been a help, sergeant. Thanks."

"Wish I could do more. You folks have fun over there in Colorado."

Gotta love small-town police forces, Tate thought. Back East, exchanging information and evidence between jurisdictions usually required bullying, cajoling, court orders or major favors being called in.

Tate relayed the new information to the sheriff. Gil leaned back in his chair and steepled his fingers beneath his chin.

"Farrah Montgomery," Gil said thoughtfully. "You think this woman was kidnapped?"

Tate frowned at the notes he'd written. "It fits with what we have. Sort of."

"That rocket scientist downstairs sure ain't no G-man," Gil said. "And if it was the feds having a shoot-out with O'Malley and Robertson, we'd know it, right?"

Tate had been involved in one kidnapping for ransom, assigned to interviewing witnesses and following up telephone numbers. From what he'd seen, the FBI had been cool, professional and completely in charge. Their number one priority was recovering the victim alive. No heroics, no hotdogging and they'd used the local police force with maximum effectiveness.

Maybe the feds operated differently in the West, but he doubted it. Confiscating case evidence and alienating local law enforcement didn't seem like the best way to recover a kidnap victim.

"Yeah, we'd know it. Unless this is something bigger."

Gil snorted. "What's bigger than kidnapping...?" His chin and eyebrows raised. "Organized crime?"

Tate shrugged. "Las Vegas casinos, expensive bird dog, a high-priced attorney for a hired hitter, the FBI. It isn't much of a stretch. If it is organized crime, I have a feeling the feds will be knocking on our door next."

A knock on the door made them both jump.

Bill Yarrow stuck his head into the office. "Sheriff, Mr. Johnson just left."

"Without talking to me? Who does he—"

"He'll be back. Said he needs to make some phone calls." Bill grinned. "Guess he doesn't trust us not to eavesdrop. Should I put our boy back in his cell?"

"Nah. Let him stew in the closet."

The station didn't have a formal interrogation room. When they needed to question a suspect, they used a storeroom crowded with metal filing cabinets. It was cramped, hot and intimidating. Prisoners were handcuffed to a metal table that was bolted to the floor. Local attorneys, who had to use it for conferring with clients, called it the torture chamber.

Tate considered it an excellent place for miscreants to ponder their sins.

"So what's our next move?" Gil asked.

"Make some inquiries with the Las Vegas police," Tate said. "Maybe I can locate Farrah Montgomery and she can tell us why Bernadette had her Lincoln."

"That was a rhetorical question, boy," Gil said. "Our next move is letting the FBI know what we have. If it's organized crime, I don't want any part of it."

Tate grunted. "I love Quantico. Best labs, best forensic scientists. But dealing with the feds one-on-one makes me insane. They won't share information, they take all the credit for busts and witnesses have a bad habit of refusing to testify on a local level when the feds convince them to save it for the big time. They'll appropriate all our evidence, and we'll never see it again.''

Gil leaned both hands on the desk and stared into Tate's eyes. ''Good. I'll gift wrap the whole damned circus for them.''

''Yeah, yeah.'' Grumbling to himself, he stalked out of Gil's office. He could feel Gil's grin on his back.

Diana waved him over to the map.

''Find it?'' he asked.

''Maybe. It was so long ago.'' She looked past him to the door. She lowered her voice. ''I hate being judgmental, but that lawyer was creepy.''

''Did he say something to you?''

''Just stared.'' She shuddered and rubbed her upper arms. ''Talk about negative energy. He had eyes like a shark. I'm glad I don't have to deal with him.'' A mischievous grin made the skin around her eyes crinkle. ''Especially with that awful toupee he's wearing. I know it's terribly shallow, but something about a toupee hits a hot button with me. The funniest looking bald spot is ten times better than the best-made hairpiece. Anyway...'' She turned back to the map and put her finger on a spot. ''Sweetpot Lake. It strikes a chord.''

He pulled a hand over his mouth and chin, wiping off a smile. It was nice knowing she had her little prejudices and foibles, just like the rest of the mortals. ''Didn't you say it was private property? That's national forest.''

''The people who owned it could have sold it or donated it. According to this map, there are no campgrounds or even a picnic area. It could be restricted or something.''

Tate asked the volunteer deputy to come over. Roger Sommerset was in his late fifties, a native of the valley. An avid hunter, he knew the area as well as anybody. Tate asked him about the lake.

"Yeah, I know it," the man said. "Road to it is shut down. Mine hazards. Mess of old shafts in that area." His silvery eyebrows knit. "Must of been ten, twelve years back, couple of city kids got themselves killed. Caused a big hullabaloo. Folks sued the government, wanting 'em to fill in the mines." He shook his shaggy head. "Some of them old shafts run hundreds of feet. Forest service talked about dynamiting the mines, but the EPA got wind of it and said it would kill horny toads or bats or some such nonsense. So, government closed off the area."

"Then is there an old mining camp there?" Diana asked. "Buildings?"

Roger grunted in the affirmative. "What you thinking, Red? Your sister made her way up there? That's more than twenty miles from your place."

"It looks right. Tate, can we go look?" Diana asked. "Tonight?"

"Not a chance." Tate turned away from her disappointment. "We aren't going in after dark. If she's there tonight, she'll be there tomorrow."

The sheriff's wife entered the station. She carried a large, cloth-covered basket over her arm. Paula Vance was a little dumpling of a woman, with a broad, pretty face and ready smile. Gil walked out of his office to meet her. He kissed her cheek; she rubbed her nose against his.

Witnessing their affection gave Tate a tight feeling in his chest. His marriage had lasted less than four years. He'd meant to stay married forever. From the corner of his eye, he peeked at Diana. In a way he couldn't quite define, Diana reminded him of his wife. Not in appearance. Lisa had been blond and willowy; Diana was broad-hipped and red-headed to beat the band. Perhaps it was her calm self-assurance, or the easy way she had around people.

Hope was sneaking around him, hiding in the shadows like a cat, ready to pounce and infiltrate when his back was turned. Hope that the grief and guilt would end. Hope that he wouldn't have to spend the rest of his life alone. He didn't deserve hope. Just as Lisa hadn't deserved what he'd done to her.

He checked the fax machine again, even opening the lid to make sure it had plenty of paper.

"Since you won't come home no more for supper," Mrs. Vance said, "I bring supper to you."

"I would've come home," Gil said.

"Uh-huh. When the cornbread turns hard as bricks." She tossed a grin at Tate. "'Sides, this way I can eat with you. Tell you what your ornery grandbabies did in church today."

"What about my prisoner?" Gil asked.

"Like I'd forget it's Sunday night, eh?"

On Mondays through Saturdays, prisoners in lockup were fed courtesy of the Pine Tree Diner. The diner was closed on Sundays, so the task of feeding prisoners fell on the sheriff's wife.

"Hey," Gil said to the uniformed deputy, "Go put our boy back in his cell and give him some sandwiches. Since I'm feeling generous, treat him to a soda pop, too." Gil sniffed at the station's main door. "When Mr. Johnson, Esquire, gets back, he can cool his heels until after the supper hour."

While Mrs. Vance and the deputy sorted out the food, Tate told Gil about Sweetpot Lake. Gil agreed that it would be too dangerous to check out the place after dark.

"I'm worried about her arm," Diana said. "What if she's sick?"

"What if she isn't?" Gil replied. "I won't risk the safety of my men."

"All right," she muttered.

"And don't you even think about going up there alone."

"I won't."

Tate determined that he'd convince Diana to stay in town tonight. He didn't trust her good sense to overrule her concern about her sister. He hoped he could trust his good sense to keep his hands off her.

"You two go on then," Gil said. "If our boy's attorney decides it's in his best interests to chat, I'll give you a call. Otherwise, report back here in the morning. We'll run over to Sweetpot."

"Can I go with you?" Diana asked. Her big eyes held a poignant plea that was difficult to resist.

Resist he did. Tate shook his head. "It's best if you don't."

A metal door slammed. Bill walked out of the hallway. He still carried the tray of food. His face was dead white, his eyes were round and glazed. His mouth opened and closed, but no sound came out.

"Bill?" Gil and Tate said in unison.

"Escaped?" Gil whispered.

"No," Tate said. "Can't be done." The basement didn't have a door leading outside, and all the windows were barred. Also, the windows were so narrow, a grown man couldn't get his head through them, much less his body.

Bill set the tray down very slowly, very carefully. "Not escaped. Dead." He blinked rapidly. "He's dead!"

Tate and the sheriff exchanged an incredulous glance, then hurried to the stairwell. Gil Vance had never lost a prisoner to illness, injury or suicide. Tate kept thinking about the head injury Williams had suffered when locals rammed his car. A doctor had checked him out, but suppose the doctor had missed an aneurysm or blood clot or other internal injuries?

Gil's cowboy boots clattered on the cement steps and echoed in the narrow stairwell. Tate's athletic shoes thudded.

The closet door stood open. One quick look showed Tate that Williams had indeed died of a head injury, but it hadn't been caused by a car crash. The man slumped over the metal table. A neat hole, blackened by gunpowder, seeped blood from the base of his skull. Automatically, Tate sought a pulse he knew wasn't there.

"Huh," he said. "Looks like we can safely rule out suicide."

Chapter Eight

Diana stared unseeing at the small television mounted in the corner of Tate's apartment. Its faint noise and shifting light offered an illusion of company. She lay curled on the futon, a blanket fisted against her chin. She wanted sleep, she yearned for sleep. She was too afraid.

When the prisoner's murderer had walked out of the sheriff's station, he'd looked straight at her. Williams had thought she was Bernadette. She could only assume his killer thought she was her sister, too. Life was a series of tests and lessons, but what was she supposed to learn from this? That her sister didn't give a damn about the destruction trailing in her wake? Diana knew that already. That red hair was easy to spot and identical twins were exactly that, identical? She knew that already, too.

A soft knock on the door made her freeze, every muscle painfully locked. Her heart thudded as if to escape her chest.

A key scraped in the lock. Tate's dark head peeked into the room. Rigid muscles slowly relaxed.

"I'm awake," she said.

He entered the apartment. She'd never been so glad to see his massive shoulders and tall stature. She propped herself on an elbow. "Did you catch him?" Please, please, please say yes, she thought hard at him.

He sank onto a chair and dangled his hands between his legs. "He's vanished. I've got a sneaking suspicion a description won't help much. The toupee is probably a disguise. I bet he was padded, too, and wearing phony facial hair. Gil is bad off. He's blaming himself."

"Why?"

"For not checking out Johnson's credentials. Frisking him for weapons."

"How could he suspect someone would commit murder in a sheriff's station?"

He raked a hand through his hair, his dark eyes bleak. "If anyone's at fault, it's me. When we drove up, I recognized every vehicle in the lot. I didn't even question how come I didn't see Johnson's vehicle. I've gotten soft as hell living here."

"If we waste time playing the blame game, not much will get done. I take it Johnson wasn't a real lawyer."

"The real Lloyd Johnson, Esquire, was having dinner with his wife and in-laws when we tracked him down. He's not too happy a hit man impersonated him."

She vividly recalled the sick, furious sensation when Bernie had impersonated her. Identity rape. "I know the feeling. What in the world has Bernie done?"

"Let's hope the feds have better luck finding out."

"The FBI?"

"They arrived about an hour ago. I've got a bad feeling this is going to get real ugly before it gets better."

"Let's go to Sweetpot Lake. Right now. If Bernie's there, she'll be asleep. We can sneak up on her. The only way this will end is to find my sister."

"Absolutely not. I'm taking you to Ric's."

The mere thought of being alone and isolated filled her with sick dread.

As if reading her fears, he said, "You'll be safe. No way can the hitter find you there. I'll stay with you. Can you handle a shotgun?"

"I've done some skeet shooting."

"Ric's place is as safe as you can get in the whole valley. I'll be with you. No one can sneak up on us."

"What about the men who are watching my farm? Aren't they in danger?"

"Don't worry about them. They're on alert." He rose and stretched out a hand to her. She took it and stood. He rested his hands on her shoulders. "We'll have that mope picked up before sunrise, I promise."

He was lying, but it was a nice lie, and she wanted to believe him. "I'd feel better if you kissed me," she whispered.

So he did, a gentle press of his mouth to hers. It didn't last long enough to suit her, but it was enough for now, enough to keep her going.

"Let me pack a bag," Tate said. "We'll be out of here in three minutes."

Not even the thought of her goats and lonely puppy made her eager to leave the protection of the Track Shack's chunky brick and plaster walls. All she had to do was get through the night without crawling out of her skin—or being shot.

THE SOUND OF AN approaching vehicle made every hair on Diana's body lift. Her chest tightened painfully. She picked up the pump action shotgun Tate had left with her. Its deadly weight offered a small amount of assurance. She believed in the sanctity of life and that violence created the worst sort of negative energy. But protect herself? Darn tootin'!

She and Tate had spent a restless night. He had tossed and turned on the lumpy old sofa, making the trailer rock, squeak and creak with every movement. She had tossed and turned in the bedroom, her mind so filled with worries about her sister and hit men that what little sleep she snatched left her thick and logy.

Before he'd left this morning, Tate had given her a quick lesson with the pump-action shotgun. "Just point it in the general direction and pull the trigger," he'd said. He set up a bale of hay as a target. She hadn't braced it properly, and had a nice gun-butt-shaped bruise on her right shoulder to show for it. The hay bale had practically exploded, showering the field with drifting straw. Having ministered to shotgun wounds in the emergency room, she knew exactly what would happen if she hit a man.

With the weapon cradled in her arms, she stepped out of the trailer.

Ric's property was the last one on a road that dead-ended less than a quarter of a mile to the north. Because of the lay of the land, she could hear approaching vehicles long before she could see them.

She swallowed a lump in her throat. Her mouth felt filled with lint. If a strange vehicle turned onto the property, she would disappear into the forest. If anyone followed her, she'd shoot first, ask questions later.

Tippy hadn't liked the shotgun's booming roar. The puppy eyed the weapon with suspicion, and refused to leave the trailer.

"Come on, sweetie," she coaxed until he crept after her. She moved around the end of the trailer where she could watch the road without being seen.

At recognizing Tate's old Bronco, she sagged against

the metal skin. The only prayer she could muster was, "Thank you, thank you, thank you." A selfish prayer that offered little solace. Tate had promised to call if they found Bernie. That he hadn't called portended bad news.

The ancient truck bounced and rumbled up the dirt driveway. She met him in the driveway. His expression was thunderous, those dark eyes flashing. Her throat choked up and her back muscles tensed. If Bernie had died, or been shot, then it was something that had to happen. It still hurt like a knife in the gut.

As soon as his feet were on the ground, she asked, "Is she dead?"

His eyebrows lifted and his face softened. "Bernadette? No. We didn't find any sign of her."

Head hanging, she closed her eyes. Relief made her knees watery. He touched a finger to her chin, urging to look at him.

"We spent hours up at Sweetpot Lake. We had dogs, trackers. Only thing we found was an elk carcass. There's no sign anyone has been there recently."

"I was so sure," she murmured.

"There are lots of little lakes and ponds around. Lots of old mines, too. The forest service is checking them out."

"Why are you upset?"

He pushed a hand through his thick hair, leaving a few unruly tufts sticking out over his ears. A muscle leaped in his jaw. "FBI."

Still cradling the heavy shotgun, she turned for the trailer. She sank onto the metal stoop and waited for him to explain.

"We might be dealing with organized crime."

She blinked rapidly, trying to comprehend organized crime infiltrating this quiet little valley. All she knew about organized crime came from mopping up the results of street gang violence. The way they shot, stabbed, beat each other and abused drugs didn't seem at all organized to her. "Are you talking about the Mafia?"

"I don't know. Turns out your sister stole a car from one Farrah Montgomery. She owns a casino in Las Vegas, and from what I can gather, she's under investigation. I can only assume it's the mob." He lifted his heavy shoulders in a rolling shrug. "The FBI rolled in with warrants, taking everything. They even took over the shooting in the station."

She cocked her head, trying to make sense of everything. "People are trying to kill my sister because she stole a car? What does it have to do with the money we found?"

He kicked a clod of dirt. "I've been busting my butt for days. Collecting evidence, making calls, coordinating techs. Risking death by bees! And the feds waltz in and take everything without so much as a thank-you-very-much." He looked ready to spit. "Thieves!"

She repressed a smile. The situation wasn't funny, but Tate's need for control was. He had yet to learn that true control lay in surrender. "This means we can concentrate on looking for Bernie, right?"

"For what good it will do. All we can do is charge her with stock theft. The feds will probably give her immunity from that."

She was too relieved over the fact that a marksman hadn't put a bullet in her sister's head to care much about the FBI. "Are you hungry? I made chicken and dumplings."

He clamped his hands on his hips. "It's my case, damn it. I did the legwork. I'm handling things just fine without the feds."

"Everything happens for a reason. Even if we can't figure out what the reason is. Acceptance is ever so much easier than going into a battle you're guaranteed to lose."

He waved her off. "Don't start in on me right now. You'll soon find out how much fun the FBI can be. They want to talk to you."

"Me, why? I already told you everything I know."

"The feds think we're a bunch of small-town hicks. Figure I don't know a witness interview from a hole in the ground." He barked a humorless laugh. "I didn't tell them where you are."

"Protecting me or getting even?"

"Both." He finally deigned to notice Tippy who was sitting at his feet and beating up a dust cloud with his tail. Tate crouched and flopped the dog's ears. Laughing, he avoided Tippy's tongue. "Did you say chicken and dumplings?"

"It can be ready in twenty minutes." She handed him the shotgun. "Does this mean I can go home?" She hungered for her comfortable bed and familiar noises. She worried about her chickens and bees.

He looked over his shoulder at the goats. They lay in the corral, soaking up the sunshine and chewing their cuds. "Chances are, the hit man did his job and split. I don't want to play the odds with you at risk. With so many tourists in the area, it's impossible to tell the good guys from the bad guys."

"What about the Shack? I missed work today. As busy as it is, I hate leaving you in the lurch."

His gaze went distant again. "I'll rearrange schedules. Is that going to be a big problem? I know your sister took all your cash."

Dear, sweet man. If only he knew... She laughed, receiving a curious look. "I tend to get in trouble when I'm bored. That's usually a problem for others." She pulled open the trailer door.

Tate followed her inside. His nose wrinkled. Mingled with the savory scent of stewed chicken was the sharp smell of vinegar. She'd scrubbed the place, top to bottom, and washed the windows. It was still shabby and small, but now it was sparkling clean.

"Can I go to the laundromat? The grocery store? I'll wear a hat and sunglasses."

"Hold on a day or two."

"I suppose. Are you still on duty?"

"Nope, I'm back on regular schedule." He fingered his uniform tie. "Mind if I change clothes?"

She bit back the impish urge to ask if she could help. "Go ahead. I'll finish up supper."

He put his hand on the bedroom door, but paused, frowning. His eyes looked black in the shadow of his brow. "If you want, I'll stay out here at night. I can get somebody to stay during the day."

"I'm fine during the day, but have to admit when the sun goes down, it gets pretty spooky. I wouldn't mind you staying." She canted her head at the sofa. "That's really too small for you. I'll let you stay only if you take the bed."

He quirked an eyebrow. His cheek twitched. "Alone?"

A thump rocked her belly. He was kidding, but then again, maybe he wasn't. She didn't want him to be. "None of us are ever truly alone."

TATE STEPPED OUT OF THE tiny shower stall and scrubbed with a towel. He'd actually slept well enough to feel refreshed and clear-headed. He was still angry about the FBI's high-handedness, but he did concede that the Maya Valley's small sheriff's department was not equipped to handle assassins and organized crime. He stepped into a pair of briefs, then cracked open the door and peered into the bedroom. It was empty and the door was closed. Wreathed in billowing steam, he gathered his uniform.

He was tying his tie when he began noticing an aroma of peppers and onions and that buttery oil Diana used for cooking. He heard singing. He couldn't remember seeing a radio in the trailer, but it sounded like the soulful pipes of Mama Cass belting out *Dream a Little Dream of Me*.

He opened the door. Diana stood before the stove, waving a spatula over a frying pan as if it were a conductor's baton. Swinging her hips, her wild hair swaying, she sang. Her sweet, sultry voice made his jaw drop.

He was learning more about Diana in a weekend than he'd learned in a year.

She noticed him and smiled. He regretted the loss of her singing.

"I made coffee. Have you time for an omelette and biscuits?"

"Whole wheat biscuits, right?" Last night, she'd served dumplings made from whole wheat and oats. He'd never seen such a thing and had been reluctant to eat them. Dumplings were supposed to be pillowy and white. She firmly believed that white flour was dead food, robbed of nourishment. Once he got over the texture, the dumplings hadn't been too bad. He could probably get used to her cooking.

She set a big cup of coffee in front of him along with a cloth-covered basket of biscuits, butter and honey.

"If you treated your husband like this, I'm surprised he let you go." As soon as the words were out of his mouth, he felt like an idiot for the cavalier comment.

Her sunny smile reassured him. "I didn't treat him like this. I was much too busy to bother with cooking. Our marriage was more of a business arrangement. We enhanced each other's careers." She lifted the pan off the stove and slid a fluffy omelette onto a plate.

"How long were you married?"

She set the plate before him. His mouth watered at the sight. She used eggs from her own chickens, and the yolks were so rich they were practically orange. The omelette was filled with green peppers and onions, and the edges were crispy, just the way he liked it.

"Technically eight years, but we were separated for almost two years." She tipped her chin, her smile amused. "If either of us had ever sat down and taken the time to think, I doubt the marriage would have lasted more than a month."

Usually he kept his curiosity in check, but in the intimacy of the trailer, engulfed in the aromas and taste of the food, he wanted to know more. "So what broke you up?"

She filled a bowl with oatmeal and brought it to the table, taking the chair across from him. She dribbled honey onto the cereal. "First Mother took ill, and I had to take care of her. Then I got ill."

"I thought you said he's a doctor."

"A plastic surgeon. A very good one, too. The prettiest breasts in Arizona are his doing." She spooned oatmeal into her mouth. Her eyes looked gray this morning, like an overcast sky, still and solemn. "Don't think he's the villain. We were equals in our relationship. Besides, he didn't leave me, I left him."

Food lodged in his throat. He knew all about bad husbands who ignored and neglected sick wives. "Why did you leave?"

She cocked her head. She must have heard more in the question than he'd intended to reveal.

"I mean, shees, that's none of my business. Sorry for prying." He focused on the food, eating fast.

"You aren't prying," she said. "I'm flattered by your interest. I must say, you're the most non-intrusive bartender I've ever met. You actively avoid hearing other people's stories. Why is that?"

Because learning others' secrets meant sharing his own. "I'm not a nosy guy."

She laughed. The husky sweetness of it made him want to sigh. Over the last few months he'd grown used to the sound of her laughter. He'd miss it terribly if she were gone.

"How can a cop not be nosy?"

"It's different when it's on the job." He slathered butter on a biscuit. She used the real stuff, no margarine.

"How long have you lived here?" she asked.

"Going on five years." He put the buttered biscuit on his plate.

"And still so much the outsider. No one knows who you really are. I only know that because there are a lot of women who are real curious about you." Her gaze dipped seductively. "Can't say as I blame them."

"Don't pump me for information, Red. Call it a favor, okay? One thing we have in common, we both live day-to-day. The past is past, the future is unknown." Her even gaze was hard to take. He felt churlish and small. "You accused me of running. Okay, you got me, you're right. I'm running as fast as I can. But it's my monster in the closet, not yours. I don't feel like sharing."

"I don't mean to upset you."

He leaned back on the rickety chair and shoved a hand through his hair. "It's not you…it is you. I don't want to spill my guts, but you make me want to."

"There might be a good reason."

"Because I allegedly have the hots for you?"

She shook her head, never losing eye contact. "Our souls are encased in flesh for a purpose. In order to understand connection, we have to experience separation. But we're never alone, not really. When we have a need, the universe provides the means to fulfill it. All we have to do is accept what's offered."

His chest hurt, as if she reached inside him and squeezed his heart.

"Some wounds heal by themselves. Some don't. Especially wounds of the spirit."

He cleared his thick throat. "No offense, Red, but I don't need your help healing anything. I don't need anybody."

"Perhaps I need you." She grinned and filled her spoon with oatmeal. "Eat your eggs before they get cold."

He finished eating, silent, but aware of her watching him. Studying him. He didn't believe for a second that she needed him. She was as self-contained and self-confident as anyone he'd ever met. Needing her? The question shook him to the core. Even if he did need her, he didn't deserve her. He tried to muster anger at her, some defense against the effect she had on him. The best he could hope for was physical distance.

He made sure his equipment was in order. He grunted his thanks for breakfast.

When he sat behind the wheel of the Bronco, he made the mistake of looking back. She stood in the trailer doorway, arms crossed, her curls dancing on a light breeze.

Back in New York, there had been a major crimes investigator who was legendary throughout the Boroughs—throughout the entire Eastern seaboard—by virtue of his interrogation techniques. Dubbed the Professor, he wore thick glasses that magnified his eyes into hard-boiled eggs and had ears like satellite dishes. He looked fussy and soft, but put him in an interrogation room with the most hardened gangbanger and the perp would spill his guts. Always. A miracle man.

Tate considered interrogation skills a gift, like being able to draw or turn your tongue upside down. Diana had the gift. He suddenly realized she'd been working on him for months, slowly chipping away his defenses, digging holes under his walls. She was a brilliant interrogator, as canny as the Professor.

Chapter Nine

Bernie stroked the gelding's nose. He was a nice little critter, mouse gray with black legs, mane and tail. He had enough quarter horse in him to make his head especially pretty. His hide shone like wax from the hours she'd spent grooming him. "Are you bored, too, buddy?" she asked.

The one danger she hadn't considered when she headed for the hills was that hiding out was a big, fat, bone-numbing, brain-frying bore. Sure Farrah had been a high and mighty muckety-muck, but what was done, was done. By now she must have dropped off those murderous chumps' radar. Time to move on. Farrah's bully boys couldn't chase her forever.

Anger tightened her forehead. Bernie and Farrah had some fun times. Who'd have thought a rich chick like her would have such a slummy side? Farrah had been a good person. Generous, sweet, always ready to laugh. It was like they'd been best girlfriends all their lives.

Bernie had told Farrah everything. The nastier the story, the scummier the characters, the better Farrah liked it. She'd lapped up prison tales like a cat eating tuna. She must have told somebody about Bernie's family. How else could those chumps have known where Mom once lived?

Bernie sighed. She missed Las Vegas, the noise, the

lights, the people. It was the best place she'd ever lived and that bozo Tim made it impossible for her to ever go back.

No more men. They were the real jinxes in her life. Tim had fooled her into thinking he was smart. Smart like a starving dog, nothing more.

She shoved her hands into her back pockets and paced. A grove of aspen trees formed natural palisades on two sides of her camp. She'd used pine branches and rotting boards from an old miner's shack to make a lean-to. Her camp was small and tidy, hidden by terrain and foliage. She was proud her woodcraft had come back so easily.

"The second coming of Daniel Boone," Dad used to say about her. It was the only nice thing he'd ever said to or about her.

She lifted her gaze to the sky. If she had to, she could live here all summer. She had a good water supply and the mountains were full of campers. Night raids kept her well-stocked with fresh food. She even had a nice little Walkman to listen to, when she could stand the static from the lousy radio reception.

Absently, she rubbed her aching arm. The wound wasn't hot anymore and the stiffness was nearly gone. Diana had done a bang-up job of cleaning it up, plus she had an iron constitution and always healed well. Even in prison where the high-carb diet seemed designed to keep the inmates fat and dull, she'd thrived physically.

"I'm going bonkers," she told the horse. He lipped the ground, in search of sparse grass stems. "Should have borrowed some of Diana's books."

She hunkered into a crouch and picked up a twig. She traced idle designs in the dirt. Diana—who'd have ever dreamed she'd give up the cushy life to live in Dad's old vacation shack!—would have discovered Tim by now.

Maybe even figured out the Buick had been stolen. So how long until life got back to normal?

Imagining her sister discovering Tim, she sighed. She felt bad about the mess, but Diana could handle it. That's what she did best—handled things, cleaned up messes, made the world right. A wave of nostalgia swept through Bernie. Diana was a genuinely good person, always had been even in the days when she'd acted like her sweat didn't stink. She'd mellowed, a lot, changed into a whole new person. If they hadn't been twins, Bernie wouldn't have recognized her own sister.

That Diana was strong hadn't changed. She'd always been the strong one. The smart one. Daddy's little darling, always making him proud.

Too bad, she thought, that all this craziness was going on. She liked the new, improved Diana. Or maybe the *old,* improved Diana. It was like she was the kid she'd once been, all wide-eyed and curious and fun-loving—before Mom and Dad turned her into a performing poodle. It would have been fun to get to know her again. They could act like real sisters.

She sketched a circle in the dirt. In a few days the moon would be full. She could make it to the shack in one night. The bees would be snug in their little bee beds; Diana would be snug in hers. Take the money and run. A quick detour to Phoenix to sign paperwork and tell Mom's legal beagle where to send her inheritance, then off to Mexico.

She'd buy a necklace or something to send to Diana. A good quality piece with real jewels to make up for the hassles. Diana would like that. No hard feelings between them.

With any luck at all, she'd make another good, best girlfriend like Farrah. Having a girlfriend had been better than any relationship with a man. Men were bad news, definitely the cause of all her bad luck. She closed her eyes and lifted her face to the sun, envisioning tall, fruity drinks and white-sand beaches and hours of girlish laughter. Life was going to be so sweet.

DIANA HAD BEEN WITHOUT a telephone since moving to the Maya Valley. She didn't miss it. As a physician, she'd been a slave to her pager. In hindsight, she realized she hadn't been communicating on the telephone, she'd been avoiding human contact, avoiding having to look people in the eyes and deal with them. It was easy to maintain professional coolness when speaking to a disembodied voice.

Still, it was weird to not know any telephone numbers. She called directory assistance and at the computerized prompting asked for the town of McClintock. She asked for Marlee Crowder's number. A voice gave it to her, and she jotted it down.

She pondered what she wanted to do. Tate had specifically instructed her to not leave Ric's place. Remembering the look on that murderer's face while he strode calmly out of the sheriff's station squashed all desire to step off the property.

Finding Bernie was the only way out of this mess. She punched in Marlee's number.

"You've reached the number of Dr. Marlee Crowder. Small animal clinic hours are 7 a.m. to 3 p.m. Monday through Thursday. If this is an emergency, please press one now. If this is not an emergency, please leave your name and telephone number and I will get back to you as soon as possible. Thank you."

Diana waited for the beep, then left the number of the borrowed cell phone. Marlee had been born and raised here, a member of the McClintock family, which had given the town its name. She knew everyone for miles around.

Marlee returned the call in fifteen minutes. "Diana!" she exclaimed. "Is everything all right? Are you okay?"

Diana chuckled. She'd never heard the vet sounding so frantic before. "Safe and sound."

"Are you sure? I mean, gosh, with everything going on. The whole town is walking on pins and needles. The hardware store had a run on dead-bolt locks. You can't buy ammunition anywhere. It's sold out. It's scary. Are you still up at Ric's?"

"Yes. And I know you're terribly busy, but I could sure use your help."

"I'm only a few miles from you. I just finished turning a breech foal in a mare and I could use a break. I can be there in ten minutes."

"I'll put on some coffee for you. Oh, and do you have a good map of the area handy?"

"Somewhere. I'm on my way."

In less than fifteen minutes, Marlee's big white pickup turned into the driveway. The vet stuck a wiry arm out the window and waved. She parked behind Diana's truck and jumped out. She placed her hands in the small of her back and arched, letting her head roll backward.

"Rough delivery?" Diana asked.

"Would have been easier if the owner had called me before the mare was in trouble. Almost lost her and the foal." Marlee Crowder was tall and lean, her hands strong and her face open. Diana considered her a true wild woman, far more wily and wise than her youth warranted.

"You look stressed out, lady," Marlee said. "I'm not sure I like your color."

The vet was the only person in the valley who knew Diana's complete history. They'd had many enjoyable discussions about holistic healing, spirituality and doctoring both animals and people. She was the only person Diana allowed to fuss over her.

"I am stressed."

"I know how rumors and stories get spread around here. Hard to tell truth from fancy, especially when folks are spooked. Do you mind telling me what's really going on?"

Diana hooked her arm with Marlee's and led her into the trailer. She poured coffee and told her friend about Bernie's arrival and disappearance, the corpse in the car, the men who'd raided the beehives and their respective deaths, and the hit man who thought she was Bernie.

"Gawd... It's like a movie."

"I wish it were a movie," Diana said with a sigh. "I'd turn it off. That man looked right at me." A shudder rippled down her spine.

Marlee looked around the trailer. "At least Ric came through for you. He's always good in a pinch."

Ric Buchanan was Marlee's brother-in-law, and the two were as tight as blood siblings. Marlee's close, loving family always filled Diana with yearning. Her birth family was lost to her, it was too late to have children and even marriage seemed unlikely. "Tate's been a lifesaver, too. Literally."

"So what can I do for you?" Marlee asked. "Do you want to come to the ranch?"

"I'm safer here. Besides, I don't think your mother will appreciate having my goats around."

"Mama keeps goats as pets for her show horses." She lifted her shoulders in a quick shrug. "You really should. Mama has more room than she knows what to do with, plus her house has a security system. Plus there are tons of people around all the time."

Diana considered Bernie's pursuers. Her driveway had been full of vehicles, but that hadn't stopped those men from searching her house or tracking the briefcase to the beehives. A street filled with people hadn't stopped that man from trying to shoot her. Being in a sheriff's station hadn't stopped the hit man from committing murder. She couldn't bear it if anyone else was harmed because of her and Bernie.

"Tate thinks I'm safe right where I am. I trust him."

Marlee waggled her eyebrows. "I bet you do. Anything I should know?" A not-so-subtle inquiry about Diana's ongoing interest in Tate.

"When I have something to report, I'll tell you."

"I don't know why you bother with him, Diana. I honestly don't. Yeah, he's eye candy, and when he smiles even my sensible little heart goes pitty-pat, but he's a player. He's dated at least a dozen women that I know of. He won't get serious about any woman until he's sixty and realizes he has no one to fetch his slippers. You can do better."

"I thought you liked him."

"I do. I just like you better and don't want you hurt."

"There's more to Tate Raleigh than you see on the surface."

"Oh, I'm sure." She leaned back on a chair, and her smile turned wicked. "Like, I wouldn't mind peeking at what's underneath his shirt."

Diana covered her mouth to stop giggles. "Very nice. Trust me." She waved a hand. "But quit talking about him. I have a problem."

"Did you see him naked?"

"Dr. Crowder, may we discuss business?"

"If you promise to take pictures next time, Dr. Dover." She hooted a laugh. "So what do you need help with?"

Diana explained about Sweetpot Lake and how she'd been so certain Bernie might be hiding there. "She left all that money at my place. She must be waiting until the coast is clear. Maybe it's another place I'm remembering. Do you know of any fishing ponds or lakes, privately owned, with old mining ruins nearby?"

"All the fishing I ever did was in the Maya River. But I do know someone who might know. Edward Keil. He's an old-time mountain man. He knows more about the area than anyone."

"Will he talk to me?"

Marlee held up her hands. "Not a chance. He's paranoid and convinced the government is out to get him. The only way to reach his house is on foot or horseback, and if you aren't careful, he might shoot you."

"Then why did you even mention him?"

"Mama has known him since she was a girl. She and I sort of take care of him. We ride up there every spring to make sure he survived the winter. Things like that. He's crotchety and eccentric, but I like him."

"I do believe I'm seeing a sweet side to you, girl."

"Ah, cut it out." Marlee checked her watch, and her nose wrinkled in concentration. "It takes about two, two-and-a-half hours to ride up to his place from the trailhead. Maybe I can go tomorrow morning."

Diana noticed Tippy lift his head and cock an ear. She opened the door and leaned outside.

"What's the matter?" Marlee asked.

Diana heard an approaching vehicle. Rather than waste time coaxing the dog, she snapped a lead onto his collar. Then she picked up the shotgun. "Somebody is coming."

Marlee stood. "Tate?"

That didn't sound like the asthmatic old Bronco, but it

could be a cruiser. "We better wait outside in case it isn't."

Marlee gave the shotgun a pointed look. "I have a rifle." She hurried to her pickup. She pulled a rifle from a rack and a box of ammunition from the glove box. The women moved behind the trailer where they could watch the driveway without being seen.

A beige SUV slowed at the driveway entrance. Diana's heart climbed into her throat.

"Recognize it?" she whispered to Marlee.

"I was hoping you did. Oh, my, here it comes."

Marlee grabbed Diana's arm in a steely grip. "We're not taking any chances. Into the woods. Now!"

"DEPUTY RALEIGH, MIGHT I have a word?"

A polite enough question, but coming from an FBI field agent, it sounded more like an order. Tate briefly considered ignoring the man. He'd come to treasure the folksy atmosphere and informality of the small-town sheriff's department. It hadn't been until he left New York City that he realized how much he despised bureaucrats, endless rules and regulations and watchdogs in every corner. The agent in his suit and tie represented red tape and slavish devotion to memos and flow charts.

The rebelliousness lasted only a few seconds. Gil Vance was right. McClintock couldn't afford a major criminal investigation that spread across several states and possibly involved organized crime. Interstate crimes were the FBI's jurisdiction.

"Yes, Mr. Albright?"

The agent indicated the briefing room. Looking glum, Gil was already in there, seated at a table and folding a message slip into a tricorner hat. After Tate walked inside, the agent closed the door.

"Agent Albright would like you to bring Diana in," Gil said. The pink paper hat fit on the end of his index finger. He was angry.

"You have her statement," Tate told the agent.

Albright smiled tightly. Of medium height, he was a slender man with the ropy build of a long distance runner. Heavy eyelids shaded his eyes. He turned a sheet of paper around on a table so Tate could see it. "Aliases," he said. "Bernice O'Malley, Bernie Smith, Marie O'Malley, Diana Dover."

Tate picked up the list and scanned the long list of Bernadette's assumed identities. "Diana said her sister impersonated her before. So what?"

"The sheriff informs me that Ms. Dover keeps to herself. It's rare to see her in town on the weekends."

"She's my employee. She works Monday through Friday at the bar I own. What she does on the weekends is nobody's business but her own."

The agent perched on the edge of the table. His expression seemed appropriate for a kindergarten teacher addressing rowdy charges. "Have you actually seen Bernadette O'Malley? Has anyone?"

Tate laughed and swung his head side to side. "Diana impersonated her sister and arranged for the stolen Buick and Robertson's corpse as a diversion. And oh yeah, she made a horse disappear, too. Interesting theory. Tell me, Mr. Albright, do you also investigate X-files?"

"Bring Diana in," Gil said. "We can clear this up with a simple fingerprint check."

Tate took one step closer to the man and straightened his shoulders. The agent flinched. "You took all our evidence, sir. You know everything we know and more. Why are you still here?"

"To apprehend O'Malley, deputy."

"Ha! What's Bernadette's connection to Farrah Montgomery? What's the connection to organized crime?"

"As I've already explained to the sheriff, it's my belief that O'Malley and Robertson are involved with Farrah Montgomery. It is also my belief that Montgomery has ties to organized crime. As for Ms. Dover, it is standard operating procedure to interview family members. In my experience, they always know more than they think they know."

"Well, duh," Tate said in a deliberately mocking tone. "Thanks for telling me what I already know."

"Tate," Gil warned.

"In my experience," Tate continued, "Feebs like to play spy versus spy games, and to hell with local law enforcement or private citizens. What exactly are you after?"

"I'm sure I don't know what you mean, deputy."

Like hell you don't, Tate told the man with his glare. This case was starting to stink like a kennel of wet dogs. "It's my belief," he said, imitating the agent's condescending tone, "that it isn't Diana's information you want. You want her because she's Bernadette's twin. She's bait to nab the hit man. Or is it Farrah Montgomery you're after?"

"You're mistaken, deputy. Ms. Dover is a witness, nothing more. I'll take every precaution to ensure her safety."

"If you want information, I'll talk to her. She's not setting foot in town until the coast is clear." He reached for the door.

"I read your report, deputy," Albright said. "Diana Dover is a licensed physician."

Albright's tone made the short hairs prickle Tate's neck.

"As you should be aware, doctors are required by law to report gunshot wounds. I must have missed seeing in your report where *Dr.* Dover reported Bernadette O'Malley's injuries."

"Whoa, whoa!" Gil exclaimed. "You don't come in here threatening citizens in my town, Mr. Albright. I don't look kindly on malicious prosecution."

"See what I mean, Gil? He wants to stake her out in the middle of Main Street. Who are you trying to catch, Albright?"

"Diana didn't break the law and you know it," Gil said.

"Failure to report, harboring a fugitive, conspiracy? She doesn't sound all that law-abiding to me."

The sheriff rose and tossed the paper hat at a trash can. He turned for the door.

The agent jumped to his feet. "Sheriff Vance, I am conducting an authorized investigation in which you are obligated to grant me full cooperation."

Gil exchanged a hard look with Tate then faced the agent. "Have you met Judge Elias Woodman? He's our local circuit court judge. He decides what's authorized and what's not around here. Give him a call. Just be sure to tell him I said hello."

"This is not in your best interests." Albright's face had turned bright red.

"I've spent the last fifty years deciding what's in my best interests," Gil said. "I don't need your input." He walked out and Tate followed. Gil entered his office and invited Tate to join him. He closed the door. "This is serious business."

"No kidding."

Gil pulled a slip of paper from his desk drawer. He

pushed it across the desk to Tate. "I made a discreet inquiry. Found out who Williams called from here."

Tate read the paper. Sparkle City casino, Las Vegas, Nevada. Poor dumb mope. Thought he was calling for legal aid, and ended up arranging his own execution. "Did you show Albright?"

Gil smiled tightly. "Forgot. I called the casino, asked to speak to Farrah Montgomery. She's unavailable. When I identified myself, I was mysteriously disconnected. So Bernadette and Robertson heist Montgomery's car. Only nobody reports the theft and Montgomery is missing in action. Now we got a hit man convention in town."

Tate knew Gil had more to tell. "And?"

"Your friend in Arizona called. First, no ballistics matches on the .22 we sent. Second, he pulled a nice palm print off the screen door at the murdered woman's house. Surprise, it belongs to O'Malley."

So Tate had been right. Bernadette had sought her sister and mother, and an innocent woman's death was a direct result.

"Third, Diana's mother used to live in one of those compound communities. The kind with guard houses and expensive security. A guard reported that a woman matching Bernadette's description tried to talk her way into the compound. She was asking for Ruth O'Malley. Within minutes after the guard ran her off, two men asked for the same address, same name. Only get this, the descriptions don't match Taylor and Williams."

"Sounds like an army is after our girl." He laid a hand on Gil's telephone. "Let me make some phone calls. If I can't get anything from Nevada, I have a few sources back in New York who might shed some light on what the feds are after."

Gil indicated permission with a wave of his hand. "Speaking of calls, Oscar is looking for you."

Tate groaned, eyes closed. His evening bartender must be having a fit over rearranging work schedules to make up for Tate's and Diana's absences. He couldn't afford to close the Shack during the day; he depended too much on the lunch crowd. He especially needed to stay open now. All this commotion had made the Shack a popular place with everyone dropping in for a dose of gossip. He hated taking advantage of a crisis, but he might make enough money to offer some breathing room.

He dialed the Shack, and hoped someone was around to answer the phone.

A heavily accented voice said, "Track Shack Bar and Grill. *¿Qué?*"

Tate didn't recognize the voice. "This is Raleigh, who is this?"

The man replied in rapid-fire Spanish, of which Tate didn't catch a word. Then he caught a shout, "*Tía* Consuela!"

"Where you at?" Consuela demanded a few seconds later. She sounded more cranky than usual. Tate could barely hear her over the clanking, shouts and laughter in the background.

"I'm working. Who's there with you?"

"Jesus, Jorge and Lupe and Dulce. Susan came in, too. Been running at a gallop since we opened. What, you don't care no more about this place, eh?"

A flash of brilliance struck him. "You're in charge."

"What?"

"You are now officially promoted to manager. Hire as many of your grandkids, nieces and nephews as you want. Coordinate the work schedules with Oscar. Deal with suppliers. You know what needs done. It's all yours."

Silence answered. That was a first. He grinned, wondering why he hadn't thought about this before. While he still had the advantage of surprise, he added, "I'll drop in when I can, but I trust you to take care of everything."

"Okay," she said, subdued.

"Are you sure this is all right by you?"

"*Sí!*" She slammed down the phone, making him flinch away from the earpiece.

Openmouthed, Gil stared. "You put Consuela in charge of the Shack? You'll have to stage a coup to wrestle it away from her."

"Can't be helped." He chuckled. "I should have done it before. She knows ten times more about running a restaurant than I'll ever learn in a lifetime."

"If you're really thinking about selling, why not sell to her?"

Tate rubbed his thumb against his first two fingers. "*Dinero.* She can't afford it."

"Is that what she said?"

Tate hadn't asked. He'd assumed she didn't have the money. He shoved the idea aside. He'd think about the Shack later. At the moment he had some calls to make.

"I bet Albright will have a warrant for Diana by close of business today. Let's hope by then we know what we're up against and how we can protect her."

Chapter Ten

Diana crouched behind a lodgepole pine, and peered through the budding foliage of a scrub oak. From this position, she had a good view of the trailer, the driveway and a dusty Blazer with Nevada plates. A man sat behind the steering wheel.

Diana was positive she'd never seen him before.

Marlee cradled a rifle against her chest. She looked more excited than scared.

Diana wrinkled her nose at the trailer house. "I forgot the darned telephone. I'm so out of the habit of keeping it with me. Give me yours."

Marlee lowered her face and peered upward, sheepish. "I left it in the truck."

"We're a hopeless pair," Diana whispered.

Marlee peeked around a tree trunk. "So what's that guy doing anyway?"

Diana hadn't a clue. "We need to get out of here. Find a telephone." She looked around at the thick forest and rocky, hilly terrain. The nearest house was half a mile down the road, but it was a vacation cabin and Diana hadn't noticed any signs of occupation. They could set off to the east in the hopes of finding a house or ranger station or forest road.

"The river is that way? Right?" She pointed east.

"Uh-uh. You aren't thinking about cutting cross-country, are you? Aside from the fact that the bears are out and hungry, if we end up out after dark...no thanks."

The car door opened. Both women tensed. Diana kept a hand on Tippy's muzzle so he wouldn't bark. The man looked to be of average height and weight, wearing khaki trousers and a bright red polo shirt. He looked younger and smaller than the hit man who'd pretended to be an attorney, but as Tate had said, the hit man most likely wore a disguise.

He walked up to the trailer and knocked on the door.

"Do assassins knock?" Marlee whispered.

"Have to check my handbook," Diana muttered. She guessed the distance from their hiding place to Marlee's pickup at about forty yards. "I bet he drops the act and goes inside. When he does, we can make it to your truck. Are you game?"

Knocking on the metal door echoed off the trees. He turned from the door, shaded his eyes with a hand and looked around. "Hello?" he called. It echoed, *o-o-o*.

Marlee sat back on her heels. "Hmm. Maybe he's a lost tourist."

"Or that's what he wants us to believe." Her conviction wavered when the man stepped off the stoop and headed for the barn. He kept calling hello. The goats trotted to the fence, bleating and baaing eagerly. The man reached through the wire and scratched a goat behind the ears.

"Must be one of those soft-hearted hit men." Marlee giggled, then slapped a hand over her mouth. "Wouldn't he be trying to sneak up on you?"

The man knocked on the barn door. When that resulted in nothing, he ambled back to the driveway. He cocked his head as if examining Marlee's truck. He placed a hand on the hood.

Marlee's truck engine would still be warm. Awash in a fresh wave of fear, Diana stiffened.

He cupped both hands around his mouth and yelled, "Mrs. Dover? Hello!"

Diana's heart hammered her chest. Her palms grew greasy where she gripped the shotgun.

He returned to the SUV. Instead of driving away, he leaned against the front bumper and pulled what appeared to be a notebook from his pants pocket. He hunched over, writing.

"I can shoot him in the leg," Marlee said.

Diana guessed her friend was only half-joking. She examined her options. Wait him out, and hope he didn't have a partner even now sneaking up on them through the forest. Risk heading into the forest and hope they didn't run into a bear or get lost. She glanced at the shotgun. "Let's draw him out."

"How?"

Diana jutted her chin toward the barn. "I'll sneak behind the barn. You hide in the trees. I'll call him. If he pulls a gun, *then* you can shoot him in the leg. If he doesn't, we'll get the drop on him. Can we do this?"

"I'm not the one who preaches peace and non-violence," Marlee said. "The question is, can *you* do it?"

"You bet I can." She lowered the shotgun to the ground, then tied Tippy's leash to a tree. "Down," she commanded and pushed on his nose until he lay on his belly. "Stay." He watched her with anxious eyes. She prayed he wouldn't start barking.

The women sneaked from tree to tree, always watching the man. He seemed prepared to wait all day for her. Marlee found a hiding place about thirty feet from the barn.

Diana went farther until she was out of the man's line of sight. Only then did she race across open ground and behind the barn. Her heart pounded as if she'd run twenty miles rather than twenty feet. She wiped first one hand then the other on her shirt, gripped the shotgun and inched along the barn wall.

She glanced at Marlee's hiding place. Green shadows concealed the woman. Diana pumped a round into the shotgun's chamber. The *ka-chack* echoed and the man jumped away from the Blazer.

"Hello!" she tried to call, but it came out a squeak. She cleared her throat, then shouted, "Hello!"

"Mrs. Dover? Hello?" He shoved the notebook into a rear pocket and strode across the grass. His hands were empty and his expression was eager. "I'm Patrick Coles with the National Press. May I—"

Diana stepped from behind the barn, the shotgun leveled at his chest.

Coles gasped, stumbled backward, tangled in his feet and went down so hard his teeth clacked. His mouth opened, his face reddened, but no sound came out even though his throat was working frantically.

In her peripheral vision Diana saw Marlee step out of the woods, her rifle aimed at the intruder's head.

"Hey! Hey!" he shouted and reached for his shirt pocket.

"Keep those hands up!" Marlee was now close enough for him to smell the gun oil on the rifle barrel.

"God! I'm a reporter, I have credentials. I'm not the law, Ms. O'Malley! Oh, God! Don't shoot me!"

"Turn over," Marlee ordered. "On your face, arms out. Do it, or I'll blow off your kneecaps!"

Diana arched her eyebrows. She'd always known her friend was gutsy—she had to be in order to doctor cattle and horses. She had never realized how truly gutsy Marlee was. Impressive. "Do what she says."

Careful to keep both hands in view, the man struggled to turn over onto his elbows, then sank to the grass and spread his arms.

"If he moves an eyelash," Marlee said, "pull the trigger." She tucked the rifle beneath her left arm then carefully patted the man's sides, pockets and legs. She removed the notebook he'd been writing in and a wallet. She stepped back. "Keep your hands out and roll over."

His face was dead white. He looked to be perhaps twenty-five, maybe a youthful thirty. Grass stained his khakis. Marlee patted his shirt front and trouser pockets for weapons. Then she backed away, the rifle again at ready.

"He's clean."

"Should we tie him up?" Diana asked.

"I don't know who you think I am, but I swear, I'm harmless, Ms. O'Malley." He tried a smile, it was thin and quivery. "Mrs. Dover?" he directed at Marlee. "It's not what you think. Honest to God."

Great, Diana thought. Hit men were actually mistaking her for Bernie.

Marlee flipped open the wallet. "Patrick Coles, Las Vegas, Nevada." She handed the wallet to Diana.

Diana scanned a driver's license, credit cards, a National Press employee identification card and a library card. They looked legitimate, but how would she know? "How did you know where to find me?"

"I told you, I work for the National Press, Ms. O'Malley. Can I get up? I think I'm on an anthill. Please?"

"All right, on your knees, but put your hands on your head." Diana backed a step. He struggled onto his knees and laced his fingers atop his head. He tried a wan smile, which neither woman returned.

"I'm an investigative reporter. For the past year I've been working on a story about Farrah Montgomery."

Marlee looked as intrigued as Diana felt. "Go on."

"Is this a joke?" he asked Diana. "You know why I'm here."

She loosed a long breath. If this man actually was a reporter working for a large syndication, then maybe he could help get out the word that she, Diana, was not and never had been her criminal sister. "I am *not* Bernadette O'Malley."

He blinked rapidly.

"I'm Diana Dover. Bernie is my sister."

He looked between the women, uncertain and suspicious.

"Bernadette," Marlee said, "is gone, *pfft*, vanished into the mountains. So if you're a hit man, you've got the wrong sister."

His hands began a slow slide off his head. Marlee brought up the rifle with the ease of an expert. He locked his fingers. "I wasn't sure there was a Diana Dover. O'Malley used the name as an alias. You're really sisters then?"

"Identical twins. On the surface anyway. So why are you here? Unless you do want to kill Bernie."

"I told you, I'm working on a story about Farrah Montgomery. Three weeks ago, she vanished. None of her people are talking. Nobody is confirming anything. And let me tell you, in Las Vegas discretion is rarely considered valiant. I heard from an inside source that Montgomery was kidnapped. There was a ransom drop, but it went wrong, and they didn't recover Farrah. A lot of people think she's dead."

Diana's belly tightened most unpleasantly. She lowered the shotgun. "Half a million dollars in ransom?"

"Something like that."

"So everyone thinks my sister kidnapped Farrah." She drew a deep breath to steady herself. "And committed murder."

"Yeah. But the law is the least of your sister's worries." He narrowed his eyes and peered closely at her face. "You look a lot like her."

"I told you, we're identical twins. Much to my dismay at the moment."

Marlee cleared her throat. She looked skeptical about Coles's story. "How did you find Diana?"

"It wasn't hard. I talked to the old guy over at the *Bugle* office. Frank...whatever."

"Carson," Marlee said. "I know for a fact he wouldn't have told you where Diana was."

"He didn't. He told me about Robertson and the man who died from bee stings and the man who was killed in the sheriff's station. I did some research, and found out who you are, Mrs. Dover. Or who you said you were— whatever. Anyway, I stopped in at a diner and overheard people talking. They mentioned Buchanan's place. Public records showed me where it was. It's all on the up and up. I didn't do anything illegal."

Ah, the charm of small towns, Diana thought. "Never mind that. How did you even know Bernie was in the area?"

He gave her an *oh please* look. "I picked up the story off the wire. Make that multiple stories. Your sister has been involved in shoot-outs, there's a possible connection to a murder in Phoenix, and a murder here and now a fugitive search."

Diana hadn't read a newspaper, other than the chatty

local weekly, in over a year. She'd forgotten how small a place the world could be. "Do you know who's sending people after my sister?"

"I have a good idea. Farrah's father is Douglas Montgomery." He nodded as if he expected them to recognize the name. He seemed rather disappointed when they didn't. "He's an international arms dealer. He started out legit, making billions by supplying small countries with weapons of war. But then he got political. If the allegations are true, he's outfitting terrorists. Police agencies around the world have been trying to catch him for years."

"Oh, my."

"The FBI believes he's using Farrah's casino to launder cash and get it out of the country."

Oh, Bernie, look what you've done... "So where is this man?"

"Nobody knows." He grinned as if sharing a naughty secret. "Nobody has actually seen Montgomery in over ten years. Some say he committed suicide, some say he lives on a secluded island, others claim he's hiding out in the Middle East. What is a fact is that Farrah is his only child. Even phantoms care about their kids."

"So he isn't after the money, he wants revenge."

"It's possible." He shrugged as if to say, *That's very bad.*

The shotgun suddenly felt very, very heavy—and very, very inadequate. "We have to call Tate. He can find out if this guy is who he says he is." She turned a tight smile on Coles. "No offense, but I don't like getting shot at. So until the law arrives, I'm tying you up."

He groaned and began lowering his hands. Both women whipped weapons to their shoulders. He locked his fingers atop his head.

"Okay, okay—jeez! No wonder Montgomery hasn't gotten to you. You ladies are mean."

IF THE SITUATION WEREN'T so serious, Tate would be laughing his head off. A peek at Gil showed the sheriff was fighting a smile. Like a pair of banditas, Marlee and Diana toted weapons. Patrick Coles was trussed up on a kitchen chair. Both hands were tied behind his back and his ankles were secured to the chair legs. The man looked relieved to see uniformed officers.

"And to think I was worried about you, Red." Tate nodded at the man. "So what's your story?"

Patrick Coles started talking, the words tumbling out of his mouth like water from a hose. While listening to the reporter's tale, he and Gil examined the contents of Coles's wallet.

Tate didn't much care for journalists. His comments had been taken out of context and misquoted often enough to put a permanent bad taste in his mouth. At the same time, he respected them, especially investigative reporters. Some of them were as accomplished in detective work as the most experienced cop. Since shady types would say things to reporters they wouldn't dream of telling the police, many journalists had better sources than the cops did.

Gil asked, "So how exactly did O'Malley get close enough to Montgomery to kidnap her?"

"Farrah has a weakness for strays." Coles looked warily at Diana. "Hookers, strippers, addicts, ex-cons. She takes them in, cleans them up, buddies around with them. Kind of a weird hobby. Or maybe it's her trashy side." He smiled at the law officers, guy to guy. "Who can figure women, right?"

The story accounted for the money, the bugged briefcase and the army on Bernadette's tail. Tate wasn't certain he was falling for it, though. Something about the reporter bugged him. He seemed too eager.

"I think Farrah is dead, and her father knows it."

"May I search your vehicle?" Tate asked.

"Anything. Look, I'm on the up-and-up. I've been working this story for months. I can't state with full assurance that it is Douglas Montgomery behind the hit men. I am confident in saying that if he is, he won't stop until he gets what he wants."

Tate untied the man, but snapped on handcuffs and led him outside. He put him in the back seat of Gil's Range Rover. Gil got on the horn to dispatch to run checks on Coles's identification and vehicle registration.

"I'll search his car, sir," Tate told Gil. He glanced at the women, and grinned. Coles must have peed his pants when they leveled weapons at his head. Gutsy gals, the both of them.

He searched Coles's Blazer. It was a late model, but there was nearly a hundred thousand miles on the odometer. The interior was littered with fast food wrappers and notes written on cocktail napkins, torn phone book pages and receipts. There was a box of cassette tapes, labeled by date, the oldest being a little more than a year old. He had eclectic taste in music, judging by the melange of country, rock and roll and classical CDs scattered on the passenger seat and passenger side floorboard. There was a very expensive camera and a cheap vinyl carryall carelessly stuffed with clothes. Tate found a cell phone with number storage capacity. He scrolled through the listings, finding numbers for law enforcement agencies, research services, Chinese restaurants and pizza delivery, and a large number of female names. He recorded all the numbers to check later.

He didn't find a weapon, ammunition or anything more dangerous than a screwdriver.

"Well?" Diana asked. Marlee echoed the question.

"He's a slob, but I don't think he's a killer." He backed out of the Blazer and showed them a photograph. Bernadette, dressed in a funky silver jumpsuit, posed arm-in-arm with a dark, elegant looking woman. Both of them mugged for the camera. Bernadette was thinner than Diana and her hair was tamed into a smooth, shoulder-length bob, but the resemblance was phenomenal.

"She really does look like you," Marlee said. Then she laughed. "Except for that outfit. Tacky."

Diana wasn't smiling. Her brow twisted, her expression pained. "That must be Farrah. They look like friends." She turned away and covered her face with a hand.

Marlee patted Diana's back. "Hey, girl, are you okay?" Then her eyes widened and her cheeks reddened. "I have such a big mouth. I'm sorry."

"It's not you, hon. It's the whole thing." She skittered away from the photograph as if it might bite her. She shoved her hands in her pockets. "I know Bernie is selfish and short-sighted and…criminal. But a murderer? A heartless killer? We shared a bedroom until we were ten!"

Marlee wrapped an arm around Diana's shoulders and led her friend toward the trailer.

Tate passed a hand over his face. Diana's pain shook him to his core. Professional distancing wasn't working. He doubted if it ever would where Diana was concerned.

"YOU CHECK OUT, MR. COLES." Tate removed the handcuffs and replaced them in the case on the back of his belt.

Coles rubbed his wrists and smiled without rancor. If

anything, he seemed as excited as a kid before a baseball game. "Does this mean you'll give me an interview?"

Gil rolled his eyes.

Tate laughed. "Reporters are all alike. No such thing as tragedy, just photo ops."

"Look, I'm a big believer in you scratch my back, I'll scratch yours. I have a lot of information you can use."

"If we need information from you, sir," Tate said, "we'll take you down to the basement in the sheriff's station."

Coles gulped, his eyes shifting up and down as if just now realizing how big Tate actually was. He sidled a step toward the sheriff, but Gil growled deep in his throat and the reporter froze.

Tate signaled for Gil to step away, out of Coles's earshot. He ignored the frustration on the reporter's face. In a low voice Tate said, "This whole thing stinks. Did the FBI mention international terrorists or kidnapping?"

"Not that I recall. Think that boy is feeding us a line?"

"Or Agent Albright is. Doesn't it seem funny to you that Albright isn't all that interested in the fugitive search?"

"Has crossed my mind."

"Albright has access to helicopters, National Guard, hell, infrared cameras and night-vision scopes. So why hasn't he offered them?"

Gil stuck his thumbs in his gun belt. His brown face took on smooth, bland, thoughtfulness. Then he blinked, once, twice. "Well, now, could be he's trying to gaff himself a big fish."

Tate eyed the reporter. The man's ears were nearly swiveling on his head. He was probably salivating over the prospect of a big story. "Let's say Albright isn't interested in Farrah Montgomery. Let's say he is after the father. Bernadette must seem like manna from heaven to him. The perfect way to draw the man out.''

''You mean draw him to our town.''

Tate rolled his shoulders in a lazy shrug. ''How many assassins would you let screw up before you got mad and went in yourself?''

''So why does Albright want Diana? He wouldn't dare try to pass her off as her sister.''

''Worst casing it, he might. Or he'd let Montgomery's boys have a crack at her, so they can fail again.''

''What's our best plan of action then?''

''First, we get Diana out of here. We need—''

Gil put up a hand. His dark eyes were blank and hard. ''Diana Dover is a private citizen. It is absolutely none of my business where she goes.''

Tate took the hint. Hiding Diana was his job, and he was never to speak of it to Gil. In protecting her from the FBI, they risked their jobs and quite possibly their freedom.

Then louder, designed for the reporter's ears, Gil said, ''How about this boy and I head on back to town? We can have a cup of coffee and a chat. You finish up here.''

''Got it, chief.'' He looked around at the trees. A sick sensation settled in his gut. If Coles spoke the truth and Montgomery was as rich and powerful as claimed, then the world might not be big enough to hide Diana.

Chapter Eleven

Diana downed a glass of cool water. The well water had a faint mineral taste that tingled against her salivary glands. She could see out the tiny louvered window over the kitchen sink. Tate's cruiser was parked behind Marlee's truck. The sheriff and the reporter had departed, with the sheriff driving behind the reporter to make sure he made it all the way to town. She was exhausted. There had been entirely too much excitement lately, and what it was doing to her body worried her.

Tate touched her back. "Are you all right?"

"No. I'm scared and I'm frustrated. I'm worried sick about Bernie. I'm even more worried about McClintock and what this could do to our town." She turned her head enough to see him. His concern eased her heart a little. "I was ready to shoot that man. I don't like what that says about me."

"It says you're smart," Marlee stated firmly. "So what now, Tate? If Coles found her so easily, then this place isn't safe."

Anger added itself to Diana's inner turmoil. In the Maya Valley she'd found peace and a sense of safety she'd never dreamed possible. She wanted it back.

Tate glared at the door. "The FBI is a problem, too. Albright is threatening to get an arrest warrant."

"For who?" Diana drew her head warily aside. "Me? Whatever for?"

"Trumped up garbage. Nothing he can make stick, but that's not the point. You're a means to an end."

Marlee snapped her fingers, and her eyes lit up. "I know where she can hide. Daddy's lodge."

Tate startled. Having no idea what her friend talked about or why Tate reacted so strongly, Diana sank onto a chair. She let a hand drop onto Tippy's head. He'd forgiven her for tying him up in the forest, but he still stayed far away from the weapons. His nose was icy against her palm.

"What's wrong with the lodge?" Diana asked.

"It's where Elaine's first husband was murdered. And my father died there, too." Marlee paused as if judging Diana's reaction. "Granted, it's creepy as all get out, and it has no electricity or heat. But, it's isolated on McClintock Ranch and there's a chain across the driveway. You'd have to be a native to find a way through the forest to get there."

Tate pulled his chin. He looked worried. "What about your mother? Or your sister? Elaine will freak out if she finds out anyone is in the lodge."

"So we don't tell her. We don't tell anybody. We can tell everyone you've left town. Gone on vacation to Mexico, or Canada."

Diana liked the sound of being someplace where she could gather herself and regain her serenity. "What about my animals?"

"Take Tippy with you. I'll take the goats to the ranch. I swear, nobody will mind having them around. The lodge is perfect." Marlee checked her watch then her beeper.

"I don't have any appointments today that can't be postponed. You and I will switch vehicles, and you can wear my hat. That way if anyone spots you on the ranch, they'll think you're me."

"And if some bad guy thinks *you're* me?" Diana shook her head hard. "We can't risk—"

"Oh, come on! Your pickup looks like a thousand others around here." She patted her light brown hair, which was cut in a short practical style. "No one would ever mistake me for you. Besides—" she patted her rifle as if it were a faithful pet "—I can take the eye out of a bullfrog at a hundred yards. I'm not scared."

Tate's shoulders shook with silent laughter. "I have a better idea. We leave your pickup here, Red. It might throw off anyone snooping around. I'll get you to the lodge. You're sure no one will stumble onto her, Marlee?"

"The cattle have been moved out of the north pastures, so nobody will be on the roads up there. Mama hasn't set up any logging operations or brush-whacking. We've got no guests looking to rough it. Unless somebody parachutes onto the roof by accident, no one will ever know."

Tate picked up the cell phone he'd loaned to Diana. A frown creased his broad forehead. "Cell phone transmissions are easy to capture. We have to keep communication to a bare minimum. All right, we can do this."

In less than an hour, the three had Diana's belongings packed and the goats loaded in Marlee's pickup.

Diana hugged her friend. "You're the best. See you in about an hour."

Marlee trundled off with the bleating goats. Diana opened the back door of the cruiser and whistled for Tippy. The pup leaped eagerly into the back seat, where he sat with a happy grin in a cloud of drifting white hairs. She turned to Tate.

"Is this going to get you into trouble?"

He smiled. Such a lovely smile with his dark eyes sparkling and a hint of a dimple in his cheek. He chucked her chin with a knuckle.

"My duty is to this valley. Protect and serve. If the feebs want to catch terrorists, good for them. But not at the expense of people I care about."

She touched his tie, giving it a little tug. "Ah, so you admit you care about me?"

"Don't start, Red." His smile faded. "Of course, I care." He cupped his large hand against her cheek, a gesture so tender it made her throat tighten. "All the years I've been a cop, and I never got personal with a case. It's a job, and I'm good at it. I'm good at leaving it behind. Coppers who can't detach, who get personal, they burn out, go crazy. I never did that." One finger gently caressed her cheek. "Damn it, this is personal. You know I don't want to care this much about you."

"It's a human tendency to resist that which we need the most." She could stand here and stare into his beautiful eyes all day long.

"Straight up, okay? No games. We're friends, good friends. That's kind of weird for me, because—" he shrugged "—I don't know many women who are friend friends. Know what I mean?"

She guessed where this led, and tamped the urge to argue. He needed to say what he needed to say.

"You're right. I do think you're sexy. I've thought about asking you out. I even dream about you. But I don't want to wreck our friendship. I don't want to hurt you."

Or himself.

She pressed her hand over his and closed her eyes. The

irony of the situation didn't escape her. As a young woman, when her body was firm and unscarred, when her sexuality was at its ripest, she'd never felt the tug of love or lust. Her husband had been more of a business partner than a soul mate. Lovemaking was a way to relieve stress, not share intimacy. She'd had neither the time nor the inclination toward what she'd mistakenly thought of as frivolity. Now here she was, middle-aged, battle-scarred, past the age when men ogled her on the street or lusted after her in their hearts, and she'd found a man who put a flutter in her heart and a thump in her belly. The very first time she'd looked into those velvety brown eyes, caught a whiff of his vibrantly masculine scent, was captured by his smile, she'd known he was *it*.

What she lacked in gorgeous femininity, she'd gained in wisdom. Wisdom counseled patience. "I understand."

"It's not you." Worry strained his voice. "It's me."

"Okay."

He used both hands now to hold her face. She couldn't have stopped staring into his eyes if she'd wanted to—which she didn't. "Damn it, Diana, I mean it. You keep looking at me like that…I'm only human. We'd be a disaster. You'd end up hating me. I'm not good enough for you."

"But you still want to kiss me. Hold me. You feel the connection."

His big chest rose and fell in a heavy breath. His hands were warm against her skin, his palms work-roughened, but tender. "Yeah."

"You may as well kiss me, then. Or we'll never get out of here."

He huffed a dry laugh. "You make me insane." But he kissed her, soft and sweet, a close-mouthed kiss of barely restrained passion. When she slid her arms around his waist, she felt him trembling. He lowered his hands to her shoulders. She touched the tip of her tongue to his lips. Electric. He reacted as if it felt electric to him, too. She liked that. She liked the way his scent seemed to darken, liked the slight thrust of his groin against hers, liked the coiled power thrumming through his big body.

She would have liked a whole lot more, but he was far from ready to surrender.

"Gotta quit this," he muttered and stepped back, still holding her shoulders. His eyes were black, hot and gleaming. "Got a job to do." His voice had roughened. He released her, giving her a wary look as if fearing—hoping?—she'd jump him. He pulled a trooper hat from the cruiser. "Tuck up your hair, put this on. You're riding shotgun, and I mean that literally. If we run into trouble, I expect you to follow orders. Got it?"

"Yes, sir." She grasped her hair and twisted the mass of it against the back of her head. She pulled the hat down low.

He finally smiled. "You look goofy."

"You look mean."

"I am mean. God help any dumb bastard who makes a run at you. Get in."

She couldn't remember the last time anyone had acted so concerned about her. Perhaps no one ever had. She loved it. Just as she was falling in love with him.

TATE STRODE INTO the sheriff's station. He wasn't worried about running into Agent Albright or his buddies, since Gil had given him the all clear. The sheriff was also aware that Diana was safely tucked away—somewhere. He wouldn't ask.

Gil was in his office, filling out budget reports. "Run

for sheriff,'' he said without looking up from the paper-work.

The non-sequitur baffled Tate. "Excuse me?"

"I've been doing this twenty-six years. Started out on the volunteer roster, then when King McClintock took office, he sent me through the police academy in Denver. I was undersheriff for more than fifteen years. Lord, but that's a big chunk of life gone." He put down his pencil and rested a cheek on his palm. "I walked into my house last night and the place was full of grandkids. I yelled at Little John for jumping on my easy chair. What kind of life is that, eh? A man making babies cry because he's wore out from working a job he's too old to be working."

Tate rubbed the back of his neck. He shifted uncomfortably from foot to foot. It wasn't like Gil to complain.

"You're the best cop I've ever met, Tate. You're too damned smart to be running a broke-down old bar. Election is coming up in November. I don't intend to be on the ballot. So run for office. The pay is lousy, the hours are worse and the paperwork will turn your hair gray. It's the perfect job for you."

Gil was serious. Tate sat and rested a foot on his knee. He folded his hands over his chest. "No one would vote for me. Most people still call me 'that New York boy.'"

Gil snorted. "Sheriff's election is nothing more than a formality. Shoot, ain't had a contested race in as long as I've been voting. Only reason they hold an election at all is 'cause that's what the charter demands, and the county commissioners are too busy bickering about street lights and new seating for the rodeo arena to change it."

Odd hunger filled Tate. He loved this town. Even more depressing than losing the bar, was the idea of having to move away for the sake of a job. "I'll consider it. Later. Right now, where's Coles?"

"Deputy," Gil said in a voice loud enough to carry into the main station room, "the Bernadette O'Malley case is now in the hands of the FBI. You will keep your nose out of it. Unless they ask directly for your input, you will not discuss it in or out of this station. Do you understand?"

This, Tate decided, was what he loved best about this small-town police force. The sheriff upheld the law, but if the law was at odds with what was right, Gil always went with what was right. In a massive, many-layered, bureaucratic organization the brass tended to forget the difference between wrong and right, and cared only about staying out of trouble.

Maybe he would run for sheriff.

The secretary rapped her knuckles on the office door. She looked as if someone had shoved dirty socks up her nose. "Sheriff? Agent Albright is here to see you. *Again.*"

"Tell him to cool his spurs. I've got business to finish up." As soon as she stepped away, he whispered, "Dollars to donuts says he's got himself a warrant."

A knot in Tate's guts jerked tight. He and Gil played a dangerous game. They could end up under investigation, or worse.

Gil rose, his smooth Ute face placid and thoughtful. With a flick of his finger at Tate, he walked to the door. "Deputy Raleigh, I've had non-stop complaints from bicyclists over on Whitehorn hill. Go convince speeders to slow down. And convince those damned cyclists that traffic rules apply to them, too."

"Roger that, sir." He nodded at Albright on his way out of the station. The feeb wore a hard, smug smile that confirmed in Tate's mind the existence of an arrest warrant.

Tate hoped like hell Gil was able to convince the FBI that interrogating Tate about Diana's whereabouts would be a waste of time. Because then he'd have to break the law and lie. And from what he'd heard, federal prison was a nasty place to be.

GIL VANCE, TATE DECIDED, was a genius.

The Maya Valley was long and narrow, the length of it running north to south. Grant Road was the only paved road connecting to a major highway. There were plenty of ranch and forest roads heading off east or west, but they were gravel-topped, narrow and, depending on the weather, not always passable. Outsiders tended to stick to asphalt. Whitehorn hill was at the south end of the valley and Grant Road curved up and over it, offering a magnificent view of the Maya River and a heart-thumping scare to anyone who ignored the caution signs. It turned steep on the north side, so vehicles headed toward McClintock had to drop into low gear and brake. From the vantage point of a turnout at the bottom of the hill, Tate could easily record the make, model and license plate number of every passing vehicle.

On a sunny summer day like this one, out-of-town traffic consisted mostly of recreational vehicles inching down the hill and four-wheelers looking for some off-road action in the foothills surrounding the valley.

Tate considered hired assassins to be predators. Not especially intelligent, but clever enough to learn from their mistakes. After the fiasco at Diana's farm and again on Main Street, hit men would realize their big-city street tactics wouldn't work in this country. The next hitters could be disguised as tourists or campers or fishermen. They'd be more subtle in their mode of attack.

There were quite a few bicyclists wearing alien-head

helmets and fluorescent spandex. Tate enjoyed a good workout as much as the next guy, but huffing and puffing over hills at this altitude struck him as just plain dumb. Instead of flagging reckless bicyclists or speeders, he flipped his lights to let them know the law was watching. He focused on recording passing vehicles.

He listened with half an ear to radio traffic. A quiet day, which was a good thing since dispatch was conspicuously not contacting him. Good old Gil, keeping him off the FBI's radar.

The telephone rang. Tate's heart lurched. Diana was under strict orders not to use her borrowed phone unless it were an emergency. It was Gil. "Your shift is almost over, right?"

"Yes, sir."

"Thought you might like to know, Albright and I attempted to execute a warrant. Can't seem to find Ms. Dover though."

"Huh." Tate grinned.

"Ran by her farm, too. If you happen to hear from her, tell her the chickens and bees are doing fine. I collected a couple dozen eggs. I'll drop them off at the Shack."

"If I see her, that's what I'll tell her."

"I was sitting here looking over time logs. You have a couple of vacation days due you," Gil said. "We've got a use it or lose it policy around here. You better take those days."

Albright must have blown his eyeballs when he realized Diana had slipped away. Tate hated leaving Gil to take the heat.

As if reading his mind, Gil said, "I mean it."

"Yes, sir."

"I'm giving Agent Albright my full cooperation and to

show him what a good old boy I am, he and his cronies are having supper at my place.''

Translation: when Tate dropped off the cruiser and logged out of the station, Albright would be otherwise occupied. ''Yes, sir.''

At six that evening, Tate pulled the cruiser into the station lot. He went inside, logged out and handed the vehicle list to the dispatcher. He didn't need to tell her what to do with it. All rental cars would be red-flagged.

''Have a nice vacation,'' she called when he was walking out.

He loved this town.

He headed over to the Shack. The number of people clogging Main Street dismayed him. So many strangers, any of whom could be a hired killer on the prowl. He slipped in through the bar's back door and entered his apartment. It struck him as even shabbier than usual. Drab, utilitarian. The house where he'd grown up had been cluttered and colorful and full of life. When he got married, the first thing Lisa had done when they moved into an apartment was embark on a frenzy of curtain making, picture hanging and furniture arranging. He'd teased her about nesting, but their pretty home had made him proud and humble at the same time.

Diana's house was homey and comfortable and pleasing to the eye. A place to leave the troubles of the world behind. Sanctuary.

''Cut it out,'' he growled at the yearning in his soul, and peeled out of his uniform. He removed all insignia and his name tag, then dropped it in a bag for the laundry. He packed an overnight bag with clothes, toiletries and extra ammunition.

He entered the kitchen.

Consuela had the place humming with her young relatives. Cooking food filled the air with steam. The dining room sounded packed.

He called Consuela's name. She turned around, her smile as dazzling as it was shocking. He couldn't recall her ever smiling at him. Her cheeks were flushed, her apron was filthy, and she looked so radiantly happy he felt certain a doppleganger had shoved the real Consuela into a closet and taken her place.

"Is everything going all right?" he asked.

"Couldn't be better!" She practically sang.

It hit him that she'd been waiting for this opportunity, most likely for years.

"I'll be out of the loop for a while. Can you fill out the time sheets. I'll pick up—"

"You think I can't handle payroll? You don't trust me?" She pulled a sizzling basket out of the deep fryer. She waved him off as if he were a stray dog begging food.

Chewing over how useless he felt, and whether that were a good feeling or a bad feeling, he left the Shack.

Suspecting the FBI might put a tail on him, he drove the short distance to Walt Buchanan's carpentry shop. He pulled the Bronco around back where Ric Buchanan's Jeep was parked. He entered the building.

"Mr. Tate!"

He smiled at Ric's daughter. Jodi sat before the keyboard of a computer. "How'd you sneak that contraption past Walt?" he asked her.

"I finally wore him down," the teenager assured him. "His accounting system is positively archaic. He keeps receipts in shoe boxes. I told him I'd input everything and set up a system so simple that even he can use it."

"Sounds good. Is your dad around?"

"In the paint booth." She jumped to her feet. "I'll get him."

Poor Ric, he thought. Jodi was nearly six feet tall, a golden-haired stunner who grew more beautiful by the day. Ric didn't allow her to date, but he was fighting a losing battle in keeping besotted boys from sniffing around. She pounded on the door hard enough to be heard over the noise of the fans and air compressor. Wearing a respirator, Ric opened the door. At spotting Tate, he pulled the mask off his face.

"Hey," he said. "What's up, jarhead?"

Tate crooked a finger. "Need a favor. Can I switch vehicles with you?"

Ric dug into his jeans pocket and pulled out a ring of keys. He worked a key off the ring and tossed it across the shop. Tate caught it with an overhead swipe. He took his Bronco keys off his ring and laid them on a workbench. It amused him that Ric asked no questions, but that's how he was. If something needed doing, Ric just did it.

Jodi fingered her chin, her eyes wide and innocent. "I'm learning how to drive. Can I practice in your Bronco?"

"Jodi," Ric warned.

"Fine by me," Tate said. "It's not like she can do it any damage."

"Thanks a lot," Ric muttered.

Tate had heard Ric's horror stories about teaching his daughter to drive. Jodi was as bold and reckless as she was beautiful. Ric swore that every lesson shaved five years off his life. "I owe you, man. Gotta go."

He drove off in the white Jeep. If anyone spotted it on McClintock Ranch, he or she would assume it was Ric or Elaine and think nothing of it.

He reached the rutted, weed-choked driveway leading to the lodge. A sturdy chain blocked access. He left the

Jeep parked and slung his overnight bag over his shoulder. He dialed Diana's number, let it ring twice, then hung up, waited a few seconds, then dialed again and let it ring three times. The prearranged signal would let her know he was here. He stepped over the chain and walked up the driveway.

The rustic old lodge came into view. Shaded by towering pines, it was squat, dark, and rather malevolent looking. Even with the front door standing wide and the shutters open, it didn't look inviting. He wondered if this were such a good idea after all. Bad things had happened at this place. He shoved such superstitious drivel out of his head.

He heard metal thunking against wood. He dropped his bag on the front porch and followed the noise around the building. He opened his mouth to alert Diana to his presence, but the sight of her stopped him cold.

With her back to him, she was splitting firewood. Her chambray work shirt hung from a tree branch. The wide straps of a sports bra was all that covered her back, proving her figure was as nice as he'd always imagined. Her back was smoothly muscled, shiny with sweat, so pale it seemed formed with mother of pearl. Her jeans snugged over the swell of her hips and rear, but gapped erotically at her long, slender waist.

A shaft of sunlight caught her hair, copper fire, rich gold, colors he hadn't even known existed. She bent over to pick up pieces of wood. His groin tightened.

Damn it, he did want her, all of her. It didn't matter that he couldn't remain emotionally detached from her. It didn't matter if she could see beneath the surface, see into his heart, read his thoughts, recognize the pain. He wanted her body and soul—even if it meant letting her get close.

Tippy burst from the weeds and barked, running toward him.

Diana squealed and spun about, the axe clutched in both hands.

He held up his hands. "Sorry. Didn't you hear my phone signal?"

She blew a harsh breath and lowered the axe. The sports bra was far more modest than most bikini tops. For a while it had been the fashion for female joggers to wear them without a shirt. Still, as he approached, he made a point of keeping his eyes on her face. She swiped sweat from her brow.

"You startled me. I didn't hear you drive up."

"The chain."

She rested the axe against the chopping stump and reached for her shirt. He couldn't resist a quick peek at her breasts and belly. He had a thing for bellies. None of that washboard, boyish look for him; he liked them soft and round. Pretty navels were the height of sexiness.

Her belly was pale and looked as smooth as silk.

Something was wrong. His mind couldn't quite register exactly what it was. Her breasts were small, or at least, one breast was small, a mound against the stretch cotton. The other side of the bra puckered like an empty sock.

Diana canted her head and lowered both arms, the shirt dangling from her fingertips.

It was rude and obnoxious to stare, but he couldn't stop.

She raised a hand to the empty side of the bra. "I had a mastectomy."

He gave himself a shake. His neck and ears burned.

She slid her arms into the shirt sleeves. She was smiling. "I thought I was okay with losing a breast. That I accepted my body and how I look. But I've been self-conscious about showing you my scars. Shoot, I've been downright scared.'' Her fingers trembled while she buttoned the shirt. ''Are you grossed out?''

Now that she was covered up, it was easier to look at her. ''What…what happened?''

''Breast cancer. I was fortunate. A mammography caught it in the very early stages, before it had metastasized—spread through my system. Unfortunately, it was an aggressive form and my oncologist didn't believe a lumpectomy would be enough. So I had a radical mastectomy, then chemo and radiation treatment. It worked. I've been cancer free for over four years.''

All he heard was ''cancer.'' The Big C, the destroyer, that stinking ugly monster that ripped through healthy flesh and killed beautiful women and ruined lives. His throat felt as if it were swelling shut. His heart pounded so erratically, painfully, he knew he was having a heart attack. He clutched his chest and stumbled away.

''Tate?''

He couldn't breathe. Gasping and choking, he made it around the house and onto the porch. He slumped heavily on a step. He choked and rasped for breath. An elephant was sitting on his chest.

Diana grasped his chin. ''Good lord, you're dead white. What's the matter?''

''Chest…hurts…''

She picked up his wrist and pressed her fingers against the pulse point. She asked for specific descriptions of his pain and encouraged him to breathe deeply, slowly. ''I'm calling an ambulance.''

''No!''

''You might be having a heart attack.''

''Don't care…no…ambulance.''

She ran into the lodge and returned carrying a glass of water and aspirin. She ordered him to take the aspirin and drink all the water. She grabbed his telephone off his belt and began punching in numbers.

He snatched the telephone out of her hand and threw it as far as he could. It landed in a weedy patch of tall brown grass. She stared openmouthed at him, speechless for once.

"Cell transmissions, emergency calls...picked up. No!"

"You are such a stupid, *stupid* man!"

She grasped his arm and helped him to his feet. Leaning heavily on her, he clutched his chest. Sweat dripped off his face. He was dying.

Chapter Twelve

"Anxiety attack."

Tate stared at the doctor. Anxiety? The chest pains had stopped during the ride to Durango. By the time he entered the emergency room, he felt perfectly fine. Embarrassed as all get out, but fine. Still, the doctor had insisted on running tests. Now he held a long ECG strip as if Tate could make sense of the jagged print-out.

"You're in remarkable shape, Mr. Raleigh," the doctor continued. "The heart of a twenty-year-old. Do you lift weights? Run?"

"Yeah," Tate said, numb over the diagnosis.

"It shows. Just to be on the safe side, I'd like to schedule a stress test. You are nearing forty."

Curtain rings rattled and Diana peered into the treatment room. She'd fussed and fumed at Tate all the way into Durango. Her anger touched him as much as it irritated him.

The doctor lowered the ECG strip and peered at Diana. The bemused look on the man's face made Tate remember the flyers sent to every hospital and clinic in the southern Colorado and Four Corners area. He guessed the FBI had added their own wanted posters.

"May I help you?" the doctor asked.

"She's my wife," Tate said. "Honey, I'm okay. No heart attack. I can go home."

The doctor patted Tate's shoulder. "Schedule the stress test. If you have another attack, give me a call. There are drugs available to treat anxiety." He flashed a curious smile at Diana, then hurried away.

"I'm so relieved you're okay," Diana said. "But throwing that phone away was the dumbest thing I've ever seen anybody do. And believe you me, buster, I've seen a lot of stupid things."

"Give it a rest, Red. We've got bigger problems. I think the doctor recognized you."

"Oh." Her eyes widened. "Oh! That's why that orderly…"

He buttoned his shirt and slid off the exam table. "What orderly?"

"He gave me a real funny look then practically ran away."

"Running to a telephone," Tate growled. He grabbed her elbow and hustled out of the exam room. He'd have told her to keep her head down, but with all that wild red hair bright as a beacon, it wouldn't do any good.

They passed the main desk. "You filled out billing information, right? I didn't give you my insurance card."

"I used a credit card." Her face was paler than usual, as if realizing she'd made a mistake.

God save him from innocents. "Let's hope the orderly calls the cops and not the feds." He straight-armed through the emergency room door.

Diana glanced over her shoulder and stumbled. "There he is!"

Tate broke into a run, hauling Diana along with him. He demanded the Jeep's keys and urged her to get in. He slid behind the wheel. The orderly's white uniform made him easy to spot in the dark parking lot. He appeared to be looking for Diana.

Tate started the engine, but didn't turn on the headlights, hoping the glow from the parking lot lamps wasn't enough to illuminate the license plate. He left the lights off until he was well away from the hospital.

Diana twisted on the seat, staring unhappily behind them. "I was so worried about you, I forgot all about Bernie."

"I should have thought of it. Nothing to do now but hope for the best."

He didn't breathe easy until they were out of Durango and on the highway toward McClintock. He breathed easier still when they turned off the highway without a copper appearing in the rearview mirror. The orderly must not have gotten the license plate number. It still didn't put them in the clear.

As if reading his thoughts, Diana said, "This is crazy. You and Gil are going to get in trouble. I'll turn myself in. I haven't done anything wrong."

"Can't risk it."

If anyone was in danger of arrest, it was Tate. This just kept getting better and better.

She hunkered down on the seat, hugging herself. He turned on the heater. "I'm really glad you're okay. You scared me."

"I don't want to talk about it." A stupid anxiety attack. He couldn't believe it. In the marines, he'd earned the reputation for having ice water in his veins. As a New York City homicide detective, he'd never burned out the way so many others had. Mr. Cool. The man who never lost his head.

"You don't have to be embarrassed."

"I'm not embarrassed," he mumbled.

"Do you want to talk about what happened?"

"No."

"It'll help." She rubbed his shoulder. "It's the mastectomy, isn't it? I shocked you."

Her silence seemed a palpable thing, nudging him, worming its way beneath his reluctance. He'd driven nearly ten miles before conceding that she wasn't going to fill the silence with chatter.

"Cancer," he said. The word was bitter. It choked him and made his heart rate rise.

Lights from the dash barely touched her face. Her eyes were dark, gleaming. "Mmm."

"I never had an anxiety attack before. I thought I was dying."

"They'll do that to you. What is it about cancer that makes you anxious?"

He'd never talked about it. Not to his friends, his family or a priest. No one. Guilt over his cowardice festered inside him like a boil, pulsing and painful. Diana would probably be disgusted to know his shame. Or worse, she'd pity him for his weakness.

There was a dirt road up ahead. He slowed, then turned onto it. He killed the motor and lights. He listened to the hot engine *tick tick tick*. Without the lights of civilization, the night was inky, the sky overwhelming in its vastness.

"I didn't know you had cancer."

"I don't anymore. Is it ugly, revolting?"

Something in her voice made him look at her. "You think you're ugly?"

Shifting on the seat so as to face him, she showed her palms in a *you-tell-me* gesture. "My ex-husband thought so. He insisted I have reconstructive surgery. That's what he did, erased flaws, repaired imperfections." She sighed and clicked her tongue against her teeth. "I'm not certain exactly why I refused. Partly I wanted the reminder, sort of a badge of honor for finding myself, for finding God. I was humbled by all I'd gained. But mostly, I suppose, he made me angry. He saw me as flawed, mutilated, an imperfect thing that must be repaired or I was unworthy.''

"He must be a real jerk," Tate said.

"It's the way he views the world. The path he must explore. Anyway, other than medical professionals, no man has touched me since my divorce. No man has looked at me, made love to me." She placed a hand on his forearm, letting it rest without pressure. "I almost had myself convinced that I wasn't afraid of what others would think when they saw the scar. But then I met you...I was very afraid."

Now he was a double-dirty low-down dog. "I don't think you're ugly. Not ugly at all."

"I gave you a panic attack."

"I'm—I'm—"

"Shh," she whispered and pressed a finger against his lips. "Don't apologize. Never apologize for how you feel. In a way you did me a big favor. Revealing myself was a huge step and I survived. I feel bad for shocking you, but I'm not hurt or depressed or angry. I can handle your opinion."

He rested his forehead against the steering wheel. "It's not you, Red, I swear it isn't. It's me." He swallowed the lump in his throat. "My wife died of cancer."

She pulled back, sitting taller. "I'm so sorry."

He stared out the window at the billions of stars and waxing moon. "I let her die alone."

"What happened?"

Her gentle question held neither condemnation or horror. He couldn't look at her. "Her name was Lisa. She was only twenty-eight. God, but I loved her. The first time

I saw her, she crawled into my head and set up house-keeping. She was a research librarian. Worked at the New York Public Library. I came up with some really screwy questions just so I had an excuse to talk to her." He tapped his head. "Smartest person I ever met. We were married for four years. We were saving money to buy a house. Then she started losing weight. Hurting. By the time they diagnosed ovarian cancer, it had metastasized into her liver, lungs and bones."

"Oh, Tate..."

He knuckled his burning eyes. "The treatments were terrible. Left her puking, all her hair fell out, her face swelled up. Nothing they did touched the cancer. It just grew and grew, eating her up. I couldn't handle watching her die, seeing her all shriveled and yellow, always in pain. Even touching her hand made her scream. So I...worked. I pulled every minute of overtime I could get. I buried myself in cases. Even went through old files, dead cases, anything to keep from witnessing her agony."

His gut ached. His heart was racing again. He deserved a real heart attack.

"Her mother called me. 'It's time,' she said. I sat at my desk and typed up a report. Typed it real careful, checking for mistakes. When I finally got home, it was all over."

She snuffled. He whipped his head about. Her face was shiny with tears.

"Don't cry for me, dammit! She loved me, needed me and I let her die alone. I'm garbage."

She fumbled around the unfamiliar vehicle, then finally wiped her face with her shirt sleeve. "Once upon a time, I never cried. I was rather proud of myself. I considered it a sign of strength. Avoiding one's emotions isn't strong at all. It's fear, pure and simple. I'll weep for you, if I must, and for Lisa, and for myself."

He pushed open the door. In the dome light, he glimpsed her reddened eyes and tear-streaked cheeks. He jumped out and slammed the door. He shoved his hands in his pockets and stared at the sky. Deep breaths of crisp air cleared his head a little. He expected Diana to get out of the Jeep, to pester him into talking, to lay on him a bunch of silly platitudes like Band-aids on a broken bone. He stood in the cold for a long time, until it became clear she wasn't going to do anything except wait.

Something inside him said she did understand, that she didn't condemn him or consider him a horrible human being.

Shivering, he slid back behind the steering wheel. He started the engine. He shoved the transmission into reverse, and backed onto the road.

Driving past small farms and ranch houses, he felt oddly lighter. Confession had relieved him, at least a little. He wondered if Diana would give him funny looks from now on. Wondered if she'd drop the kidding around about sexual tension. Wondered if she still found him desirable.

THE CHAIN ACROSS THE driveway was down.

"You didn't unlock the chain, did you?"

"No," Diana replied.

"Stay." He cut the engine and killed the lights. "If you hear me shout, disappear. Got it? The Jeep will block the drive. You just run like hell."

With his Glock in hand, the safety off, Tate cat-footed up the driveway. He stepped carefully, aware of ruts and weeds and broken branches ready to trip him in the dark. He recognized the pickup parked in the yard. Marlee waited on the porch. Tippy sat beside her, ears raised, letting Tate know he'd been heard. A pair of lanterns sitting on the porch railing lit up the front of the house.

He breathed a long sigh of relief. He hurried back to Diana. Together they drove up to the lodge.

"Where have you been?" Marlee demanded. "I've been here over an hour. I couldn't reach you by telephone. I've been worried sick!"

Diana hugged her friend. "I'm sorry. We had a little incident."

"What kind of incident?"

Diana exchanged a look with Tate. "The less you know…" She let the comment dangle, allowing Marlee to imagine what she pleased. "I really am sorry. I should have left a note."

Marlee shot a glare at Tate that said she figured it was his fault. "I brought groceries and stuff. Extra blankets, some camping gear. I started a fire for you, too. It's pretty cold up here. What are you doing with Elaine's Jeep?"

"I switched vehicles with Ric," Tate said. "Thought it might be safer. Have you heard anything?"

"I haven't been to town. Do you want me to snoop around?" Marlee nodded eagerly. "See what people are saying?"

"Absolutely not."

"Oh, all right." She gave him a hopeful look as if he might change his mind. "I'll swing by tomorrow."

Tate sat on the porch step, watching Diana and Marlee walk to the pickup truck, talking in soft tones he couldn't hear. Were Diana anyone else, he'd suspect she was gossiping about his cowardly past. He knew, sure as sunrise, she'd never bring the subject up again. A comforting thought.

Marlee drove off. Diana picked up a lantern. "I'm starving."

He picked up the other lantern and followed her inside. The last time he'd been inside the lodge, he'd been collecting evidence for a homicide. Since then, somebody had cleaned the place. A big cotton rug covered blood stains on the wooden floor. All personal effects—books, papers, an old fashioned dial phone, hunting trophies— were gone. He set the lantern on the dusty surface of a desk. A fire crackling in the big stone fireplace made the place seem almost comfortable.

Diana sorted through grocery sacks.

He approached her from behind and settled his hands on her shoulders. She stilled in what she was doing. Her hair smelled of honey and shampoo.

"I'm embarrassed. I don't think you're ugly. Or revolting or any of that."

"Thank you."

"I didn't freak out because of you. The way you look."

"I know."

"The cancer…I can't go through that again. What I did to Lisa…"

Lisa hadn't actually been alone. Her parents and brother had been there, so had every member of Tate's family. When he'd walked in, they'd all murmured their sympathies, wept with him, but he'd felt their contempt for his cowardice. No one ever mentioned his desertion, but it was always there. He saw it every time he encountered them. It followed him, ever present, a cloud of guilt and shame. He even felt it at work, saw it in the eyes of other detectives, heard it in the voices of his friends.

He'd taken the first opportunity to get out of New York, away from his family, away from Lisa's death.

She waited a few beats. "What you did was pretty bad. But understandable."

He flinched. That was the last thing he'd expected her to say. "I don't understand it."

"It's hard watching a loved one in pain. Especially pain that's so difficult to manage."

"I've seen people die. I'm no stranger to pain. What I did was pure cowardice. I let her down. I loved her, but I deserted her. Now I can't..."

"Forgive yourself?"

"Yeah.

"I know the feeling." She turned to face him. He let his hands dangle at his sides. "I still haven't forgiven myself for keeping Bernie away when Mother was dying. Forgiveness isn't as easy as some would have us think."

She surprised him again. He'd expected, oh, you didn't do anything wrong, your guilt is misplaced, Lisa was so out of it because of the drugs that she didn't know you weren't there anyway, blah blah blah. "So, uh, how does a person go about forgiving himself?"

"It's a two-step process. First, you have to make amends. Maybe that's what this is all about for me and Bernie. Dealing with her is how I'll make amends."

"How do you make amends to somebody who's gone?"

"Sacrifice, good deeds, helping others. Living a godly life." She tilted her head, staring into his eyes. "You gave up everything, didn't you? Your home, family, friends, a job you loved. Even God."

He backed a step. "Don't go there. I don't want anything to do with a god that fills a woman up with cancer. A woman who never did anything mean to anyone, never said a bad word. A genuinely good person. It got so bad even a draft of air on her skin was agony. What kind of freaky god does that?"

"God doesn't do it. These frail, fragile animal bodies

we inhabit are the price we pay for the experience of living.'' She tapped the center of her chest. ''Our spirits are imbued with all of God's love, and generosity and power and wisdom. Free will is our birthright, to do with those godly gifts whatever we wish. God isn't Santa Claus, or a zookeeper.''

Shaking his head, he turned away. ''You honestly believe that.''

''I do. I also believe that everything is a gift. Every breath we take, every idea, every occurrence. Even those things we fear or consider a tragedy.''

Incredulous, he rubbed his nape. ''Are you saying cancer was God's gift to you?''

''Yes.''

''You're nuts.''

''It's a possibility.''

''How can something that horrible be a gift?'' He practically shouted. His ears burned. He'd never met anyone who so flustered, infuriated and engaged him—except for Lisa.

She resumed unpacking groceries. ''I woke up from surgery. There was no one in the room. It hit me hard that here I was a respected physician, I drove a Mercedes, my husband's and my combined annual income was in the seven figures. I lived in a million-dollar condo, furnished with expensive antiques, with a full-time housekeeper. Yet, I woke up alone. My marriage was empty. I hated my work. I had no friends, no family. For years and years anger sustained me. Anger at my father for his perfectionism. My mother for emotional blackmail. My sister who wouldn't act right no matter what I did. That anger manifested itself in breast cancer. On that day, in that lonely room, for the first time in over twenty years, I wept.''

Dumbfounded by her brutal revelation, he sank onto a chair.

"I cried a lifetime of tears that day. I was empty. In that emptiness, I realized I wasn't alone. The knowledge was so clear, so profound, it was blinding. Right at that moment, for the very first time in my entire life, I knew what it felt like to be unafraid. *That* was my gift."

"Wow." He leaned forward, his elbows on his knees. His intellect said she was nuts, but his gut told him otherwise. "So you gave it all up? The husband, the money, the job?"

"I gave up all that was meaningless." She smiled. "It's an abundant world. I'm not deprived."

"Huh. So, uh, you said forgiveness is a two-part process. What's the second part?"

"The assertion in total confidence that you will never commit that particular sin again."

He stared at his hands and loosed a rueful laugh. "Then it should be easy. Because I'm sure as hell never putting myself in the position to ever do that again."

STEALTHY NOISES ROUSED Tate. He'd been up and down throughout the night, investigating every creak and rustle. The lodge had only one door—he slept in front of it. The windows were painted shut. Even so, the persistence of both the FBI and the hired guns made him nervous.

Adding to his sleeplessness was knowing Diana was in the other room, snuggled in a musty old bed. Her puppy shared the bed with her. Lucky dog.

A lantern in the kitchen nook had its wick turned down so the glow was soft. Thin morning light seeped through the dirty windows. Diana crouched before the fireplace. She had a blanket wrapped around her shoulders. She poked at embers, fed them sticks until they caught fire and added a log. Along with the wood smoke, he thought he smelled coffee.

Her legs were bare. They were as beautiful, as long and strong and shapely as he'd always imagined. As sternly as he told himself to behave, his body had other ideas.

She moved toward the kitchen, the thick socks on her feet whispering against the wooden floor. Firelight outlined the long, smooth muscles in her legs.

"Good morning," he said. It was growing unbearably hot inside the bag.

"I didn't mean to wake you."

A tiptoeing mouse could have awakened him. He fumbled around for the sleeping bag's zipper and lowered it until he could wriggle his shoulders free.

"What time is it?" he asked.

She crouched beside him. Bundled in the blanket with her hair sticking out every which way, he wouldn't have been surprised if she broke into some kind of shamanistic chant.

Why she was so damned sexy, he couldn't imagine. His male parts were doing enough imagining for ten people.

"It's probably around six. I'm up for the day. If you want the bed, take it."

Bed. Don't say bed, he pleaded silently. He stretched and rolled his shoulders and neck. Goosebumps prickled his back. "I'll get up." Might as well. In this state, he'd never get back to sleep.

Diana eased past him and opened the door enough for Tippy to slip out. In passing, the pup licked Tate's chin. Diana gathered his jeans. "I'll warm these for you."

Icy denim might be just the thing to cool his ardor. "Not necessary."

"It'll be like wearing ice packs. Stay where you are for a few minutes. I'll get you some coffee." She draped his jeans over the back of a chair so they hung near the hearth. She did the same thing with her jeans.

He sure couldn't leap out of the bag. Not with an erection.

Then she shrugged off the blanket. All she wore was a man's shirt, the tails hanging to mid-thigh, and the socks. Lace teddies and garter belts couldn't best the eroticism of a woman wearing a man's shirt and nothing else.

"Brr," she said when she brought him a cup of coffee. "I ought to crawl in there with you."

He nearly choked. The way she crouched put her knee within kissing distance. A nice, nice knee. He forced his attention onto the coffee cup. It smelled heavenly—he wanted to smell her, bury his face in her hair, rub her body all over his. "How'd you make coffee without electricity?"

She bent closer. He avoided her eyes. "Is something wrong? You sound funny. You aren't catching cold, are you?"

He sounded horny and desperate, neither of which he wanted her to know. As the rising sun penetrated the surrounding forest, it was growing lighter in the cabin. Any chance he'd had of retaining some dignity while he retrieved his clothing was long gone.

"Drink your coffee. You're grumpy." She left him. She adjusted the wick in the lantern, and the cabin filled with light. Abruptly, she turned, staring right at him— catching him staring at her.

She *knew*. And she liked it.

He slammed the cup onto the floor and ripped down the zipper. He wasn't shy, he'd never been shy, and besides which, she was a doctor. A mature woman who'd been married. She knew perfectly well that a healthy man's sexual response was instinctive, automatic and completely beyond his control. She watched his every move. Lurching to his feet, he almost tripped in the now tangled sleeping bag. He kicked it aside and snatched the coffee off the floor. She wanted a show? He hoped she got a good eyeful.

He glared at her over the coffee cup. She wore a grin he knew too well. A look that said he was an idiot, but she thought he was cute anyway. His feet were freezing. The rest of him was burning up.

Picking up a cast iron Dutch oven, she said, "There's no hot water. I'll have to warm some up so we can wash." She filled the pot with water, then sauntered past him, her hips swaying. She hung the pot from a metal hook that swung into the fireplace.

"You better quit teasing me." His feet were frozen and his tongue was burnt. Neither sensation came close to the desire raging through his blood.

"Why?"

"Because—because—" His brain blanked. "Because I said so."

She dropped her gaze to his crotch. "That's pretty lame."

He couldn't disagree. He held out a hand. "Give me my pants."

Still smiling that infuriatingly sexy smile, she brought his jeans. "No games, right? I want you. From what I can see, the feeling is mutual. Is it mutual?"

"Yeah," he muttered. "Damn it." He pulled the jeans from her hand, let them drop to the floor and gathered her into his arms.

Chapter Thirteen

"You can touch me," Diana said.

Tate made a guttural noise, and his hips rolled beneath her thighs. They'd made it to the bed—somehow—barely. Once his hot mouth was on hers, time and space lost meaning. Theirs had been a frantic dance of fumbling and groping and grasping, and he'd finally lifted her off her feet and swept her onto the bed.

The first shock of icy bedding had brought a squeal from her, but now she was so hot they could be making love in a snow field and she wouldn't care. She straddled him, her body thrumming in a controlled burn, her senses saturated by the feel and taste and smell of him. She ran her hands over his chest. He wasn't buff-cut or grotesque like a body builder, but beautifully solid, his muscles supple. She wove her fingers through the crisp hair whorls on his chest.

His hands paused on her belly, fingers splayed, spreading fire. Between the main room and the bed, he'd lost his briefs and she'd lost her panties. He'd unfastened all but one button on her shirt, baring her belly, but concealing her chest. His fingertips teased the arch of her ribs, as if seeking a breast to fondle, but he kept stopping short.

She wanted him to touch her breast. She ached for him,

yearned for him, wanted his mouth and tongue devouring her.

The button remained fastened.

He lowered his hands, a slow, sensual sweep into the dip of her waist and over the swell of her hips. A moan rose in her throat, and she rocked against his erection. Arousal almost hurt, a sweet pain, full and pulsing and urgent. When he grasped the sensitive juncture of her thighs, a shudder rocked her, and she arched her spine.

"Ready, baby?" he whispered. His smile could slay a battalion of Amazons. It certainly slew her. He had a hand between her legs. Tremors gripped her again. She fought to keep her eyes open, wanting—needing—to see his face. A flex of her thigh muscles raised her, a cautious thrust and he was home. His eyes rolled back in the sockets, and his hips rose to meet hers.

"I take it that feels good, hmm?"

"Oh…oh my." His fingers tightened, so powerful, so erotic. His thumbs pressed either side of her mound, unbearably sweet. She rocked, he thrust and eventually a rhythm found them.

She couldn't stand it. Orgasm hit so fast, so powerful, it was almost embarrassing—if she had the wits to feel embarrassed. Instead she cried out, swept away, her joints disjointing and her spirit soaring. He bucked beneath her and made a strangled sound. His jaw was clenched and cords stuck out on his powerful neck.

She fell forward, burying her face against his neck. Aftershocks trembled through her. Cold air made itself known. As if reading her mind, he tugged blankets up over her back and shoulders, then slid his hands beneath the shirt so they rested against her damp skin. They breathed in unison, deep and satisfied.

He nibbled her ear. "Grateful?"

It took her a few seconds to remember the crack she'd made about Ben Franklin calling older women not only experienced, but grateful. She chuckled. "Very. You're quite a stud."

"I'm grateful, too." He kissed her neck.

Lazily, but with care so as to keep them connected, she managed to straighten her legs so she lay full length atop him. The hair on his legs tickled. She could feel the thump of his heart. Its strong beat soothed her and she drowsed.

"I'm sorry," he said.

Her eyelids fluttered. Her mind was nowhere, so it took a few seconds to figure out what he said. "About what?"

"Not…touching you…you know."

She lifted her head. It was a cloudy day and fog wreathed the forest and curled around the lodge. Daylight was pearl-colored. Even so she saw the chagrin. She fought the urge to sigh. She wasn't offering him therapy, and he had nothing to prove—not to her anyway. If the mastectomy scar bothered him, then it bothered him. He didn't have to apologize or force himself to do what he wasn't ready for. She sure didn't want to give him another panic attack.

"Seems to me, you touched me pretty good."

"I really do think you're beautiful." It almost sounded like a plea.

God save me from guilty men. "And I think you're gorgeous." She planted a kiss on his nose. "If you don't want to look, that's okay. If you don't want to touch, that's okay, too." She wanted to tell him she loved him, but no sense scaring him any more than he was already.

"I feel stupid."

"I'm after your body, not your brains."

His laugh rocked her. Laughter which ended too soon. "Does it hurt? The scar, I mean."

"No."

"How do you know the…it won't come back?"

"I don't." With a sigh and a sense of loss, she struggled upright. He let her go without argument. Sitting cross-legged beside him, she buttoned the shirt. "All I have is today. It's all any of us have. Whatever happens in the future will happen, whether I worry about it or not."

"But statistically…"

She sighed again. "I'm healthy, college-educated, don't smoke or drink and I eat a low-fat, low-protein diet. Statistically, I should live to ninety." She cupped his chin. "Oh, Tate, I wish I could assure you with a hundred percent certainty that the cancer will never come back. But I can't."

He pulled his face away. "I just…I know what it does."

This was the cold fire of fear he needed to walk through. She scooted off the bed. "I forgot all about the water. I hope the pot didn't boil dry."

He followed her out of the bedroom. The sight of his nakedness turned her knees weak. Waves of desire rolled through her pelvis.

He found his underwear and snatched his jeans off the floor. "Diana, please, I'm sorry. I know I should get over it."

She used tongs to swing the Dutch oven out of the flames. Water bubbled and steamed. Not enough for bathing, but at least he could shave. She pulled on her pants. They were toasty warm, even hot in places.

"You want a guarantee from me," she said. "I can't do that. It's impossible. It would be like me demanding you not get shot by a bad guy." She grasped his hands. Head hanging, feet planted in a wide stance, he looked like a man about to mount the gallows. "Believe it or not, I don't take your fears personally." He lifted his head just enough for her to see the whites of his eyes. "I don't. I don't consider your fears unreasonable either. What happened to your wife, to you, was a terrible thing, a tragedy. You'd have to be heartless not to suffer some traumatization."

"I couldn't watch…she was in pain… I couldn't do anything."

She knew exactly what he meant. As a physician, she'd protected herself from the misery of others by armoring herself with a shell of professional detachment. When her mother fell terminally ill, however, the shell had cracked. Helplessness to alleviate the suffering of a loved one hurt even more than the loss.

She squeezed his fingers. "Look at me. Please." Hesitantly, he did so. His gaze was bleak. "You have to deal with this. I can't do it for you, as much as I wish I could. But you aren't alone. Okay?"

"I'm a coward."

"Now you're just feeling sorry for yourself." She squeezed his fingers again and tried to tease him into a smile. "A coward wouldn't be risking his life and livelihood for a waitress."

"Yeah, I—" His head snapped up. "Ric! Oh, jeez!"

"What's the matter?"

"If that orderly got the license plate number of the Jeep and reported it, Ric will get in trouble. Where's my phone?" He snatched a phone off a desk, punched buttons, shook it, then tossed it down with a grunt. "Battery's dead. Where's mine? What did I do with it?"

"You threw it into the bushes. Calm down. I'll find it. Finish getting dressed."

TATE DROVE THE ROUGH back roads off ranch property. The fog was so thick in places it was akin to pushing through gauze curtains. Even though it wasn't raining, dripping trees kept the windshield wipers clacking. He had to pass through several gates, and each time he left the Jeep, moisture condensed on his skin.

Such slow going gave him too much time for thinking. He shouldn't have made love to Diana. There had been none of the detached pleasure he'd felt with other women, none of the separation of body and heart. This wasn't affection, or a mutual good time, or even scratching an itch. He was falling for her, hard—he'd fallen already.

She had cancer.

He turned the radio on as loud as he could stand it. The only station coming in clearly was the morning farm report. Anything to distract from death and dying and his shameful cowardice.

He drove a roundabout route to the ranch's main entrance. In the distance he could just barely make out semi-tractor trailers idling at a weigh station where cattle milled in holding pens. A tractor plowed a field. Cowboys on ATVs rumbled along a fence line.

Cancer. He shuddered and flipped the heater on high. She claimed she was cured, but how could she know? How could anyone know that vicious mutant cells weren't even now lodging in her tissues?

His jaw tightened and blood pulsed in his temples. It wasn't fair. His diaphragm tightened, and his heart was jittering. He ground a knuckle against his breastbone as if he could still his racing heart through pressure.

He couldn't go through it again.

Catch the bad guys, life would return to normal and things would be as they were. He and Diana would be friends, nothing more, nothing less.

He was lousy at lying to himself.

He reached Ric and Elaine's house. Windows glowed in welcome.

Elaine Buchanan met him at the front door. A petite woman, she always made him feel like an oversized oaf. Even in jeans, a flannel shirt and a faded old cardigan sweater she carried herself like royalty.

"Morning, Elaine," he said with a nod. "Is Ric around?"

She pushed open the screened door. "He's in the shower. Come on in."

He followed her into the cheerful kitchen, which was redolent with the aromas of baking biscuits and frying sausage. She handed him a large mug of fresh coffee and bade him sit at the table. "How's Diana?" she asked.

He noticed a montage of framed photographs on a shelf. Many of them were of Elaine's first husband. Bobby on horseback, Bobby posing with Jodi or Elaine or all of them together. Tate wondered if the reminders bugged Ric, then immediately discounted the idea. Bobby and Ric had been good friends. What really made him curious was how Elaine could stand the constant reminders of what she'd lost.

"Diana's fine."

She wanted to ask more, know more—curiosity shone on her face. She probably knew Marlee had helped Diana; it probably drove her crazy that her sister knew something she didn't. She wasn't the type to pry, however, and Tate was grateful. At the same time, he wished they had a closer relationship so he could ask how she'd recovered from grief. Elaine had loved her late husband. How had she managed to get on with her life, to love again, risk again?

Ric entered the kitchen. He didn't look all that surprised

to see Tate. He kissed his wife and poured himself some coffee. "What's up, jarhead?"

"Need to trade vehicles again." He placed the Jeep key on the table. "Had a bit of an…incident last night. You might be getting a visit from the FBI."

Husband and wife exchanged a look.

"Just tell the truth. No sense you taking any heat on my account."

"Are you in trouble?" Ric asked.

"Working on it." He felt bad about involving his friends. It was a small consolation that Ric honestly did not know anything. He gulped coffee, enjoying the pleasant burn of it going down his throat. He stood. "I'd tell you more if I could, but it's best if I don't."

"Is there anything we can do for you and Diana?" Elaine asked. "Or can Mama do something? She's got heavy-duty connections, you know."

Tate grinned. Not even the FBI would dare mess with Lillian McClintock Crowder. "Just keep your eyes and ears open. The sooner we take Bernadette O'Malley into custody, the better. I need to go."

"Stay safe," Elaine said. "Tell Diana if she needs anything, give a holler."

He gave her a jaunty salute and left the house.

The fog had lifted a little by the time he reached McClintock; Main Street had a misty, watercolor look. Dark storefronts and empty sidewalks made it seem like a ghost town. He kept a close watch out for any suspicious activity. As he cruised past the Shack he did a double take and stomped on the brake.

He gaped openmouthed at the big front window. Even though the bar wasn't open, all the lights were on and he could actually see into the dining room! A man on a ladder was painting the glass. Tate whipped around behind the business and found Consuela's old Plymouth parked in his spot.

Managing the place was one thing. Taking over was quite another. He stomped inside. The heady aroma of roasting chilies greeted him. Spanish conversation and laughter filled the kitchen, which happened to be full of Consuela's relatives.

"What the hell is going on?" Tate demanded.

Consuela eyed him as if he were a pesky salesman. Tate stomped to the batwing doors and stared at the dining room. A pretty little girl of about ten or eleven was smoothing a tablecloth. Bright white, yellow and green cloths covered all the tables. Neon beer advertisements and tacky memorabilia had been removed from the walls. Young people scrubbed the floor, washed the walls and polished the mahogany bar. A young man stood on a ladder and painted the glass. The *clear* glass.

"What happened to the window tinting?" he asked.

"Pfft!" Consuela said with a dismissive wave of her hand. "Ugly and peeling and old-fashioned. Couldn't get it clean. We scraped it off."

His mouth fell open.

"Miguel is an artist," she said proudly. "He is making the window beautiful. Customers will come in just because his paintings are so wonderful!"

He sought an argument against the improvements but couldn't think of a single one. Shaking his head, he wandered back to his apartment. Consuela had left a shoe box on the table outside his door. It was filled with receipts, invoices and cash. She'd completed the payroll and placed orders for supplies.

Inside his apartment, he sorted through the shoe box. Business was booming. He'd have to deal with it later. He crouched before the small safe tucked beneath the sink in the kitchenette. He spun the dial, pulled it open and started to slide the box inside. A small framed photograph lay inside the safe. It was a snapshot of Lisa he'd taken on a visit to Coney Island. A breeze was flipping her sundress, and she was pushing down her skirt à la Marilyn Monroe.

She was laughing, her cheeks pink with sunburn. It was the way he wanted to remember her. He couldn't bear memories of the shrunken, pained, drugged creature she'd been at the end.

He stared at the picture, waiting for the pain to overwhelm him. It didn't come. Instead there was a bittersweet sadness and the certainty that Lisa had been a gift. He hadn't had her long enough—he'd wanted a lifetime—but he treasured what they shared. She'd been a generous woman, never harboring grudges, always willing to kiss and make up after an argument. Always quick to forgive.

She'd have forgiven him for not being there when she died.

He carried the photograph in both hands to the crate that served as a bedside table. He cleared away books and wiped off dust with his forearm. He placed the framed picture on the table, adjusting it until it looked right.

He locked the cash and receipts in the safe.

Lisa's picture drew him again. Not only would she have forgiven him, she'd have found a way to encourage him to forgive himself. That was the way she'd been—the way Diana was now.

His dad used to advise, "Don't argue with your mother, son. Women are always right. Get used to it."

Wise man, his father.

Tate called Gil and reached the sheriff at home. He told him about the orderly at the hospital in Durango.

"No one reported any tips from the hospital or any-where else. What were you doing at the hospital?"

Tate hunched into his shoulders. No way did he want his boss to know he'd suffered an anxiety attack. "Don't worry about it. Are you sure nothing came in? I'm posi-tive that guy recognized Diana."

"Damn it, Tate, if you're injured, I have a right to know."

"Forget about it. The important thing is, I was driving Ric's Jeep. I don't want the feebs hassling him."

"I'll keep them away. Are you sure you're all right?"

Tate rolled his eyes. His own parents had never fussed over him the way Gil Vance did. "I'm perfectly fine."

Gil grumbled, then said, "Judge Woodman threw out the warrant for Diana's arrest. None of the charges fall under federal jurisdiction." He chuckled, an evil sound. "Woodman reamed Albright a new one. If I were you, I'd stay the hell out of McClintock. All Albright needs is an excuse and he'll hang your head on his wall."

"I'll take that under advisement."

Tate packed extra clothing and threw in batteries for his cell phone, shells for the shotgun and a .38 snub-nosed revolver. He made a quick stop in the kitchen. "If anyone asks, you haven't seen me," he told Consuela.

"See who?" she said with a sniff then snapped her fingers at a teenager. The girl handed Tate a heavy gro-cery sack. It was filled with carry-out containers.

Touched, he said, "Thanks."

"You paid for it. Now get lost."

He loaded his bag and the food in the Bronco, and drove out of town. He got stuck behind a line of behemoth recreational vehicles chugging up a steep grade. The or-derly at the hospital gnawed at him. He'd definitely rec-ognized Diana.

Lines at the station must have gotten crossed. Or else the orderly had contacted the Durango police and they'd failed for some reason to act immediately.

An open stretch came up and he gunned the accelerator, passing two RVs before he had to veer back into the right lane to avoid a cattle truck barreling down the hill. He passed the third RV and picked up speed. The engine blew an angry-sounding bang and the truck shuddered and shimmied. Tate let up on the gas. The shimmying stopped, but the engine ran rougher and louder than usual.

"Don't die on me now, you old pig," he muttered and turned up the radio's volume to drown out the distressing noise.

The phone rang. Tate turned down the radio and answered. It was Gil.

"Did the tip come in?" Tate asked. "Can you keep it—"

"I've got nothing from Durango," the sheriff said. "This is better. We got a break."

Tate snapped to attention. "Bernadette?"

"Couple of campers up at Fox Den Draw caught her pilfering their food box. This morning they reported it to a forest ranger."

Tate nearly whooped. He'd half-believed that Bernadette had been eaten by wolves or abducted by aliens. "Is she in custody?"

"Not yet. But the ID is positive, and the campers claim she's on foot. Which means she's hiding not far away. I'm coordinating a search party as we speak."

"I'll be there—"

"Like hell you will. You're on vacation. Besides, Albright is right outside my door. He's sweating under a protective vest and rarin' to go. He might accidentally shoot you."

"But—"

"No buts. Let me handle this. The real beauty of it is, Fox Den is on state land. So when we pick her up, the state police will have initial custody. Albright will have to haggle with them. That'll make him appreciate what nice guys we are."

"What about Coles? Will you tip him off?"

"I don't know. He's a squirrel."

Tate knew what Gil meant. Something about the reporter rubbed Tate the wrong way. That he couldn't pinpoint why the man made him so itchy, bugged him. It was probably that Coles was so darned eager.

The turn-off onto the ranch was just up ahead. "Keep me posted."

"You got it." Gil rang off.

The Bronco's engine died each time Tate had to stop to open a gate. It restarted easily enough, but black smoke billowed from the tail pipe. When Tate finally limped up to the lodge, he breathed a little prayer of thanks.

The fog had lifted completely, but the sky was low and gray. Despite it being June, they could be in for snow. Or the clouds might burn off by noon and the temperature could soar. He'd given up even trying to predict Rocky Mountain weather. His shoes squashed on the soggy ground when he locked the chain across the driveway. Wood smoke hung heavily in the sodden air.

He carried his belongings onto the porch and used his foot to knock on the door. Diana opened it.

"My goodness," she said, eyeing the Bronco. "What did you do to that poor thing? It sounds terrible."

He'd told himself he'd keep things cool. One look into her shining eyes and he was lost. His insides jumbled with longing and memories and sexual heat.

"Are you coming in?" she asked, a note of caution.

Having his arms full saved him from making a fool of himself. Otherwise he'd have her on the floor right now. Merely looking at her made him hard.

"Tate?"

He forced his feet to move. He struck something solid and Tippy yipped. That snapped Tate out of his stupor. Diana grabbed the grocery sack before he dropped it. He crouched to apologize to the puppy, who proved ridiculously eager to forgive.

"Talk to me! Did something bad happen?" Diana carried the sack to the kitchen nook. "What's wrong? Oh no, it's because I used a credit card at the hospital, isn't it?"

"No! Sorry." He closed his eyes a moment, gathering his wits. He wasn't the brightest bulb in the chandelier, but he wasn't stupid either. Except, apparently, around Diana. "Actually there's good news."

"They found Bernie? She's alive?"

"She's alive and Gil thinks they can find her."

She dropped gracelessly onto a chair. She twisted her fingers on her lap.

He related what Gil had told her. She patted the base of her throat and her eyes glazed with tears.

"It's okay, honey, I swear. Nobody is going in with guns blazing. They're pros." He patted her shoulder. Which turned into a caress and then she was in his arms, her shoulders hitching and her hot breath seeping through his shirt. "It's okay, it's okay."

She snuffled loudly. She wasn't crying, but she was close. "I was so afraid she was dead."

He rubbed her back and stroked her hair and called himself the worst sort of cad for being so aroused. Her hip shifted, her belly rubbed against his and her hands slipped over his shoulders and around his neck. When she lifted her face to his, a gun to his head couldn't have prevented him from kissing her.

And kissing her. He kissed her generous mouth, trailed his questing mouth over satiny skin, the taut jut of her cheekbones, her petal-soft eyelids. A whimper rose in her throat, a tiny sensuous sound that he homed in on like a predatory bird. He backed her against the desk. She tore his shirt out of his jeans. Anxious little noises she made drove him over the edge. He hoisted her onto the desk. Her fingers tortured his belly while she fumbled with his belt.

He swayed drunkenly away from kissing her. "Crazy," he breathed.

Her eyes were glazed, her cheeks flushed. "Yeah." She jerked at her shoelaces and practically threw her shoes across the room. In a flash, she had her jeans and panties around her ankles, and she was grabbing for him again.

The sex wasn't sweet, it wasn't tender—she blew his mind. If she had inhibitions, she'd left them at the door.

In the aftermath, he panted against her shoulder. His feet were on the floor, one of her glorious legs was draped over his shoulder and he held on to her generous butt to keep her from sliding off the desk.

"Da-ahm," he breathed.

"That was…pretty…good…" She chuckled.

"This can't be comfortable for you."

"It's not, but my bones have dissolved."

His knees were cramping. He shrugged until her leg was off his shoulder and she could wriggle higher onto the desk. He couldn't resist her gorgeous belly. White as milk, and with a honeyed smell he wanted to bottle. He licked her navel. She giggled.

"We shouldn't be doing this, Red." Lord, but she was a true redhead. He was getting hard again.

She hooked her hands behind her head and grinned at him. "You'd rather do what? Play cards?"

He pushed up on his arms, looming over her. Two buttons on her shirt remained fastened, covering her chest, her scars. It hadn't been deliberate to miss those buttons. Or maybe it had. Shame damped his desire. "I'm hungry."

"Ah, fuel for the machine." She urged him to move away. Stretching like a cat, she languorously slid off the desk and onto her feet. Working her fingers against her scalp, ruffling that magnificent mane of hair, she strolled into the kitchen nook.

No jeans.

No panties.

Just shirt tails swaying over her derriere and long, shapely legs. No shame in this woman, no self-consciousness. The slow roll of her hips said she welcomed his hungry gaze.

She was gonna give him a heart attack for real. He tore his attention away and went in search of his clothing.

"How long will it take Gil to apprehend Bernie?" she asked. She pulled carry-out containers from the grocery sack.

"She's probably exhausted, hungry and maybe sick. I don't think she'll resist capture."

She loaded plates with still-warm huevos rancheros and corn muffins. "What will the FBI do to her?"

He formulated a reassuring reply, but then caught the twist of worry in her brow. What she wanted to ask was, did the FBI mean to use her sister as bait to catch a terrorist? "I don't know. Once she's in their custody, it's all over for us."

She brought plates to the table. Mumbling about making fresh coffee, she turned her back on him.

"That reporter could have been blowing smoke about Montgomery. Making himself look important. I don't care how good his sources are, I bet he doesn't know the whole story."

"If she did kidnap and murder that woman, she could get the death penalty."

He couldn't sugarcoat this. He didn't try. "It's possible. Best casing is, we're talking a life sentence in a federal penitentiary. There's nothing you can do for her."

"I know." She filled an enameled coffeepot with water and fitted a basket inside. After fiddling with the flame on a small propane camp stove, she joined him at the table. "When Bernie and I were little girls, we played a game. I'd say, I was going to be a stage actress. She'd top it, saying she was going to be a star. I'd have a million dollars, she'd have a billion. The last time we played, she lost her temper. She screamed at me. She said no matter what I did, she was going to make sure she was more famous." She sighed heavily. "In hindsight, it seems horribly prophetic."

He felt bad for her. "My youngest brother went to jail once." As soon as those stupid words were out of his mouth, he felt like an ass. Doubly so when she cocked her head and wrinkled her nose. He groaned. "I'm sorry, I…"

"Trying to make me feel better?" She patted his hand. "I'm very sad about my sister. You'd think I'd be used to the heartache by now." She ate a few bites, but didn't seem interested in the food. "Why did he go to jail?"

"Busted the cap off a fire hydrant. He and his buddies were hot."

At least she laughed. Small consolation.

He wished there were something he could do to ease her worry. All they could do was wait.

TATE HUNKERED INTO A crouch and poked at the logs in the fireplace. Ashes fell off embers and pitch crackled.

Diana sat on a rocking chair with a blanket tucked around her legs and feet. A novel lay open on her lap. "You're prowling around like a caged animal. Why don't you read a book or something?"

He paced to the window. Earlier it had snowed. Big, fat, clumpy snowflakes that melted as soon as they touched the ground. Then it had rained for a short while and now the sky was rapidly clearing. A brisk wind rocked the treetops and whistled around the chimney. He paced back to the desk and checked his phone. He had a good signal. Gil hadn't called.

He peeked over his shoulder at Diana. Worse than boredom, he was all too aware of her. Her honeyed scent filled every corner of the lodge. Her hair beckoned his fingers. If he stayed still, he thought about her mouth and kissing her and the way her hands felt moving over his back. She soothed him, relaxed him—hypnotized him! If he wasn't careful, he'd end up at her feet with his head on her lap, as pitifully eager for her attention as the dog was.

He wished he'd brought some weights. A good, hard workout would ease his restlessness. He clipped the phone to his belt. "Come on, Tippy. Let's get some more firewood."

He dawdled outdoors. He threw sticks for Tippy and straightened stacks of lumber from a fallen-down stable. He did some pull-ups from a stout branch and found a good-size stone to hoist and warm his muscles. Only when his shoes were soaked through and his feet were freezing did he return to the house. Tippy shook himself, flinging water. Giving Tate a chastising frown, Diana pointed at a ragged towel hanging near the door. He caught the squirming puppy and rubbed him down. Then he removed his shoes and damp socks, and sat on a rug before the hearth. The heat from the low flames stung his cold feet, but felt good. Tippy lay beside him.

At least with a soggy dog practically under his nose, Diana's scent wasn't driving him crazy.

"Tell me about your family," Diana said.

"Not much to tell. Just everyday, average folks. Parents still live in the house where I grew up. Everyone likes to eat."

Her mouth quirked. "I can't imagine everyday, average folks producing you."

He had to consider what she said before deciding she complimented him. He shrugged. "Dad's a retired fireman. Mom is convinced retiring will mean more work, so she's still at the hospital. She's a pediatrics nurse."

"You must have grown up in a very safe household."

He laughed. He couldn't even remember how many times he and his brothers tumbled down the stairs—on purpose or on accident. As kids, they'd fought constantly, usually physically, and played dangerous pranks. And there was all the stuff they did on their own—bike riding, skateboards and hitching rides on the bumpers of delivery trucks. All of them were sports nuts, too, which meant the emergency room was practically their second home. "Right. I have three brothers and two sisters. That all of us made it to adulthood is by accident, not design. We were rotten."

"All those brothers and sisters, amazing. Your mother must be quite the lady."

"She's cool." A pang of homesickness surprised him. "Meaner than a junkyard dog, though. Dad was the softie in our house. 'Wait 'til your mother gets home' was the phrase that put terror in our hearts." He smiled at the memories. All of the Raleigh boys and girls took after their father in height. On a few occasions Mom had stood on a chair in order to face down a miscreant child.

"Have any visited Colorado?"

"Dad hurt his back on the job and long road trips are out of the question. Even an airplane ride is too much for him. My brothers and sisters are busy with families of their own. I'm the only one who's ever lived outside New York."

"Do you miss the big city?"

"Sometimes. But I was a cop for a long time and there are a lot of things I never want to see again. Muggers, junkies, gang members. The stupid, senseless things people can do to each other." He leaned back on one hand. "I don't miss the noise either. When I first got here, the quiet drove me crazy. I couldn't sleep. Now that I'm used to it, I doubt I could go back again."

"I feel the same way about Phoenix. An emergency room physician sees bad stuff, too."

"Do you miss being a doctor? Waitressing is quite a step down for you."

"Not really. I like the Shack and the customers are the best. I've made a lot of good friends." She pushed the floor with her heel; the chair squeaked. "When I was a doctor, I was terrified of making a mistake, terrified of looking like a fool. The only time I ever felt comfortable was when I was in my office, doing paperwork with the door closed."

He tried to picture her uptight, tense, impatient, fearful. He couldn't reconcile the image with the calm, gentle woman he'd come to know.

The telephone rang. Both of them startled. Her book thunked on the floor. He fumbled the phone open.

"We found her camp," Gil said.

Tate guessed by the sheriff's disgusted tone that they hadn't found Bernadette. "And her?"

"Gone. If we hadn't been looking so hard, we'd have missed the camp altogether."

"Did Montgomery's people find her?"

"Only if they're neat freaks. Place is clean as a whistle. Only way we're sure it's hers is because she left behind an empty prescription bottle of painkillers. They're prescribed to Diana."

"Any idea what direction she's headed?"

"A downpour wiped out her tracks and search dogs aren't having any luck picking up a trail. Damn it!"

"So what now?"

"Keep sitting tight. We've got a full scale search spreading out, and the state boys are trying to wangle a helicopter to help out. I'll keep you posted."

Deep in thought, Tate disconnected the call. He turned to relay the information to Diana.

"She's gone again, isn't she?" she asked.

"Yeah. Let's hope she runs into our people before she runs into Montgomery's."

Chapter Fourteen

Diana couldn't sleep. Worry raced circles through her mind like a frantic animal chasing its tail. She lay in the darkness, staring out a window into the night. Tate had an arm draped over her belly and a leg on her thighs. Each deep, slow breath ruffled against her hair. The scent of their lovemaking overrode the musty, mousy smell of the saggy old mattress.

She should have been comfortable, should have been at peace. She was exactly where she'd wanted to be for a long, long time—in Tate Raleigh's arms.

Instead she fretted about Bernie. Her sister wasn't a ghost, she wasn't psychic. So how had she known to desert her camp one step ahead of the law?

Tate claimed she'd been spotted stealing from campers. Diana didn't believe that had spooked Bernie. Her sister always seemed surprised when she was caught doing something, as if it never occurred to her that others noticed her crimes. Besides, if Bernie had fled in fear, she wouldn't have left the campsite so clean.

Wind swayed the trees, casting crazy shadows across the window. Branches scraped the roof with skittery sounds that made her shiver. She wished the window had a curtain to block the bright moonlight and the shadows it caused.

The moon!

"Tate, wake up." She shook his shoulder.

He grunted and mumbled, then snapped to an alertness that startled her. "What? What's the matter?" He fought the too-soft mattress and groped under the pillows for the weapon he'd stashed.

Diana hopped off the bed and hurried to the window. The moon, huge and silver, turned the night into a high-contrast study of black and gray. "I know where Bernie's headed."

He knuckled an eye. "What are you talking about?"

"Bernie broke camp. She wasn't panicked, she took her time. I bet it's because of the moon. Look at that sky. It's practically as bright as day. It's the perfect time to go for the money. Isn't it?"

"You think she's going to your place? She has to realize people are after her."

"It would make sense to Bernie. All she has to do is give Smoky Joe his head and he'll go home. Being on horseback gives her the advantage. She'll see any searchers long before they see her. I'm telling you, she's gone after the money."

He joined her at the window. He watched for a few seconds, then turned for his pants. Enough moonlight streamed inside for him to find them easily.

While he contacted the sheriff, Diana dressed warmly. She intended to be there when her sister was caught. She gathered a thermal undershirt and flannel shirt for Tate. When she handed them to him, he was finished talking to Gil Vance.

He pulled the thermal shirt over his head. "Gil agrees with you."

"Let me go with you," she said. "Please."

"It isn't safe."

"It's my house. I have the home field advantage. Please, Tate, once the FBI gets their hands on her, I may never get a chance to talk to her again."

"Don't ask this, honey. Things could go wrong, get messy. You don't want to see that."

She didn't want to see a shoot-out, her sister gunned down, men she knew wounded. She refused to believe it would come to that. "Please. She's my sister, all I have left. Please."

Eyes closed, standing stiff and rigid, he seemed in pain. Perhaps he was. She felt bad for his turmoil, but she desperately wanted, needed to see her sister. If she were there, she felt positive Bernie wouldn't do anything stupid to get herself killed.

"You'll stay out of the way. Follow orders."

"Oh, yes, sir." Silently she prayed for Bernie, for Tate, for them all.

TATE RUBBED HIS HANDS briskly, then jammed them under his armpits. It was small consolation that the wind had died. The night was, as Diana had pointed out, so still and quiet a person could hear the mountains sing. The stillness worked in their favor. Not even a cat could sneak up on Diana's farm.

The waiting wore on Tate's nerves. He'd always hated stakeouts, sitting, fighting sleepiness, boredom, fidgeting. This was the first stakeout he'd ever pulled in Colorado, and it was as numbing as any in New York. There were four of them: Gil, Tate, Deputy Bill Yarrow and volunteer Moe Sherwood. Moe's pickup was parked in Diana's garage, so Bernadette would think it was Diana's. All other vehicles were hidden off the property. They operated on total radio silence, and cell phones were turned off. No talking amongst themselves, no moving around. Gil and Tate were posted at the barn. Moe and Bill waited near the house. All four were armed with shotguns and powerful flashlights.

The high point was that Gil had tipped off the reporter, Patrick Coles. He'd told him to keep an eye out for Albright and the reporter could end up with a major scoop. A national story about Bernadette's arrest and the FBI's custody of her should convince Montgomery once and for all that he wouldn't get what he wanted in McClintock.

Gil wasn't happy about Diana's presence. She'd agreed to stay in the house, out of the way. Tate trusted her to not interfere, no matter what happened.

Diana. He shifted his weight from foot to foot, working out the pins-and-needles sensation. He was falling in love with her. He hadn't meant it to happen. He'd been resisting her for a long, long time. Imagining life without her filled him with aching pain.

She didn't act as if he were a miserable, cowardly dope, but she had to be thinking it. He couldn't even bring himself to touch her breast, couldn't make himself look at her scarred chest. One of these days she was going to get damned sick of his cancer phobia.

Gil touched his shoulder and Tate snapped to attention.

The moon now nearly touched the western mountains and the eastern sky was beginning to lighten. It was darker now than it had been an hour ago and Tate could barely see his own hand in front of his face. He followed the shadow of Gil's arm, pointing north.

Then he heard it. The clip-clopping of horse's hooves, drawing near. Along with pounding hooves came the jingle of hardware and squeaking leather.

Tate picked up the shotgun in his right hand and the flashlight in his left.

"Wait," Gil said, the barest whisper. "No rider."

Tate couldn't imagine how Gil knew that, but trusted the man. Sure enough, Diana's horse trotted around the house and toward the barn. That Bill and Moe weren't reacting meant they realized Bernadette was pulling something. Tate's respect for the Colorado lawmen hiked a notch.

They kept waiting. Tate imagined Bernadette was waiting, too, to see what kind of reaction the horse received. The sun was rising. She had to make her move soon.

Finally, they heard the noise Gil was waiting for. The metallic scrape of the bee enclosure gate latch. Gil touched Tate's arm, urging him to the left. The two spread out, flanking the bee enclosure.

Tate spotted her stealthy shadow. He raised the shotgun. When she had both hands on the beehive, Gil, who was standing behind her, turned on the light and yelled, "Freeze!"

For a heart-stopping second Tate watched her hand hover as if she debated going for a weapon. Don't do it, he urged silently. Dear God, don't do it.

"Put your hands on your head," Gil ordered. "This is the sheriff. You are under arrest."

She laced her fingers atop her head. Tate turned on his flashlight and set it on a boulder so it shone directly on Bernadette. He rested the shotgun against the stone, then drew his handgun. He entered the bee enclosure. From the corner of his eye he spotted a few bees reacting sluggishly to the light. He patted her down and found a .38 in one coat pocket, and a folding knife and a loaded clip for the handgun in the other pocket. He checked her waistband

and ran his hands down her legs in case she had something in her boot tops.

Aware of bobbing flashlights announcing the arrival of Bill and Moe, he handcuffed Bernadette's arms behind her back.

He could hear the bees now. A low warning hum. He grabbed her upper arm and hustled her out of the enclosure.

Gil shone the flashlight in Bernadette's face. Her resemblance to Diana staggered Tate. Knowing they were twins was one thing, but seeing her in the flesh was an eye-opener. Her hair was short and her face was thinner than Diana's, but if he saw her walking down a street, he'd be uncertain which sister she was.

"Bernadette Marie O'Malley?" Gil asked.

She grinned crookedly, seeming resigned. Tate wondered if she'd be so smug if she knew the FBI had the half a million dollars. "You got me. You guys don't still hang horse thieves, do you?"

Even her voice was like Diana's, low and slightly husky. Spooky.

Tate recited the Miranda warning.

"Yeah, yeah, I heard it before. So I guess Di is pressing charges. Oh well, guess you caught me red-handed. I'm bad."

Tate wondered if she'd forgotten about Tim Robertson and the stolen Buick, or figured if she didn't mention it, neither would they. It didn't matter. She was in custody with no blood spilled. In a short while, she'd be the FBI's problem. He and Gil marched her around to the front of the house and had her sit cross-legged on the ground. Gil directed Bill and Moe to bring up the hidden vehicles, then he pulled out his cell phone.

The house windows lit up and the porch light came on.

Diana stepped outside. Gil took his phone conversation out of earshot. Tate nodded at Diana to let her know she could approach.

Bernie grinned up at her sister. She acted like a kid who'd been caught filching cookies. "Hi, there."

"How's your arm?" Diana asked.

"Right as rain. You did a bang-up job. I think you're a better doctor than Daddy ever was. He had a lousy bedside manner." She batted her eyelashes at Tate. "I didn't really steal your horse. I always meant to bring him back. You didn't have to call the cops. There isn't a scratch on him."

"You always were good with animals."

"So, uh, why don't you tell the Incredible Hulk here to take off the bracelets. They don't match my ensemble."

"Oh, Bernie, this isn't about you stealing Smoky Joe."

Headlights appeared over the hill, and the sheriff's Range Rover rumbled into view. Bernie's smile faded. Tate guessed she was finally getting that this was a lot more than a domestic dispute between sisters.

"Honey," he said to Diana, "your horse went into the barn. Go take care of him."

Bernie watched her sister walk away. "Honey?" she said to Tate. "How do you rate that you can get away with calling her names? She hates that kind of stuff. Must be 'cause you're so darned cute. Or tell me, are you the reason she's so mellow these days?"

Her teasing amused him and gave him a better understanding of how she'd flim-flammed her family all these years. She was a charmer.

Gil walked up to them. "Albright's ticked. Says we should have notified him before the capture."

"Looks like we'll get our hands slapped. Too bad."

Gil hunkered into a crouch and rested his elbows on a

knee. He studied Bernadette as if she were an exotic insect. "A whole lot of people are looking for you, Ms. O'Malley."

"For little ol' me? I'm flattered."

"Mind telling us what's going on?"

She looked from man to man. Tate noticed the real physical difference between the twins. Where Diana's expression was open and gentle, this woman was sly, always on the lookout for an advantage. "Going on?" she said innocently. "I can't imagine what you mean."

Gil turned a wrist enough to see the faintly glowing face of his wristwatch. "In about fifteen or twenty minutes, the FBI will arrive. They're going to take you into custody."

Her smile faded and she worked her shoulders as if the handcuffs were hurting her. "FBI? How come?"

"You tell us."

"I'm not telling anybody anything until I have a lawyer."

Those words ended the interview. Gil was legally bound to stop all attempts to elicit information or a confession. He rose.

"Huh," Tate said. "Last mope who asked for a lawyer in this town got himself a bullet in the brain."

"She's invoked her right to counsel," Gil said. "Drop it."

"I'm not talking to her, sir. I'm talking to you. Do you think the FBI will protect her or dangle her like a worm on a fishing pole?"

"Hey! What's that supposed to mean?"

Tate wondered if it were possible that Bernadette didn't know who she'd crossed. "Wait for your mouthpiece, Ms. O'Malley. Here," he grasped her arm and hauled her to her feet, "Let's get the inventory over with. Call it a favor to the feds since they've been so helpful. Anything in your pants pockets that will cut or stick me?''

"The FBI is asking for me by name? For real? Did I make their Ten Most Wanted list?''

Tate pulled a wad of cash, several matchbooks and a set of keys from her pockets. She stank of wood smoke and sweat. He stood in front of her to count the cash. Two hundred and eighty-six dollars. The keys intrigued him. There was a set for a Lincoln, and a few that might be door keys. One, however was tiny like a luggage key and another was for a safe-deposit box. The key fob was a fancy silver bar with turquoise chips spelling out stylized letters: FKM.

"I'm guessing the cash came out of Diana's cookie jar. But who owns the keys?''

"Those are mine.''

"What does FKM stand for?''

She pressed her lips together.

"I'm not going to question you, Ms. O'Malley. So you just sit back down and listen.'' He helped her to the ground. "You're in a lot of trouble. The feds aren't the only people looking for you. Two armed men came to this farm. One died, the other was murdered by an assassin after we took him into custody. His assassin is still on the loose. I have reason to believe that there are other men searching for you, and they have committed murder.'' He looked to the sheriff. Gil's face was bland, tacitly giving permission for Tate to continue.

He dangled the key fob. "Farrah Montgomery. Missing and presumed dead. We found the ransom money, Bernadette. The briefcase was bugged. You led those thugs straight to your sister's home. One of them mistook her for you. Did you have any idea who Farrah Montgomery was before you kidnapped her? Murdered her? Do you get who she is now?''

"I didn't kill her." She begged with her eyes for understanding. "She was my friend. Best friend I ever had. I never hurt her."

"Where is she?"

She lifted a shoulder. The cockiness had fled and she chewed her lower lip.

"Is she dead?"

"What will you give me if I talk?"

Gil planted his fists on his hips. "This isn't an auction, Ms. O'Malley. Besides, it's out of our hands. If you want to make deals, you'll have to deal with the FBI."

"Then I better shut up."

"This isn't a joke," Tate said. "Your sister could be in danger."

"Diana?" She made a hissy noise through her teeth. "She's like a cat. Always lands on her feet. Leads one of those charmed lives, you know? Nothing bad ever happens to her."

Tate clenched his fists. He wanted to shake her. "Does the name Douglas Montgomery mean anything to you?"

Her eyes narrowed. She was sizing him up, trying to guess how much he knew and how he could use it against her—or vice versa. Finally, she pulled a facial shrug. "Farrah's daddy. Sweet old guy. What does he have to do with this?"

Tate snapped his head around and faced Gil's shocked expression.

"What?" Bernadette scowled. "What's the big deal? Me and Farrah went to her place in Lake Tahoe and he flew in. Had his own Learjet. We partied, had some fun. For an old guy, he's pretty hot in the sack. He even invited me to his island for a vacation. He's way rich." Her scowl deepened. "Oh. Guess he's mad about Farrah being…out of touch."

"You actually saw Douglas Montgomery."

"Every inch of him." She winked. "A nice suntan hides a lot of wrinkles."

Tate pulled Gil to the side. "If that reporter told the truth, then Bernadette is one of the few people who can ID Montgomery."

"You think the feds will use her to reel him in?"

"That's exactly what I think." Tate rubbed his scratchy eyes. Every muscle ached from the tension of the stake-out. "We need to get her out of here."

Moe Sherwood walked up the driveway, his big yellow hat pulled low on his forehead. "Can't get that rustbucket to run," he said. "Engine will turn, but then it dies. I about killed your battery."

Tate breathed a curse. When he asked for the keys, Moe said he'd left them in the Bronco. If he were lucky, Tate thought, someone would steal it.

Diana walked around the house. She wore a thoughtful expression and had her hands in her pockets. In passing, she glanced at her sister, but said nothing to her. "I don't have coffee," she said to Tate, "but I can make tea." The men shook their heads and mumbled, "thanks but no thanks." Shrugging, she entered the house.

"She's mad at me," Bernadette said, a woebegone look on her face. "It's not like I did anything to her."

Tate never had understood the criminal mind. He sure didn't get how Bernadette could act so clueless about the damage she wrought. He followed Diana into the house.

She leaned a hand on a kitchen counter and the other hand covered her face. Soundlessly, she sobbed, her shoulders shaking.

"Ah, honey, it's okay," he said, feeling helpless and

stupid. He awkwardly patted her back, unsure if he should hold her or leave her alone. She solved his dilemma by turning into his arms and burying her face against his shoulder. He rubbed her back and held her until her shaking subsided.

"Sorry," she said, breathlessly. "I was so afraid she'd try to run or shoot it out with you. So scared. Now that she's safe, it's such a relief."

"I know, I know." He lifted strands of hair off her damp face. "She's alive, healthy. Like you said, she chose her own path."

She nodded. "I didn't want her to escape. I'm glad she's in custody. It's just hard on my heart, you know? She's going to prison for good."

He pressed his lips to her forehead.

Gil tapped on the door. "Albright is taking his sweet time. Ms. O'Malley is getting cold. I'm going to—"

"Can she come inside, Gil? I'd like to talk to her."

"That's not a good idea, Diana."

She wiped tears off her cheeks with the flats of her hands. "I doubt I'll get another chance. Please?"

After a few seconds, Gil nodded. He had Moe and Bill bring Bernadette inside. They seated her at the kitchen table. Gil and the deputies went back outside.

"I could sure use a cup of hot tea," Bernadette said. "I'm kind of hungry, too."

Without a word, Diana went to the stove.

Tate smoothed hair off his ears. It was weird seeing them together in the light. Like stereo-vision. Even the way they held their heads, slightly canted and chins up, was identical. He moved to the window. Gil was dismissing Bill and Moe. The sheriff shook hands with both. Whatever he said made Moe laugh. Both of them got into Moe's truck and they drove away. Gil opened his phone and punched in a number. He listened then shook his head and walked to the Range Rover. He reached inside for the radio mike.

Diana measured water into a pot. "Remember when you tried to call Mother? I refused your collect calls? I didn't know you were in jail. Mother wanted to talk to you, see you. It's my fault it didn't happen. I'm sorry, Bernie. Really sorry."

"Eh." Bernie shrugged. "I don't blame you. I've always been a pain in your butt."

"I had no right to keep you away from her."

Bernadette laughed. Even her laugh sounded exactly like Diana's. "Why, 'cause Mom acted all gooshy about me? Ha! She didn't like me all that much, Di. Besides, even if I wasn't in jail, I wouldn't have gone to see her." She shuddered. "Sick people creep me out. You know that."

"Mother loved you."

"I was just her way of sticking it to the old man. You're the one she loved." She shrugged again. "Why not? You were the good daughter. Mom and Daddy thought you walked on water." She turned her big blue eyes on Tate. "I like you a lot better than Dr. Jeff. She tell you about her husband? He had a stick shoved so far up his butt he could brush his teeth with it. I never could figure out what she saw in him."

"Bernie."

"What? Am I wrong? You two don't have a big thing going?"

Diana placed a hand over her mouth. She was fighting a smile. "You're incorrigible."

"If you don't have a thing going on..." Bernadette raked Tate up and down with an impertinent look.

''Maybe you and I ought to chat. I bet you're just a big boy all over.''

Tate had to turn away to choke down laughter. He caught a glimpse of Diana's face. She wore an expression that said, See why I can't resist her?

Gil pushed the door open. ''Tate, come here.'' Tate joined him on the porch. The sun had topped the mountain peaks, glazing the sky with red-gold light. ''Something is wrong. I can't get Albright on the phone. Desk clerk at the hotel said he and the other agents left twenty minutes ago.''

Tate closed his eyes. Cell phones were as easy to monitor as radios. All it took was someone willing to listen. He imagined Douglas Montgomery's goons were paid well to do the job.

His entire body itched in warning. ''We better get out of here.''

The sheriff's call letters squawked over the radio in the Rover. Bill Yarrow and Moe Sherwood had come upon an automobile accident on their way back to town. Agent Albright's rental sedan had gone off the road and into the Maya River. All three FBI agents were alive, but two needed emergency services.

Tate and Gil heard the approaching engine at the same time headlights flashed across the boulders lining the driveway.

Gil grabbed an extra shotgun and a box of shells out of the Rover. A monster SUV roared over the hill, churning dust into the morning air. Gil and Tate ran for the house.

Chapter Fifteen

"Good guy? Bad guy?" Tate asked. He watched out a window while a black Lincoln Navigator pulled up about twenty feet behind the marked Rover. The windows were tinted so it was impossible to see inside. The front bumper was crumpled. The occupants must have seen him and Gil run into the house.

Gil was already on the phone with the sheriff's station. Steely-eyed, he watched out another window.

A person stepped out of the Navigator's passenger side. All Tate could see was the top of the head.

Gil bobbed his head, trying to see better. "Can you see—?"

Gunfire erupted. Bullets sprayed the Rover. Both back tires blew and the bubble lights shattered. Diana pulled Bernadette off the chair and flat onto the floor.

A muffled whump. Window glass bulged in the frames. The Rover's gas tank had exploded, lifting the rear end then dropping it hard. The vehicle burst into flames.

Gil's mouth fell open. "My budget," he murmured. "Sons of bitches just wrecked my budget."

Tate drew back the butt of the Glock to smash the window pane. Gunfire raked the house. Windows exploded in blizzards of glass. Splinters flew from the door. Bernadette screamed and Diana threw herself atop her sister. Tate and Gil dropped to the floor and covered their heads with their arms.

Silence.

With his back to the wall, panting, Gil said, "Bad guys." He spoke into the phone. "Hear that? Machine guns. They blew up my damned Rover! We're in a lot of trouble, but damn it, don't send anyone in blind! I don't know how many there are."

Tate cautiously peeked out the window. The shooter, marked by blue smoke curling from the gun barrel, crouched behind the Navigator, protected by the engine block. Through the flames and smoke of the burning Rover Tate glimpsed movement by the garage. He duck-walked beneath the window to the other side. Slowly, he brought the Glock to the window and took aim. He pulled off four quick shots at the SUV before he ducked back down behind the safety of the thick log walls.

Gunfire blasted the house again. Bullets zinged through the door, showering the room with splinters. Art work cracked and splintered, falling off the walls. Bullets striking kitchen utensils zinged and pinged.

Diana half-pulled, half-pushed her sister into a corner of the kitchen. She tucked Bernadette there, where she was hidden from the windows. Then she crawled across the floor to a shotgun.

"Stay away from the door," Tate hissed at her.

"I am!" she hissed back.

"Two are running around the north side of the house." Gil checked the load on his pistol. "Is there a back door?"

"No," Diana replied. "But the bedroom windows are big enough to get through."

"Get over here. Watch this window. You see a face,

shoot it.'' Gil wriggled on elbows and knees to the bed-room door. Broken glass ground beneath his body and obscenities streamed from his mouth. He slowly pushed the door open.

"In the house!'' a man yelled outside. "I know you have Bernadette O'Malley. Send her out and nobody gets hurt.''

Bernadette whimpered, her eyes as round as saucers and her face dead white. "Except me,'' she whispered. "He's gonna hurt me bad.''

"Do you recognize the voice?'' Tate asked her.

"It kind of sounds like Doug.''

Tate peeked. He couldn't see anything except smoke. He prayed the burning vehicle didn't give those mopes ideas about torching the house.

"You are assaulting law officers!'' Tate yelled. "Other officers are on the way to the scene. Put down your weap-ons and step into view with your hands up.'' That ought to give the mopes a good laugh.

"Do you honestly think that will do any good?'' Diana asked.

"No. But it might slow them down a little.''

"Incoming!'' Gil snapped. He rolled to the side and fired into the bedroom. Glass shattered. A man howled.

"That will definitely slow them—''

Automatic fire raked the back of the house. Diana and Tate flattened themselves on the floor. Fortunately the bul-lets were aimed high and the log walls absorbed the rounds rather than causing ricochets. Acrid gun smoke filled the house.

"You okay, Gil?'' Tate whispered.

"Yeah.''

"Diana?''

"Shaken, but okay. I never realized guns were so loud."

"Uh, Incredible Hulk?" Bernadette squeaked. "You want to free up my hands? I'm handy with a gun. I can help."

"Shut up!" Gil and Tate yelled in unison. The woman glowered and tucked her legs tighter against her chest.

"In the house!" the man outside yelled again. "Send Bernadette outside, or I will set the house on fire. You have thirty seconds. She's not worth your protection. Send her out and you will live."

Tate risked a peek. He spotted a man behind the Navigator. Older, silver-haired, his face was darkly suntanned. Even at a distance he appeared furious. So why try to bargain, Tate wondered. "I can't do that, sir!" he yelled.

"Fifteen seconds!"

Tate glanced at Diana. He hadn't told her he loved her. He didn't want to die without her knowing it.

"Five! Four!"

Tate stretched across the splintered door and snatched the shotgun from Diana. He swung in front of the shattered window and fired. The Navigator's window exploded. He jacked another round into the chamber and fired again. The force of a blowing tire actually lifted the heavy SUV off the ground. He ducked out of the way. Automatic fire blasted the front and back of the house.

The deafening clatter stopped and Tate heard the thumping of feet. He racked another round into the shotgun just as the door burst open. He fired, chest high. A hole the size of a cantaloupe appeared in the door and a bloodied man fell inside the house. Bernadette screamed.

An AK-47 skittered across the floor. Gil dived for the weapon. A shadow filled the doorway; muzzle flashes flared. Tate threw himself in front of Gil. At the same time he pulled the shotgun's trigger, his foot struck a throw rug and slipped. He went down on his back, hard, knocking the wind out of his lungs.

The man in the doorway threw the machine gun aside and drew a pistol. Time seemed to slow for Tate. Gil groaned. Shards of glass cut into Tate's back. He brought up the shotgun, fought with the pump action, but he was moving too slow. The man was aiming, his face a blur behind gun smoke.

There was a flash of red and purple, a spray of icy water, smashing crockery and the goon fell backward. Diana had struck him squarely in the face with the prayer altar bowl.

Tate managed a breath, and his hands remembered how to work the shotgun. He rolled out of the doorway. Gil groaned again.

Before he could yell at her to stay out of range, Diana scrabbled across the floor, in front of the open door, to Gil's side. Blood and gore peppered her face, hair and shirt. A splinter stuck out of her cheek. On her knees, she dragged Gil across the floor, away from the door and windows. Tate leaped across the dead man blocking the doorway and flattened his back against the wall. His ears strained for the sound of an approaching enemy.

Sirens rose, a blessed noise. A man ran past the smoldering Rover. Tate tried to get a bead on him, but the man was too fast and Tate didn't dare step outside. He had no idea how many shooters were out there.

"Gil," Diana said. "Talk to me. Come on." She ripped off his tie and tore open his shirt. Blood gushed from his neck.

"How bad is he hurt?" Tate asked, never taking his eyes off the driveway. He couldn't see Gil's phone anywhere, nor did he know where he'd lost his.

"He'll live. Right, Gil? Come on, open your eyes."
She tore off her shirt and ripped off a wide strip of chambray. She folded it into a square and pressed it against Gil's neck. "Gil. Gil! Come on, buddy, Paula will be furious if you don't cooperate with me. She needs your help with all the grandkids. Come on, wake up."

Sirens turned into a deafening wail and the first cruiser flew over the hill. Tate tensed for the sound of gunfire. Maya Valley sheriff's cruisers and state police vehicles screamed into the yard, forming a protective circle. Tate recognized the distinctive wail of the fire truck, but it wasn't getting any closer.

Tate yelled, "This is Deputy Raleigh! There's at least one man on foot. Last spotted running north!" That one dead man and one dead or unconscious man lay on the porch was self-evident. Tate felt certain there was at least one more wounded man somewhere. "Sheriff's been hit! I need paramedics now!"

First one deputy, then another, and a state policeman left their vehicles. No gunfire greeted them.

Diana worked feverishly to stop Gil's bleeding. His eyes were open, but glazed with shock. His walnut complexion had turned ashen. Diana applied pressure to the wound.

"We need paramedics!" Tate stepped over the fallen criminals. "Get a chopper! Move!"

"HEY, TATE IS IT?"

Tate blinked stupidly at Bernadette. Tension, adrenaline, terror and rage had drained from his system, leaving him thick and slow. The *chup-chup-chup* of the Flight for Life helicopter was fading fast, flying Gil Vance and one of the shooters to the hospital. Another shooter had been loaded into the coroner's van. The man Diana had smashed in the face with her prayer bowl had a broken nose, two broken teeth and a knot the size of a baseball on his forehead. He'd pay a visit to the local medical clinic. Tate had seen to sorting out the bad guys and organizing a search for the man who'd escaped.

He slumped on a chair and stared at Bernadette. She was still huddled in a corner between kitchen cabinets. A few shards of glass glittered in her dirty hair, but she didn't have a mark on her.

"Tate?"

"Yeah."

"I think Diana is hurt."

Diana had administered first aid to Gil until the helicopter arrived. Then in the confusion he'd lost sight of her. "What?"

She pointed her chin at the ruined bedroom door. "She just went in there. I think she's bleeding."

He launched off the chair and ran into the bedroom. Through the bathroom door he saw Diana with her shirt off. She had her face close to the mirror and used tweezers to pluck splinters out of her cheek. In the mirror, her reflection was ghostly pale.

"Honey?"

She turned around. His mind briefly registered that her sports bra revealed the ravages of cancer. He focused on the bloody welts and furrows that marked her upper chest, shoulder, neck and cheek. Blood seeped in thin trickles. Splinters stuck out of her face and neck like porcupine quills.

When the shooter burst into the house and Tate fired the shotgun through the door, Diana had been in the line of fire.

"Oh my God, I shot you. I'm so sorry. Oh, honey, I never meant to hurt you."

"Yeah," she sighed. "I didn't notice...thought it was someone else's blood..." A wan smile pulled her mouth.

He held out both hands. "Come on, let's get you to a doctor. You're full of buckshot."

"I'm okay. It's just that shallow wounds always hurt more than deep ones. I want to get the splinters out before I go anywhere."

"Sit." He pointed at the toilet. "I'll get them."

She loosed a long sigh and sat. She handed him the tweezers and turned her face upward. A few splinters were close to her eye. He extracted those first. She flinched, but didn't cry out.

"Were you scared?" she asked.

"Terrified. You?"

She grinned. "I was fine until you shot me."

He winced. "It was an accident."

"I'm sure you'll find some nice way to make it up to me, right? Ow!"

"Sorry." He fully intended to make it up to her, every which way he could imagine. He'd start with repairing her house. Scrubbing blood off the hardwood floors and shampooing it out of the rugs. New windows and doors. Patching the bullet holes, replacing the destroyed art work. He'd even buy her a new leather couch and kitchen table.

"Tate?" It was Deputy Bill Yarrow.

"Back here," he replied. He tipped Diana's head and pulled a splinter from her neck. He could see the bluish shadow of pellets embedded under her skin. She was shaking and her teeth were clenched, but she sat still for his clumsy ministrations.

Bill appeared in the bathroom doorway. "We caught him." Then he noticed Diana and started. "What happened?"

She pulled a bath towel over her chest. "Tate shot me." She was shivering.

At least she was having a good old time with this. He gave her a dark look, earning a wink in reply, then turned to Bill. "Did you catch the shooter?"

Bill's face creased with merriment. "He was trying to escape in your Bronco."

Everything happens for a purpose, Diana liked to say. Tate marveled at the way things worked out. "Do you have an ID on him? Is he Montgomery?"

"Albright has all the details." His amusement faded. "I searched the Navigator top to bottom. No sign of a scanner or any kind of radio that could have intercepted our transmissions. Albright and others claim it was the Navigator that ran them off the road. Good thing the perps didn't open fire on the feds. They were sitting ducks."

"Find out where they were staying in town. There might have been more than four of them. How bad are Albright's partners injured?"

"One has a concussion, the other has possible internal injuries. Albright has a busted nose, but he refused treatment." He leaned to the side so he could see around Tate. "Paramedics said you saved Gil's life. We owe you big, Red. You're an incredible lady."

Faint color blossomed on her cheeks.

Just wait, Tate thought, until they heard how Diana had risked her life pulling Gil out of the line of fire. She might get herself a medal, or even a parade.

"Tell Albright I'll get to him after I finish here. Take care of O'Malley. Don't let her sweet talk you into removing the handcuffs."

"Roger that."

After the deputy left, Tate asked, "Are you going to tell everybody in the whole world that I shot you?"

"There are ways to shut me up, you know."

He pressed a soft kiss to her mouth. She tasted faintly of gun smoke. "Like that?"

"It's a good start." Her grin faded and her beautiful eyes darkened. Her shivering increased. Goosebumps covered her exposed skin. "I was so scared I was going to lose you."

"Did you pray?"

"Of course."

"It worked. We're okay now."

She placed a hand flat against his chest. "Yes. I think we are."

Feeling better, Tate removed as many splinters as he could with the tweezers. The deeper splinters and embedded buckshot would have to wait for a doctor.

When Tate walked out of the bedroom, Agent Albright was walking into the house. The agent's dress shirt was blood splattered, his nose was plastered and both eyes were bruised. His shoes crunched glass and he looked around at the damage as if he couldn't believe what he saw. "Your methods are messy, but effective. How is Sheriff Vance?"

Pain arced through Tate's gut. "We don't know yet."

"He's a good man. Hope he makes it."

"The man you caught. Is he Douglas Montgomery?"

A flicker of surprise brightened his bruised eyes. "How do you know about him?"

Tate rubbed at his temple. A world-class headache was forming. "I'm sick to death of your spook games. I know you suspect O'Malley of kidnapping Farrah Montgomery and that you've been hoping Douglas Montgomery would come after her. So do you have Montgomery in custody?"

Albright drew himself ramrod straight. His lips thinned. "Making a positive identification is a bit of a problem," he said stiffly. "Douglas Montgomery has never been arrested. We don't have his fingerprints on file. His only living relative is his daughter. And she's missing. Until we find her, we can't run DNA tests. The man we have in custody is carrying what looks like valid paper identifying him as Victor Morales, an Ecuadoran citizen."

"O'Malley claims Farrah introduced her to Montgomery. That she had sex with him."

If looks could kill… Tate rubbed his mouth and chin to keep from braying laughter.

"She claims a lot of things."

Tate grinned. "She seems to be a clever little thing. What are you going to do with her?"

"That's up to the federal prosecutor."

Tate caught a strained note he could only interpret as disgust. Pure orneriness made him ask, "So what are you going to charge her with?"

"At the moment, interstate transport of a stolen vehicle."

Tate got it then. Without Farrah Montgomery's body, the feds couldn't prove murder; it was highly unlikely that any of Farrah's people would accuse Bernadette of kidnapping because that would mean incriminating themselves in a string of shootouts and murders. The feds wanted Montgomery and only Bernadette could give him up. She had them by the shorts.

If the situation in the Maya Valley weren't so tragic at the moment, Tate would be laughing his head off.

Buttoning a clean shirt, her movements now stiff and pained, Diana came out of the bedroom. An angry rash covered the left side of her face. She eyed the agent warily.

Albright did a double take. "You really are twins."

"I'm certain you were informed of that, sir."

The agent gave himself a shake. He gingerly fingered his plastered nose. "I would like your permission to search this property."

"Why?" She looked around at the damage, her eyes skimming over pools of blood. "You already have the money Bernie stashed under the hive. I also turned over the clothes she was wearing when Montgomery's people shot her."

"I can get a warrant."

Diana rolled her eyes. "I'm not being obstinate, sir, and I'm not refusing. Excuse me, but I am very tired and I'm not making myself clear. What I mean is, if you are looking for something specific, perhaps I can point you in the right direction."

Tate caught his lower lip in his teeth to keep from grinning when the agent glared at him. Albright might as well be wearing a sign that said *I hate being shown up by hicks!*

"Your sister hinted that she might have something juicy she can bargain with."

"Hmm. She's probably lying."

"Searching this property will show if she is or not."

"Go ahead." She toed a shard of pottery. "It's not like you can damage anything."

Albright left the house. Diana bent to pick up a broken bowl, but Tate stopped her. "We need to get you to a doctor."

"I hate going to the doctor."

"Funny. Come on." He guided her out the door. Even more officials had arrived. Men in black Kevlar vests and hats with FBI emblazoned on the front, guarded a sedan. A tow truck backed up to the blackened, fire-foam covered sheriff's SUV. Crime scene techs gathered shell casings and swarmed over the shot up Navigator. Bernadette was in the sedan's back seat. She threw her head back as if delighted all this fuss was over her.

"Oh look at that face," Diana murmured. "She thinks this is funny." As if in reply, Bernadette laughed, drawing frowns from her guards.

Wondering who he could hit up for a ride into town, Tate held Diana's elbow to help her down the steps. She sounded okay, but she was shaky.

She stopped short. "Wait a minute. She's laughing at the FBI. That means she's sent Albright on a wild goose chase, or she's hidden her juicy item where she's convinced he can't find it."

"The beehives."

Diana shrugged. "Only way to find out is to look. I'll get my smoker."

"Can this wait?" Tate asked. "You need a doctor."

"It's all right," she said, waving off his concern. "I was getting very negative vibes off Agent Albright. That is one man who could benefit from some anger management, or a good massage. It wouldn't surprise me if he turned a fire hose on my poor little bees."

Armed with a veil and smoker, Diana calmed the bees enough to run her hand beneath the hives. She gathered quite a crowd of men and women who watched with interest, but stayed far back. Under the last hive, farthest from the gate, her fingers closed over a handle. She puffed smoke at the hive entrance, then gently worked a slim portfolio free. Gold initials, FKM, were affixed to the fastening strap.

Diana had to smile at her sister's cleverness. If not for the transmitter that had led Montgomery's people to the hives, this portfolio and the case of money would have never been found.

Leaving the enclosure, making sure the gate was securely latched, Diana handed the portfolio over to Albright. He unlocked it with the small key Tate had taken from Bernie. He opened it and peered inside.

"Holy mother of God," he breathed. He snapped the portfolio closed.

"What have you got?" Tate asked.

"If it's what I think it is," the agent replied, "it's the Rosetta stone that will bring down an empire." Gesturing for other agents to follow him, he hurried away.

Tate and Diana watched him go, then looked at each other. In unison they shrugged. Agent Albright and his Rosetta stone were out there, in the world beyond McClintock. All that mattered to Tate and Diana were each other, their friends and the mountain valley they called home.

DIANA DOZED ON THE FUTON in Tate's apartment. Tippy lay beside her, his muzzle on her hip. The normally exuberant puppy was being very quiet today, as if he recognized Diana didn't feel well.

A doctor had dug twenty-two pellets out of her skin. Digging them out and stitching up the tiny wounds hurt worse than leaving them in. What hurt even more was extracting splinters that had been driven so deeply into her body a few had pierced muscle. Her entire left shoulder felt sore and hot. Her right arm ached from a tetanus shot. Her stomach was upset from antibiotics. Overall, she felt lousy.

Light tapping on the door preceded Tate. With the door open the sound of the Track Shack's busy kitchen and crowded dining room filtered inside the apartment. If business kept up the way it was, Tate might not have to sell. Tippy pricked his ears and his tail whapped against the cushion.

"Hey, honey, how are you doing?"

"I'll live." She struggled to sit upright, and he was at her side in a flash. He eased her upright. Then he placed the back of his hand against her forehead. She chuckled at his mother henning.

"No temperature," he said.

"Oh my, that means I'm dead."

"No *fever* then." He stared into her eyes for a long moment, then kissed her, sweetly. She wouldn't have minded a not-so-sweet make out session, but he showed some restraint. "I'll get you some water." He filled a glass then shook two antibiotic tablets into her hand.

"Ick."

"Take them. Consuela is making you some soup. It'll settle your stomach."

She swallowed the pills and drank the entire glass of water.

"Need to check your dressings."

"I can do it."

"Doctors make lousy patients. Why is that?" He gestured with his fingertips. "Let's see how high you can raise your arms." She couldn't raise her elbows above her rib cage. She glowered in reply. "I thought so. Unbutton your shirt."

She wasn't wearing a bra. She glanced at the photograph of a pretty, blond woman she guessed was his late wife. It hadn't been on display when she'd been in this apartment previously. That it occupied a prominent place now told her Tate was on the road to recovery. Still, the last thing she wanted was to give him a panic attack over the cancer reminder. "You don't have to do this, Tate. I can manage. You don't really feel guilty that I caught a few pellets? I was only teasing. You saved our lives."

He frowned, his eyes downcast. "I feel bad that you

got hurt. But that's not why I want to do this. It's because you need me."

His call. She fumbled open her shirt. He eased fabric off her shoulders. His jaw tightened and his eyes went steely and determined, but he kept his attention on her chest. He peeled tape off her skin and peeked beneath a large pad of gauze. "The doc said to change the dressings if they seep. Everything looks clean. It's not too inflamed. No bleeding."

"Then I'll just change them later after I shower. Are you okay?"

"It's...not so bad." He touched the thin white mastectomy scar, a butterfly caress. "You have nice skin. Smooth."

His struggle choked her throat with emotion. This was so difficult for him, he was trying so hard to overcome the fear. For this moment alone she'd love him forever. "Thank you," she whispered.

He reached into his shirt pocket and brought out tea packets. "I'll fix you some tea."

She buttoned the shirt, an awkward task considering how poor her range of motion was at the moment. "Is there any news about Gil?"

Strain left his handsome face. "Great news. He came out of surgery just fine. I even talked to him on the phone for a few minutes. There won't be any lasting damage. He should be home by Saturday. He told me to tell you that you're invited to a Ute-Mexican feast."

The universe was being very good to them all. Thank you, dear God, thank you so very much.

"More interesting news." He adjusted the flame under the teapot. "You know that reporter?"

"Coles, yes." She frowned, realizing he'd never shown

up at the farm, despite being promised a scoop. "Oh, gosh, is he all right?"

"I doubt if he thinks so. The state patrol picked him up before he could cross the border." He grinned and shook his head as if he couldn't believe what he'd seen. "We found where the shooters were staying. No sign of any equipment that could have intercepted our phone calls. So I followed up on a hunch. Turns out Coles made a call from his motel room to the shooters."

"He was working for Montgomery?" She remembered the scene at Ric's trailer. What might have happened if she'd taken the reporter at his word? A shudder rippled through her body. "I thought he was a real reporter."

"He is. But Montgomery managed to buy him. I checked out the list of numbers I took off his cell phone. One of them matches the number written on the matchbook found in your sister's pocket."

"Whose number is it?"

"Don't know yet. The FBI is checking it out. I suspect it was Bernadette's contact in the kidnapping. And do you remember the orderly at the hospital? On the night we were there, a call was made from a payphone in the hospital to Coles's motel room. The FBI questioned the orderly. Turns out Coles spread a lot of cash around local medical facilities for tips about your sister."

She slumped on the chair. Bernie had gone too far this time. No judge would give her leniency in a kidnapping case, especially if it were proved she murdered the kidnap victim.

"I guess the FBI has already taken Bernie away. Is there a number where I can call her? I want to make sure she's okay."

"She's still in town. In fact, she won't leave until she talks to you. Albright wants to know if you're up for it."

"What? Since when does Bernie dictate to the FBI?"

Tate sat beside her on the futon and picked up her hand. "Your sister has more brass than a war college. If she keeps her mouth shut, the only thing the feds can charge her with is grand theft auto and possibly criminal negligence in Tim Robertson's death. Even if we charge her locally with grand larceny, and Arizona and Nevada add some charges, she'll be back on the streets in five years, ten years max."

"What about kidnapping? Murder? International terrorists?"

"No evidence. She's the only one who can ID Montgomery. The only one who knows where Farrah is. The only one who can testify that the portfolio was ever in Farrah's hands. It looks like Farrah was taking it to the bank to stash it. Albright hinted that the safety-deposit box and the portfolio contain enough information to take down Montgomery's entire operation."

Diana didn't know whether to laugh or despair. Only Bernie could turn a situation like this to her advantage. "So why does she want to talk to me?"

"Let's get some food into you, then go find out."

DIANA AND TATE ENTERED the conference room at the sheriff's station. Agent Albright made introductions between them and a federal prosecutor and Bernie's attorney. Bernie wore handcuffs, but she was the only one smiling.

"They're offering me immunity."

"Immunity from what?" Diana asked.

Bernie's mouth pursed in a mischievous smirk. She batted her eyelashes at the glowering federal prosecutor. "Everything."

Diana couldn't believe it. One woman was missing,

presumed dead. An innocent in Arizona was dead merely because she had the misfortune to buy Diana's condo. Five men had died. Gil was still in the hospital. FBI agents had been run off the road and nearly killed. An assassin had escaped.

And don't forget all the property damage.

It boggled her mind. That no man in the room disputed the comment said Bernie was telling the truth.

"Why?"

Bernie rolled her shoulders in a lazy shrug. She toyed with the chain linking the cuffs. "I know things."

"Ms. Dover," the prosecutor said, "your sister has agreed to cooperate with our investigation and testify against Douglas Montgomery and others in exchange for blanket immunity from prosecution on either a local or federal level."

"So why am I here?"

"If I agree to cooperate," Bernie said, "I'm dead meat. Doug is, like, one of the richest guys in the world. So they're going to put me into the Witness Protection Program."

Again, no one disputed Bernie. "Witness protection, huh?" She looked to Tate, but his impassive cop face told her nothing. "And you aren't prosecuted for anything."

"That's the deal."

Diana wanted to ask if Bernie had murdered Farrah Montgomery, but doubted if an answer would be forthcoming. "We're on this earth to experience life. To get back to God, we have to learn our lessons. We have to own what we do, take responsibility, show wisdom in the use of free will."

Bernie pulled a face. "Geez, what happened to you? Turned into a preacher or something?"

''What happens to you if you don't get immunity? If you take full responsibility for your actions?''

She snorted a laugh. ''Not take immunity? You're out of your mind, sister. First place, prison sucks. Second place, I've got a feeling old Dougie is a lot meaner than the FBI.''

Diana rose. Her shoulder ached and itched, the burn going deep. She resisted the urge to scratch. ''Then we have nothing else to say to each other.''

Bernie stretched her hands toward Diana. ''Hey, if I take this deal, I'm going to disappear. We'll never see each other again. No calls, no letters, not even a birthday card. It'll be like I never existed.''

Just when Diana felt convinced her sister could no longer surprise her, Bernie surprised her. She sounded genuinely pained by the prospect of permanent separation. Even more surprising, Bernie wanted Diana's blessing. ''You have to go where your conscience takes you.''

''Hmm. Guess your life will be better if you don't see me again. I probably embarrass you.''

''You fluster me, confuse me.'' She shook her head. ''Infuriate me. But you don't embarrass me.''

''You're still better off without me hanging around.'' She turned a dazzling smile on Tate. He jerked as if she physically touched him. ''You do have the Incredible Hulk, here. Do you treat her good, man?''

''Bernie, please. Not now.''

''This is my last chance to talk to you.'' She looked between Diana and Tate. ''Oh man, you guys are in love. That is so cool. Maybe I should work on finding some-body nice. I'm getting kind of old for bad boys.''

Bernie slumped back on the chair, her grin as saucy and unrepentant as ever. ''You know, Di, if I was strong and smart like you, I'd do the right thing. Take my lumps.

But hell with that. Immunity it is.'' Her smile faded, and
for a brief moment Diana saw the child she'd once been,
the beloved twin who'd been as close as her own skin.
Bernie's throat worked in a hard swallow. "I didn't think
you'd talk to me. I'm glad you did.''

"I'm glad, too. But I have to warn you, if you don't
learn your lessons in this life, you'll have to learn them
in the next.''

"I'm willing to wait. And I promise you, I won't waste
the money Mom left me. I'll do something good with it.''
She gestured at her attorney. "Bring on the paperwork.
I'm ready to sign my life away.''

The prosecutor cleared his throat. "You do understand,
Ms. O'Malley, that this deal is only good as long as you
tell the truth, the whole truth. If we catch you in one lie,
all bets are off.''

"Sweetie pie, with a deal like this, you're gonna hear
so many truths, you'll want to etch them in stone.''

Diana canted her head toward Bernie and asked tacit
permission from Albright. He nodded. She hugged Bernie
and kissed her cheeks. She didn't bother reminding her to
be good. It was a waste of breath. Tate took her arm, and
she headed for the door.

"Di?''

"Yes?''

"I never told you I'm sorry. For all the trouble. The
mess. Getting shot at. Your friend getting hurt. I really
am sorry.''

Bernie had never apologized for anything in her life.
Diana decided she must mean it. "Apology accepted.
Take care. I'll see you in the next life.''

Chapter Sixteen

"Are you sure you want to do this?" Tate asked Consuela.

She lifted her chin, her dark eyes filled with triumph. She looked around at the Track Shack's dining room. New vinyl flooring gleamed in the soft glow of sparkling clean light fixtures. A rainbow of neat tablecloths covered brand-new oak tables built by Consuela's oldest son. The chairs had been covered in matching upholstery by Consuela's talented daughters and nieces. Early morning sunlight outlined the window painting of a narrow-gauge coal train puffing through the mountains. Gold letters, in an Old West style, proudly spelled out Track Shack Bar and Grill. Instead of tacky neon beer advertisements, the walls were hung with Navaho blankets, Ute baskets, paintings by local artists and old mining tools.

Business had never been better. Even the crustiest old regular approved of the changes.

Consuela held out a hand for a pen. "This is my dream."

Tate nodded at the attorney, who then pointed out where Consuela needed to sign the purchase contract. With a flourish, she handed over an earnest money check. The attorney placed the check and contract in a folder.

"I'll set up the closing and let you know when and where." He shook hands with them both and left the bar.

"Why didn't you tell me before that you wanted to buy the Shack?" Tate asked.

Consuela sniffed. "You never asked."

"I'll be cleared out of my apartment by the end of the day. If you have renovations in mind, go for it." Chuckling to himself, he walked away.

"Tate?"

He turned back to her.

"You're a good man. A lousy restaurant manager, but a good man. You run for sheriff in this town." She tapped the center of her chest. "I'll vote for you. All my relatives will vote for you, too."

That would be a hundred votes, easy. "Thanks."

He practically floated to his apartment. Diana was hard at work in the apartment, packing books into cartons. "Well?" she asked.

He showed his palms. "It's done. A cash deal that will clear my debts and leave me enough to put a down payment on a new truck."

"Good for you." She pointed at a stack of magazines. "Pack or recycle?"

He slid a hand over the back of his neck. "Ric offered me his trailer. If you have second thoughts about me moving out to your farm, I understand."

"I offered because I meant it. Why are you having second thoughts?"

The time was past for any secrets between them. He swung a chair around and sat backward on it. "I'm broke. It'll take me awhile to get on my feet again. Replacing the windows and doors in your house must have cost a fortune. Plus, Consuela wants her relatives to work here, so you're out of a job. And you have doctor bills."

"You aren't seriously worried about money, are you?"
He couldn't even look at her.

"I'm not poor," she said. "I live the way I do out of choice. In fact, some people might say I'm rich." She crossed the room and cupped his face in her hands. "I know you won't ask me for money, not even for a loan. So I won't bother offering. Just rest assured that you living at my place does not cause me any kind of economic hardship."

"You're rich?"

She stroked his cheeks with her thumbs. Merry light made her eyes sparkle. "Rich is relative. In today's economy a few million is pretty piddly."

A few million. He suspected he could live to be a thousand years old, and she'd never cease to amaze him. "So why were you working for me in the Shack?"

"I told you, I wanted to be close to you." She kissed his nose. She stared into his eyes. "I want you to live at the farm for purely selfish reasons. I'm madly in love with you, Tate Raleigh."

His heart felt too big for his chest. "I love you, too."

"I know." She kissed his nose again. "I also know you will not be pushed, prodded or manipulated. If you don't want to move in with me, that's okay. I can find other ways to pester you."

He turned his head and gazed upon the photograph of Lisa. "As long as we're being honest here, I have to lay it out for you."

"Okay."

Her accepting manner frightened him in a way he couldn't define. Maybe because he didn't feel deserving. But she deserved the truth and nothing but. "I loved my wife. We were going to stay married forever. But I couldn't love her enough. I couldn't hang with her when she needed me the most.''

A line appeared between her brows. ''I don't see it that way, but I understand why you do.''

He slid a hand beneath her shirt until his palm rested against her scarred chest. The smoothness of her skin felt strange, but not unpleasant. ''This scares me.''

''I know.''

''I couldn't bear to let you down because I'm a coward.''

''I know that, too.''

''I can't make you any promises.''

''I'm not asking for any.'' She trailed her fingers through his hair. Her face was so calm and wise and beautiful he could barely bear to look at her. ''For the first thirty-six years of my life I thought only perfect people were worthy of love. That love meant making demands, forcing changes, molding people into ideals. To cause disappointment was the gravest of sins. That isn't love. It's fear. What I know now is that love is acceptance. It's surrender. Love just *is*. That you are so hot and an incredible lover is a bonus. I love you, the whole package. Whatever happens, happens. Nothing will change the fact that I love you and I always will.''

His insides felt like mush. ''And if I disappoint you?''

''Then we'll have a big fight and really wild make-up sex.''

He laughed. ''So you're willing to take a chance on me.''

She kissed his mouth then moved away. ''I'm not the one who has a problem with that. It's you.''

DIANA STEPPED INTO the shower and lifted her face to the pounding water. She and Tate had spent all afternoon worming seven very uncooperative goats. Marlee had given her specific instructions, but the execution had proved far more interesting and strenuous than theory.

"Hey, honey," Tate said. He rapped his knuckles on the shower door. "The timer went off for your bread. Should I pull it out?"

Tate knew his way around a kitchen, but the finer points of baking eluded him. She slid the door open enough to see him clearly. He was already showered and dressed in his deputy's uniform. Broad shoulders and bulging biceps strained the khaki shirt. The equipment belt fit snugly around his lean waist. Sexy. She wondered if they had enough time for a quickie before he went to work. If they skipped dinner...

He shook a finger at her. "Quit looking at me like that."

"I know how you can wipe that look off my face."

"Yeah, then I'll be late to work." He backed a step. "How do I tell if the bread is done?"

"Thump the loaves. If it sounds good and solid, it's done." She watched his backside while he walked away. Maybe when he got home they could play sexy cop and naughty prisoner. She slid the door closed.

This summer had been heaven. She and Tate had settled into housekeeping as if they'd lived together all their lives. He was even getting used to the animals. When she mentioned getting a horse for him, he hadn't discounted the idea and even acted a tad interested. The only sore point was that Tippy had decided Tate was the love of his life, and when Tate went to work, Tippy howled his misery for a good twenty or thirty minutes.

She washed her hair and soaped up her body, rinsed, then lifted her right arm over her head. She probed her armpit. All was well. She shifted to her left side. She was growing used to the pock-mark scars left by the shotgun pellets and splinters. Good thing Tate adored her butt and legs. After examining her breast, she moved her fingers to her armpit.

As soon as she touched the lump, she knew it wasn't scar tissue. Her belly lurched and her eyelids snapped open. She pushed at the tiny lump in her lymph nodes. It was solid, but she could manipulate it. When she pressed hard, it hurt, but otherwise it didn't.

Fear rose. That the lump was in her armpit as opposed to her breast could indicate an infection, or it could mean cancer cells had escaped treatment and now metastasized into her system.

"Okay, God, I'm scared, but not immobilized. What happens, happens. I can deal with it." She stepped out of the shower and dried off. Her hands trembled. She could deal with the cancer recurring. She didn't know if Tate could. She wrapped the towel around her body and walked out of the bedroom.

Tate was setting the table for dinner. He lifted a smile, but it faded. "What's the matter, honey?"

"I found a lump." She raised her arm and pointed to her armpit. Fear made the lump feel as big as an orange. She blinked back tears. "I'll go to Durango first thing in the morning to get it checked out."

His head moved in a slight nod.

When he didn't ask questions, or say anything at all, she returned to the bedroom and dressed.

They ate dinner. He told her Gil Vance had decided to officially announce his retirement. Gil had offered Tate his full support in a run for sheriff. Diana thought that was a very good idea. He'd do an excellent job.

He didn't say a word about the lump. He didn't look her in the eye.

A spiritual leader had told Diana, "True faith isn't believing in God. It's the conviction that no matter how weak, fearful, wretched, skeptical or downright disbelieving you are, you know that God believes in you."

Diana felt Tate's lack of faith in himself as if it were a dark little animal squatting on the table between them. When she kissed him goodbye, she said, "I'll always love you."

He brushed her cheek with a kiss, but failed to say he loved her back.

"PUT THAT NO-GOOD BUM on the street," Marlee Crowder exclaimed.

Diana gave her friend a dry look. Arms folded, expression stormy, Marlee leaned against a stainless steel counter in the exam room. Marlee had dropped everything to accompany Diana to the hospital in Durango. Diana sat on a paper-covered table. She wore a paper gown, tied in front, and wished the doctor would hurry up. It was cold.

"You've been outraged for hours now," Diana said. "It isn't healthy. All that negative energy."

"Why aren't you outraged? How can you make excuses for him?" She curled her upper lip. "Had to stay at the station and write up accident reports? Right. If he really loved you, he'd be here. You're too good for him. Just boot his butt right out of your house. Tate Raleigh isn't good enough to lick your feet. Ought to run him out of town!"

The doctor bustled into the room. A nurse bearing a tray followed. Short, dark and all business, the doctor turned to Marlee. "You might want to wait outside."

"I'm a veterinarian, I won't faint." Marlee clasped Diana's hand. "I'm with you all the way, girlfriend."

"Then stand on the other side of the table." The doctor scrubbed her hands then snapped on fresh gloves.

At the sight of a hypodermic needle Diana's courage wavered. This was going to hurt. She untied the gown and stretched out on the table. She turned on her side and raised her arm to expose her armpit. The doctor palpated the area, then lowered the needle.

A ruckus outside made everyone pause. "Sir!" a woman cried. "You cannot go in there!"

The door burst open and Tate, wild-eyed and pale-faced, filled the doorway. He still wore his uniform, his eyes were bloodshot and his jaw was blue with beard stubble. He looked rather insane and definitely dangerous.

"Pardon me?" the doctor said coldly.

A pair of nurses hovered helplessly behind Tate. One threatened to call security. Diana raised onto her elbow and grinned at him.

"Look, damn it, I love you," he said, shaking a finger at her. "And yeah, this scares the hell out of me. Right now my heart is about to blow up. But I love you!"

"I know," Diana said. "You don't have to do this."

"Yes, I do. So here it is, in front of witnesses, I don't care what happens. Cut you up, pump you full of drugs, whatever, I'm with you. At your side, through thick and thin. I'll quit work if I have to. I'll cuff myself to your side, but you aren't going through this alone."

"Thank you."

Marlee's mouth was hanging open. The doctor and nurse looked annoyed.

"And we're getting married, too. You don't need some bum chumping off your good will when you're sick. For better or worse, in sickness and in health. We're in this together."

She and Tate had danced around the idea of marriage.

Tate brought it up more often than she did. He'd even mentioned the possibility of adopting children. At forty-one, Diana didn't feel any pressure. She loved his company, loved him. She was content.

As far as marriage proposals went, this was pretty strange. The directness of it appealed to her, even if they did need to discuss the motivation behind his impulsiveness. "Okay."

He jostled Marlee out of the way and grasped Diana's hand in both of his. "I'm so sorry about last night. I was scared, terrified. But you're right, I have to choose. And I choose you. I'll always choose you, no matter what. Do you forgive me? Do you believe me when I say I'll never leave you again?"

She stared into his dark, tormented eyes. Suddenly, she wanted marriage, the formal commitment, the knowledge that they would be together for the rest of their lives. She wanted to hear people say, "There go the Raleighs."

"You're forgiven and I believe you." She flashed an apologetic smile at the doctor. "Um, but you really need to let the doctor do her job. Just move over a little, okay?"

"How bad is it? Has it metastasized? Are you going into surgery?"

The doctor cleared her throat. "Deputy, if you're finished entertaining us with your little melodrama, would you please be quiet and get out of my way?"

"It isn't cancer," Diana said. His befuddled expression was so comical, she had to choke down a laugh. "It's a piece of buckshot that got missed before. It's formed a cyst. The doctor is going to remove it. It'll only take a few minutes."

"It's not cancer?"

"No. I even had a mammogram. I'm all clear."

He looked from face to face. Muscles leaped in his jaw.

His ears turned crimson. "I just made an ass of myself, didn't I?"

Marlee, her face bright red, snorted into her hand, giggling about him being a romantic fool. The nurses snickered. Even the doctor had a bit of a smile.

His broad chest rose and fell in a heavy sigh. He turned to Marlee. "And I suppose you'll tell everybody in McClintock all about this."

"Not," Diana said, "if she wants to be my maid of honor."

"Oh, all right." Marlee hooked her arm with Tate's. "Come on, you big dope. I'll buy you a cup of coffee. I'm sure the doc will appreciate it."

"I think that's best," the doctor said. The hint of humor had fled. She held the hypodermic like a weapon.

Tate balked in the doorway. His dark eyes were filled with hope and relief and shining love. "You'll marry me anyway?"

"Yes, Tate."

He darted back into the exam room and kissed her hard, leaving her dazed and so happy she doubted if she'd need the local anesthetic. Then he loomed over the little doctor. "Take good care of her. I want her around for a long, long time."

Where the bond of family, tradition and honor run as deep and are as vast as the great Lone Star state, that's...

Texas families are at the heart of the next Harlequin 12-book continuity series.

HARLEQUIN®
INTRIGUE
is proud to launch this brand-new series of books by some of your very favorite authors.

Look for

SOMEONE S BABY
by Dani Sinclair
On sale May 2001

SECRET BODYGUARD
by B.J. Daniels
On sale June 2001

UNCONDITIONAL SURRENDER
by Joanna Wayne
On sale July 2001

Available at your favorite retail outlet.

HARLEQUIN®
Makes any time special ®

Visit us at www.eHarlequin.com

HITT

Harlequin truly does make any time special.... This year we are celebrating weddings in style!

To help us celebrate, we want you to tell us how wearing the Harlequin wedding gown will make your wedding day special. As the grand prize, Harlequin will offer one lucky bride the chance to **"Walk Down the Aisle" in the Harlequin wedding gown!**

There's more...

For her honeymoon, she and her groom will spend five nights at the **Hyatt Regency Maui.** As part of this five-night honeymoon at the hotel renowned for its romantic attractions, the couple will enjoy a candlelit dinner for two in Swan Court, a sunset sail on the hotel's catamaran, and duet spa treatments.

A HYATT RESORT AND SPA

MAUI *the Magic Isles™*
Maui • Molokai • Lanai

To enter, please write, in, 250 words or less, how wearing the Harlequin wedding gown will make your wedding day special. The entry will be judged based on its emotionally compelling nature, its originality and creativity, and its sincerity. This contest is open to Canadian and U.S. residents only and to those who are 18 years of age and older. There is no purchase necessary to enter. Void where prohibited. See further contest rules attached. Please send your entry to:

Walk Down the Aisle Contest

In Canada	In U.S.A.
P.O. Box 637	P.O. Box 9076
Fort Erie, Ontario	3010 Walden Ave.
L2A 5X3	Buffalo, NY 14269-9076

You can also enter by visiting www.eHarlequin.com
Win the Harlequin wedding gown and the vacation of a lifetime!
The deadline for entries is October 1, 2001.

PHWDACONT1